J. BENEDICT

IT'S NOT OVER

J. BENEDICT

IT'S NOT OVER

DEDICATION

Special thanks to my wife, the love of my life, and to God, who has given me the health, strength, wisdom, and perseverance to stay focused and finish this book. Also, a big appreciation for the help and assistance of Andrea, Steve, Tracie, and the background staff who were with me from the beginning and made this book possible.

I am no one special. I have no letters after my name. This book is a first. The chances of me ever writing another one are slim, but who knows. I do not aspire to have a book listed as a best-seller, although that would be great. I am one in a family of twelve. I came from a humble background, barely made it out of high school, and never once stepped foot in a college to further my education. At one point in my life, I had sixteen jobs in twenty years. As a retired individual, with time on my hands, I decided to sit down and write a semi-true story of one individual. I started writing this book over ten years ago, putting it aside when things came up but worked on it as time permitted. If it wasn't for the help of others in editing and proofreading this book, I never would have made it available to the public since composition and English are not my strong suits. I simply wanted to tell a story that might uplift and encourage anyone who reads, so, hopefully, they view life from a different perspective. It's not about me. If I can enrich the life of just one individual, my job is done.

INTRODUCTION

Everyone faces problems in their lives, some more than others. At that time, we tend to look at ourselves as the only one who feels or understands the suffering we are going through. For the most part, that is true. But have you considered what situations others have had to endure? Maybe far worse than you will ever experience. This book is about such a person. A courageous young woman who was placed in life's reality that bad things happen to good people. Outcast, mistreated, and emotionally damaged. From childhood to adolescence, she couldn't catch a break—a broken home, a broken marriage, and physical abuse. She could have just stayed angry, bitter, self-pitied, or even destructive. But she didn't. Her remarkable struggle to succeed and overcome will amaze you. She realized that just having faith was not enough. She had to put it to the test. Faith without works is dead. So she determined to try to live a life of normalcy in spite of her upbringing and condition. It wasn't easy; it was hard. This young lady's faith and character were being tested. Nevertheless, her faith and trust in God, although stretched at times, was ever-present. Because her faith never wavered, help came to her in various forms. She survived! The underlying lesson she learned...NEVER GIVE UP! It is my hope that you view life through a different lens, having read the experience of this young lady. She is a living example of knowing, "I will never leave you nor forsake you."

CONTENTS

Life is a journey; the path is different for everyone. Some people have it easy. They are born with a silver spoon in their mouth, while others, not so much! This was also the case for Stacy Lee Johnson, a black child born in Houston's inner-city neighborhoods.

Stacy's mother, Monique, gave birth to her at an early age. It was a teen pregnancy. Her on-and-off boyfriend, Stacy's father, was long gone. To make matters worse, Monique's family wasn't very friendly about the whole situation either. I can't blame them, though. When the first thing you're taught is to hustle and make money by any means necessary – it does that to you. Monique's mother sold drugs, and her sister worked the corners. Monique didn't grow up with a father. She didn't even know if she shared the same dad as her sister.

Addiction ran rampant in Monique's household. Any extra "product" her mother swindled, she used. She was also quite generous in sharing it with her daughter Natalia, Monique's sister, but Monique stayed clear of all of it. The copious amounts of drugs and alcohol were a recipe for disaster.

Monique wanted a change from all of this—she wanted to get away from the years of abuse and needed a break in the cycle. She had only ever seen her family struggle and face problems, both emotionally and financially. The root cause of all the problems in her life was substance abuse. Monique had enough - she was sick and tired of the same toxic cycle repeating itself, so she took a drastic measure. She dropped out of high school, skipped towns, and started a job as a waitress in a diner. After two weeks of sleeping on park benches and eating from soup kitchens, she managed to save enough to move into an efficiency apartment.

Unfortunately for Monique, the apple didn't fall far from the tree. For someone who wanted to break free from the habits she saw all her life, she eventually fell victim to them herself. What started as a few drinks after work quickly became a crippling addiction. She found an escape from her life-long trauma. Working at the diner wasn't pleasant either–minimum wage with customers too stingy to tip well. Her plan to turn her life around quickly plummeted; she just couldn't get a break. It didn't take long for the drinks to not feel "enough." To curb her new-found addiction, she needed more. She started to smoke, snort, and inject whatever she could. Little did she know, the thing she wanted to escape from – she inadvertently brought it with her.

Monique met Stacy's soon-to-be father at a local nightclub, the "Do Drop In." Monique had developed a habit where she found comfort in the bottle and companionship in the company of men who frequented the establishment. She could get her drinks for free; all she had to do was flirt back. Amongst the many men interested in Monique was Charles Yates. Charles worked as a truck driver. Although he also drove local routes, he mainly hauled products across state lines. He was charismatic and witty and managed to catch her attention amongst the dozens of other men trying their luck.

The "Do Drop In" lounge and nightclub was the best in town. It was a place where most locals and frequent visitors knew each other. If you were one of the clients, your personal life, more often than not, was made public. Everyone knew Monique from the diner, she was a clever girl, and despite only being 16 years old, no one knew this. In fact, she got herself a fake ID and passed herself as a 22-year-old. She never told

Charles this, seeing that he was 25. The only people who knew about Monique's real age were the lounge owners, although they also knew she got the short end of the stick in life and let it slide.

Another reason Charles and Monique got along well was that he hauled more than one type of "cargo" across states. The "fix" Charles could get her was better than anything she could find locally.

Charles and Monique had an on and off relationship. He wasn't around often because of his work, and Monique wasn't particularly looking for something serious. They both used each other to "de-stress," and it worked out great for them. Despite sharing similar interests, Charles's family fared a little better than Monique's. They had the occasional alcoholics, but unlike Monique's family, they stayed away from hard drugs. Charles was able to stay away from alcohol and drugs, as well. However, it was only long enough to secure a CDL license. Whatever happened after he got his license, though, is a different story. He often drank on the job, but he was fortunate enough never to have been caught. He didn't consider a few swigs every now and then a big deal with the hours he drove. Due to their different lifestyles, it was quite challenging for them to hold down a long-term relationship. Still, that didn't stop them from hooking up whenever they got the chance.

In June of 1987, Stacy was conceived in the backseat of Charles' beat up 72' Impala. Monique never told Charles about the pregnancy; she didn't even believe it herself. But when the signs got obvious, she knew it was too late to get him involved. She also knew Charles was not the type to settle down or take responsibility for a child, and she was right. A few months later, when it became too obvious, Charles left on one of his routes and never returned. On 25th March 1988, a healthy, 8lbs baby girl was born – Stacy Lee Johnson. As happy as Monique was, she knew that she could barely make ends meet for herself. How could she do it for two? Monique realized that she had no other option but to quit her job and move back home.

As cold as Monique's family was, they welcomed her return – or so they showed. Seeing how she left a year ago without a word, only to return with a baby in her arm, Monique expected to be driven off by her mother and sister. Surprisingly, Monique's family tolerated this new mouth to feed. However, this was not out of love for the baby, but because now Monique was bringing in money. Monique had gone through the process of getting state aid, which provided the state check for Stacy. Just having Monique and Stacy around was great for everyone. They got extra money only because of the baby. However, Monique could not use that money toward providing for Stacy, as whatever money she received, her family took it as "rent." Of course, this was to have more funds to fuel their habits, which had only worsened while Monique was gone. Whatever little money Monique made doing odd jobs, like babysitting and doing household chores, she used it toward Stacy.

Monique knew this environment was too messed up to raise a baby and tried her best to get help from her extended family. Aunts, uncles, cousins, and grandparents – she expected at least someone to help. Alas, it was in vain! Monique's family barely kept in contact with anyone, and the few she could connect to didn't want to keep a girl who came from a family like hers.

Having not been taught the basics of caring for a newborn and her money being used to support her habits and those of the family, Monique was left with a tough decision. She could either tough it out, straighten her life, get a job, and move out again to give herself and her baby a good life or give the baby up for adoption.

Despite how she was as a person, she was a mother first, and it is never easy for a mother to give up her child. She knew that even if she somehow managed to raise her child, she would eventually end up like her. Monique spent her life growing up in that household, advocating against all the bad habits she saw – only to fall victim to it herself. She didn't want to take this chance with Stacy. Failing at her attempt to change things, Monique knew, as tricky as it was, the best bet was adoption. Going through the hassle of legal adoption was too tedious, so she tried a different approach. In the month of January 1989, she decided how she would go about this.

Monique bundled up Stacy carefully. She remained careful not to leave any evidence behind that would lead back to her. She caught the 5 AM bus across town to St. Mary's Catholic Church. Monique was relieved that she had wrapped Stacy up well; it was a rather chilly morning. Her plan was to get there early and drop the baby off at the front door, making sure no one saw her; or worse, recognize her. She knew the baby would be found by either the priest or the parishioners arriving for service on that fateful Sunday morning. Indeed, a baby found at the Church's steps would be welcomed into loving arms – a healthy household, one Monique, unfortunately, could have never provided for her.

The Church also provided an emergency foster care program for situations like this, something Monique specifically searched for to make sure there were no loose ends. Monique placed her scarf on the Church's steps, which were cold because of the morning dew. She kissed Stacy's forehead one last time as she set her down. She picked up a rock with her sleeves and tossed it at the Church's window to break it - knowing this wouldn't leave any fingerprints behind. Monique then hurried away and hid behind some bushes across the street to watch.

A priest opened the doors in just a matter of minutes, who immediately began to look around. Perhaps, the steps were cold because Stacy started crying, which alerted the priest. He gently picked her up while continuing to look around to see who would have put this innocent infant on the steps. Without wasting any more time, he went inside with Stacy cradled in his arms. Monique, realizing how this was probably the last time she would see her baby, couldn't stop herself from tearing up.

As much as she loved her, she knew this was the best option for her. She could only pray that whoever took her in gave her a good home and an even better life. Little did she know, Stacy's troubles were just beginning.

CHAPTER TWO

Right from the time they were married, Vicky and Keith Edward had a straightforward plan for survival. Keith puts on the overalls while Vicky makes money under the table. It was brilliant, yet simple. They made their ends meet and were not suspicious in the slightest. Keith worked as a janitor at the local high school and presented a "front" for Vicky. Keith found her the clients who would buy weed off her.

Vicky brought in more cash selling weed in a week than what Keith made in a month. She was quite brilliant and called the shots around the house – whatever Vicky says, goes. Vicky easily manipulated Keith, and she cemented her control over him. Keith tried his best to "break-free" from his wife's control, but she was always two steps ahead of him. Keith soon realized that resistance was futile. It was in his best interest to do as he was told. Keith couldn't help but feel emasculated. To curb his insecurities, he found comfort in a bottle of whiskey. The janitor's closet was notorious throughout the high school to reek of cheap liquor – the rumors were correct. An alcoholic father and a cunning, manipulative mother put Wesley, their seven-year-old son, in emotional turmoil.

As the years progressed, Vicky realized selling drugs for this long without a backup plan could soon blow up in her face. She knew she had to think of another means of income, which was just as easy and paid just as good. She was clever and understood that there must be a way she could finesse the system to make it work for her. Vicky believed in the "quick, easy buck" instead of working hard. Why work when you don't have to?

Vicky grew up in the Projects in Dallas. From a very young age, she knew if she had to survive and make something of herself, she had to beat the system and do whatever it takes to benefit herself. However, getting pregnant in high school was not one of her plans. She dropped out in her senior year, right before graduation. Vicky was rather promiscuous and didn't exactly know who the father was. What she did know was, amongst the possible candidates, Keith was the one who would be the easiest to manipulate. Vicky dropped the bomb on Keith that he was the father. Being a high school senior himself and not being very bright, he followed her bidding. Vicky knew his part-time job would never be enough for her and her baby. She decided to get married to him and applied for state aid, which she received. Keith's income and the state aid were enough for them to move into a one-bedroom apartment out of the Projects. Soon after they moved into that apartment, Vicky started selling weed - even before giving birth to Wesley.

In the seven years of Vicky selling weed, she made some loyal customers. One of those customers was Gayle. Gayle and Vicky had become friends over the years. Vicky never paid much mind to it, but now that she wanted to get out of selling drugs and into doing something "safer," she asked Gayle – who, despite not having a job, *always* managed to have money to buy weed off of her.

Gayle's plan was simple, really. She adopted five children and let the state do the rest. She was paid quite handsomely in financial aid, eliminating the need for her to work. Gayle explained the details to Vicky how she "played the system." Vicky, who had made it her life's mission to do that, was immediately impressed by Gayle's income source and set out to do the same. She told Keith about her plans, and even though he objected, she paid no mind to him. When has she ever? She was convinced in her ability to con the system and knew she could devise a plot to do the same thing that Gayle did. She could care less about the children's welfare; it was the money she cherished. If she had any questions along the way, Gayle was there to help her.

Vicky contacted the local adoption agencies and filed the necessary documents to be approved to adopt children. However, there was a problem. The government would not allow a family who was already receiving state aid to adopt. Both parents had to be employed for a minimum of one year. With that goal in mind, Vicky knew what she had to do. She had to find the most comfortable job she could fool around with to satisfy the quota. Ironically, one of her "customers" set her up with a cashier's job at a local grocery store he was managing. She didn't want to draw attention and be suspicious, so she temporarily halted selling weed and worked solely as a cashier.

After a year and a half of "hard" work, Vicky was ready to bring her plan to fruition. She now returned to the adoption agency and produced the pay stubs and the tax returns to complete the necessary qualifications to adopt. This time, Vicky came much more prepared. She studied the system in and out. She knew she had to continue working a few more months because the application processing takes time. She could not quit her job during the processing period.

Three and a half months later, Vicky finally got the call that she was so anxiously waiting for. The adoption agency told her that they had a five-year-old boy, Amarion, who they needed to place in a foster home. Vicky's plan did not include foster children – because they don't end up *staying* – they are not permanent. She knew the children could be removed from her "care" one day, and the financial support would stop. Her plan was to adopt as many kids as possible – the maximum number of kids the state would allow. Vicky and Keith needed to prove they were "fit" to adopt another child. Having Wesley somewhat helped their case. Vicky was not interested in the children's well-being. The only thing that mattered to her was the money. In Vicky's mind, money ruled. She knew she did not have to *prove* that the money was spent on the children. Vicky could do whatever she wanted to with the additional income.

After pestering the agency for a month, she finally got her first adoption – Darcy. Darcy was a timid child who had lost her parents in a drunk driving accident. The PTSD had festered itself on the child, and she was too scared to rebel against any of the torment Vicky subjected her to. Vicky never intended to care for the children either way. They only needed to be kept alive to keep receiving the money; this was her mindset. It was no surprise that Darcy, as well as Wesley, became subject to abuse and neglect. To make matters worse, Vicky decided that the best way to "invest" her new income was to pick up gambling – which she quickly became addicted to. Keith could not dare intervene in Vicky's "parenting," he just did as he was told and nothing more.

CHAPTER THREE

Darcy was just the first child Vicky adopted, but she had planned for many more. She was able to earn enough money gambling to move into a bigger house, which was necessary if she needed to adopt more children.

The second child who Vicky was going to adopt was Stacy - who was now a year old. Stacy was too young to remember her mother, and Vicky never told her that she was adopted. As time went on, Vicky adopted more children and had a total of five, not that they were treated very well in the first place! Stacy was cute and smart, which perhaps reminded Vicky of the attributes she lacked. She started to sow the seeds of jealousy toward Stacy. On the rare occasions when gifts were brought for the children, Stacy was left out more often than not. She noticed that the other children periodically got new clothes and toys, not out of love, of course, but because the agency did visits to see the well-being of the children. Vicky wanted to show a positive image – that all was well. Stacy was left out of Vicky's minimal generosity. She always wore hand-me-downs.

With Keith and Vicky always fighting and equally traumatized siblings, Stacy's only friend was the television. She and her siblings sat for hours, being babysat by cartoons, movies, and soap operas – whatever their little minds got interested in the most. Vicky didn't mind them sitting in front of the TV for hours. She got time for herself to do what she wanted to – she enjoyed this freedom.

Vicky's control over her children was apparent. They did what they were told, and if they didn't do it right, they would have enough bruises to remind themselves to do it correctly the next time. The house was kept clean, and the little children made whatever food they could for themselves. Sometimes, if Vicky felt generous, she would leave $10 for pizza, but this was usually for everyone except Stacy. Despite the toxic environment that Stacy was being raised in, she was very book-smart and excelled in school. She got straight As consistently, and she was liked by both students and teachers. Unfortunately for her, things got worse by the time she turned ten.

Vicky's resentment toward Stacy only seemed to grow. Stacy was rather tall for her age, had a slender frame, and was very pretty, something Vicky just could not handle. She was a walking reminder of the things Vicky did not possess. With time, this resentment turned into pure hatred for her, and she channeled it differently. Although now she had money and lived in a decent house, it was not enough for Vicky. She became obsessed with others' success. Anyone who had more money, a nicer home, a better car, and was educated enough to have a much better paying job became her automatic enemies. She was frustrated by all of this, and she used Stacy to lash out all of this pent up frustration. She was relentless in her emotional warfare against Stacy. At every opportunity, she would degrade Stacy, her character, her looks, or her intelligence; nothing was spared! Vicky made it her mantra to remind Stacy that she would never amount to anything. She became the Cinderella of the household and the ugly duckling to her mother's wrath. The older she got, the worse it got for her. In the back of her head, Vicky knew it was only a matter of time until the adoption agency got wind of how she was treating her children. The kids were getting older, and it was only a matter of time until one of them reported her to the authorities. She didn't want to lose this easy source of income. She researched where she could continue to get an income doing nothing – she found Indiana! The laws in Indiana were much laxer than in Texas. She also found the most vital thing for her – parents who adopted children were paid more in Indiana. Fortunately for Vicky, her sister lived in Fort Wayne. She reassured Vicky that finding a suitable place to live was not a problem since Indiana was much cheaper to live in than Texas. The only person Vicky needed to convince was Keith, and that had never been a problem in her entire life.

In the summer of 1999, Keith and Vicky reported to the agency that they would be relocating to Fort Wayne, Indiana. Since the state government gave the financial aid, it was a simple procedure to document an address change so that funds would be uninterrupted. However, Stacy was devastated. She had to leave the friends she made in school behind. They were the ones who brought comfort to her challenging life. But now, she had to leave it all behind. The teachers grew fond of her, too, and all her friends were sad to see her go. Despite everyone promising to keep in touch by giving her their landline numbers, she knew Vicky would break the communication chain between her friends and her as another form of exercising sadistic control on Stacy's life. At only the age of ten, Stacy was made responsible for most of the household chores. Vicky gave her no prior instructions! Stacy was expected to figure it out on her own, but she was severely punished if the work she did had any mistakes. Stacy never learned to cook properly because of this. When she had to provide the meal, it was always a microwave TV dinner. This was all according to Vicky's plan. Not only did she spare no opportunity to berate Stacy, but she also made sure the rest of the children did that, as well. Vicky determined that once Stacy was on her own, her value in a relationship would be no more than that of a servant. She was adamant about ruining, not just her self-esteem but also provided her no help in preparing for the challenges a teenager would face.

Soon, it was time for them to move to Indiana. After Stacy said her final goodbyes, they were off. It was a long drive, especially hauling all that luggage across states. Vicky initially stayed at her sister's house while they looked for houses for themselves. They put their furniture in a storage locker.

Vicky pressured Keith to get a job to make the down payment on a rental property. Despite having much more money than him, Vicky was very stingy with it. Keith found a job after a few weeks as an assembly worker at a local cookie factory. By then, Vicky had started to get her state checks and found a casino nearby where she gambled with that money. Stacy got enrolled in St. Thomas grade school. Vicky was by no means religious or even moral, for that matter. The only reason she was enrolled there was that it was convenient for Vicky. However, Stacy looked forward to this. Her mother and father never attended Church. Stacy hoped this change would make a difference in her mother having to visit the Church. However, it didn't! Vicky's contempt for Stacy never stopped.

During the registration, Vicky met with Sister Agnes, the principal. She told her to be extra watchful toward Stacy since she was a "problem child." She further explained how Stacy would exhibit emotional distress signs due to her being a "cocaine baby." When the time came for the new student schedules to be distributed, the principal called Stacy to her office. Sister Agnes had seen her fair share of Cinderella cases, where the adoptive mother is against the child. She wanted to know if Vicky's claims were true. Sister Agnes could tell Stacy was a good child with a pure heart, who was just caught up with the wrong type of people. However, she observed that while speaking to Stacy, she became reclusive when Sister Agnes talked about Stacy's life at home. Stacy withdrew eye contact and began to fidget.

Guided by divine wisdom, a decision was made. As long as Stacy was at school, the principal proposed that she would do all that she could to help Stacy realize some sense of a stable life. She also expressed her desire to do this with all the staff members. Sister Agnes stayed cautious about confronting Vicky about her lies, fearing she may lash out at Stacy.

With the help of those around her, Stacy's stay at St. Thomas became fruitful for her. She became more sociable and made new friends. However, she was cautious not to bring this new form of life home with her, knowing the put down she would have to face from her mother.

CHAPTER FOUR

Stacy was introduced to religion during her time at St. Thomas. Neither Vicky nor Keith had any liking for religion or anything of the sort. Throughout her prior schooling, she had heard of her friends talk about "Sunday church," but she didn't really care much for it.

At St. Thomas, she had a more in-depth view of religion, where she was taught all of the doctrines and principles of the Church. However, despite all the things she learned, the thing that interested her the most was the concept of heaven and hell. Stacy already felt that she was in her own, personal hell, without the fire. But heaven? Now that's a place she wouldn't mind visiting. It sounded like the perfect place to be – all joy, no more crying, no more pain, and no more mistreating parents – just her, living forever in eternal bliss. She didn't know much about God or Jesus, but she was determined to find out about them on her own when the time came.

Time went on, and Stacy eventually graduated with a somewhat average grade score. It was a miracle in itself that she managed that, seeing the lack of support from her toxic and abusive household, which put her in a lot of emotional anguish. This, added with the household chores she was nearly buried in every day, only made matters worse for Stacy. Despite all odds, the crucial thing was that she graduated.

Although she knew most of her friends from St. Thomas would be attending the same high school, she couldn't help but wonder what type of support she would get from her new principal, teachers, and the supporting staff. She knew it was because of Sister Agnes that everything went as well as it did for her. Without her guidance ahead, it would be quite challenging for Stacy. Fortunately for her, this concern was already taken care of. Little did she know, Sister Agnes had already met with Sister Augustine, the principal of Stacy's new high school – St Benedict High School. Sister Agnes made sure Sister Augustine was well informed of Stacy's situation. She vowed to take up where Sister Agnes left off. Once Stacy finally enrolled in her new high school, Sister Augustine invited her to her office and realized the same thing as Sister Agnes, Stacy was a very bright and warm-hearted girl. She was eager to learn and improve upon herself, full of life, but very insecure about herself.

Now that she was in high school, Sister Augustine thought it was best that Stacy got involved with some school activities to gain new friends, hoping it would help her lose some of her insecurities, even if it was only a temporary fix. After Sister Augustine had a hard-fought confrontation with Vicky, she got her way. She encouraged Stacy to try out for the volleyball team and assured her that Vicky gave her permission.

Stacy never played sports in her life and became quite apprehensive; she didn't want to embarrass herself in front of others. However, she realized this was the only "chance" she's got to get out of her shell – a way to have fun with her friends without Vicky emotionally and physically torturing her. Sooner or later, she had to come out of her shell, and this was the perfect opportunity to test the waters.

By the time Stacy reached high school, her older brother and sister had graduated, found jobs, and moved out. However, Vicky had no intention of quitting her lifestyle, and as one child moved out, another moved in. Her responsibility had only increased since Vicky had adopted more children, and Stacy was now the eldest. When she brought the permission slip for her mother to sign for consent for her to play volleyball, she knew it wouldn't go smoothly, regardless of what

Sister Augustine had reassured her. Her suspicions were right; it didn't go smoothly at all.

Once Vicky found out that she had to buy equipment for Stacy, she had no intention of giving up the money she made by gambling to buy Stacy the necessary equipment; shoes, clothes, and other accessories. Vicky was furious. Spending money on Stacy? That was absolutely unacceptable for her. She held a meeting with Sister Augustine the next day to protest about not being informed about the monetary obligations. However, Sister Augustine saw right through her. She wasn't born yesterday; she knew *exactly* the type of person Vicky was by only one encounter. She knew just how to deal with her "type." Sister Augustine emphasized to Vicky how an after-school activity was essential for child development, and if this weren't allowed, she would have no other choice but to report it to the state board since, after all, Stacy was supported by the state.

To further squash any objections Vicky may have, she told her that the school will pay for Stacy's volleyball outfit, accessories and would even provide a ride after practice back home. All Vicky had to do was buy her the shoes. Vicky was backed into a corner. She knew the school was quite literally on Stacy's side, and till she turned 18, she was still bringing in money. Knowing that she had no other option, she reluctantly agreed. She signed the consent form and stormed out of the office, leaving behind a *very* content Sister Augustine, who sat in her chair with a smile on her face.

The four years of high school were Stacy's safe haven. She got time away from home, and the after-school activities kept her busy enough to stay away from her wretched life at home. She was getting her first taste of freedom, away from Vicky and the hell she had conjured up for Stacy. After volleyball, Stacy tried other sports as well; baseball, track, soccer, and even golf.

Stacy was a bit taller than the rest of her teammates. At 5'8", it was easier for her to spike the ball because she could jump higher. Her determination on the field was evident. She gave her 100% – all the time. Stacy's "hustle" on the field inspired her teammates to do their best, too. In baseball, Stacy became the first basewoman and created an easy target to throw toward. She was quite athletic and managed to catch almost everything thrown at her. However, she just didn't have the necessary hand-eye coordination to be a good hitter for the life of her.

At the track, she was also average. The hundred-meter dash wasn't her forte. Others were much faster than her. However, where Stacy lacked in speed, she made up in stamina. Her coach suggested that she do a distance run, like the half-mile or even the mile. Having tried both, she realized she could easily outlast most of the runners in a mile. She was not tops by any means, but she managed to win quite a few races. Her coach pointed out that, in almost every race, she came in no lower than fifth place, which was quite an accomplishment. Her attempts at soccer made her realize it just wasn't for her. Most of the time, she waited for the ball – which seldom came her way. With golf, her dilemma with baseball followed. She couldn't hit a baseball, and it was no different from golf. After only three attempts, she gave up. Even though Stacy had success on the field, she still battled with her insecurities off the field.

To make matters worse, no one really liked her at first at school. Many girls were jealous of Stacy, even her teammates. It was not only because of how good she was on the field but off the field, too. She was beautiful – her smile, the way she walked, and the way she talked – all exhumed elegance. No one could have guessed the type of household she came from because she carried herself very well. She was the envy of every girl, without even realizing it. She never understood why she drew so much attention, especially from the guys – she was just an ordinary girl in her own reckoning. The guys in her school didn't think that, though. They went out of the way to find *any* excuse to talk to her. Some of them who got the nerve would ask her on a date – either to one of the school dances or to watch one of the games. However, their attempts were in vain; she was interested, but knowing Vicky, Stacy knew she would never approve. Vicky barely tolerated her female friends. Stacy couldn't even imagine how she'd be with male friends. She also knew it was quite likely that Vicky would find a way to embarrass them, either publicly or privately, a chance she just couldn't take. Stacy politely denied all of their advancements. As time went on, the other girls knew Stacy wasn't a threat to their "status quo." Although she wasn't interested in dating any of the guys, it didn't stop them from trying.

Stacy's life was slowly looking up. She managed to complete and pass the driver's education course and obtain her license. It was challenging for her, being shy with little confidence. However, her instructor vowed not to give up on her, and their joint efforts bore fruit, and she achieved the first milestone in her life. Vicky, on the other hand, was utterly powerless to stop this. Knowing Sister Augustine had the complete upperhand, she could only stay angry.

Vicky's gambling addiction had only gotten worse. Although she lost more than she won, her few victories acted as motivation for her to "score big" one day. Every time she lost, though, she took out her frustration on Stacy. Unfortunately, one of her rage-bouts was on prom week, which is why Stacy never went to her prom. Although Stacy didn't get the chance to dress up for prom, Sister Augustine made sure she was provided with new clothes to wear from time to time by tactfully threatening Vicky with a state investigation.

Stacy's newfound responsibility was to make sure her younger siblings' homework was finished on time and that they ate and went to bed on time as well – basically, a full-time babysitter. Although Vicky and Keith prepared food on occasions, there had also been times when Stacy had to borrow money from her friends, so she could have the bare necessities, such as toothpaste, soap, and other essentials. Only after all of this was done could Stacy spend time trying to complete her own school assignments. This became one of the primary reasons why Stacy showed up to school without completing her own work. Her teachers understood, though. They were well aware of her situation, and as such, she was never reprimanded. This was the harsh reality of her life, but Stacy was eagerly looking forward to graduation, an opportunity for her to change her life.

CHAPTER FIVE

June 2nd, 2005. On a beautiful spring afternoon, graduation day had finally arrived. Despite all her difficulties, Stacy had managed to graduate in the top one-third of her class. The day she had looked forward to ever since she started high school was finally here. Stacy had her heart set on going to college. To make this dream a reality, she became determined to find a job and hide enough money from her mom until she could move out on her own.

Sister Augustine organized a sleepover at the school for all of the graduates. Food, games, and music were all there. Everyone was required to bring their sleepwear, a pillow, and a blanket. Obviously, the boys were separated from the girls during sleep time. Chaperoned by the school staff, the graduates had time to say their last goodbyes – some they may never see again. Stacy had gained some close friends who helped her through her struggles, and she vowed to keep them as friends throughout her life. Little did she know that she would never see the rest of them ever again, except for just one – Christy.

After graduating, Stacy got a job as a waitress at a pancake house just outside of town with the help of her closest friend, Christy. The only reason Vicky allowed her to work was that the additional funds would bring more fuel for her gambling addiction.

Knowing her mom would take all her pay, Stacy devised a plan. She informed her boss about her situation, and he vowed to help. Stacy's starting pay was only $6.35 an hour, but she asked her boss to only pay her $6.10 an hour. The remaining $.25 would be posted in a ledger until Stacy needed it, which she would request as a lump-sum amount. Just to be on the safe side, she kept her own ledger as well, which had to be initialed by her boss every week. She knew Vicky would ask for the tips, too. Whatever tips she made by the end of the shift, she gave half of them to Christy for safekeeping until she needed it.

It was hard work. Stacy was on her feet near constantly, but because of her friendly nature, and her experience from home on how to serve, she was tipped better than other waitresses. With time, Stacy confided to her co-workers what she was going through at home and her future plans. They were very moved by her efforts, and on certain days, they would give a part of their tips to her, as well.

While at work one day, Stacy noticed a rather handsome gentleman entering the restaurant, who took a seat at her station. She had seen many men come and go, but this man caught her attention for some reason.

Mitchell Elkins was raised on the west side of Chicago, in a neighborhood that saw its fair share of drugs and violence. He was a production worker in a conduit pipe manufacturing plant. The company decided to relocate to Ft. Wayne, and he took it as an opportunity to move out of the hood. He was 28 and worked ever since he graduated from high school. He wasn't very fond of school, to begin with, and barely graduated with passing grades. In fact, he disliked school so much that he vowed never to go to school for any reason, ever again. He had married his childhood sweetheart, but that only lasted for two years.

Mitchell wasn't the independent type, though. He was always on the lookout for a young lady who would do the things he couldn't – or wouldn't, such as household chores. Mitchell used his good looks to his advantage. He had been in town for two weeks and visited other restaurants and eateries in Ft. Wayne, but now wanted to see what the other surrounding communities had to offer.

Mitchell noticed Stacy; Stacy glanced at him on several opportunities as well. It was obvious he had piqued her interest. In the past, when Stacy liked a boy, she had two problems. Firstly, she was too insecure about herself and wouldn't even know what to say if the opportunity presented itself. Secondly, her mother was against her socializing and dating. Now, with her self-confidence improving and the fact that she was almost free from her mother's control, she finally had the opportunity to date.

As Stacy introduced herself, her voice was shaky. It was evident that she was nervous. Mitchell was quick to pick up on this. He even managed to glance at her hand, on which he noticed no rings on her fingers. As Stacy laid down the menu and prepared the table for him, she could feel him looking at her. She was nervous but excited. Before she could ask, Mitchell asked for a coffee. Stacy was glad that he did; she needed time to recollect her thoughts. She hurried to the kitchen to prepare it for him. It gave her enough time to relax. She took a deep breath and headed back to his table to give him his coffee and take the remaining order. Stacy noticed that he didn't take his eyes off her for even a second. Once she served his meal, she went about doing other tasks around the restaurant. However, she also caught a few glimpses of him every chance she'd get.

After a while, when she was sure he was done with his meal, she went over to his table with the bill. Before she could lay it down on the table, Mitchell eased it out of her hand and slid a $20 bill in its place. He thanked her, smiled, gave her a wink, and left. His simple gesture left Stacy stunned; she just stood there, lost in her thoughts. It was only when another customer called out to her that she snapped back to reality. His bill was a little over $8, which meant she got a reasonably decent tip. As she unfolded the bill to put it in the register, she noticed a paper slip had fallen out. Mitchell had written his phone number on it. Stacy couldn't help but blush. She quickly put the note in her pocket and went about continuing the rest of her shift. She kept patting her pocket to make sure she still had the note.

Stacy felt great. Not only did an attractive man give her his number, but she now knew she might just be able to have something substantial from it. She hurried back home and quickly finished all the chores her mother made her do. None of them fazed her today; she was too excited to feel bad. Once they were done, she hurried to her room and sat on the edge of the bed, staring at the piece of paper with a phone number and the name "Mitchell" scribbled in. She had no idea who this random stranger was, but that didn't stop her from feeling excited about the whole situation. Having never allowed herself to feel attracted to anyone, she could only wonder – was this love? Or just a silly crush!

Stacy chose to sleep on it. Perhaps a full night's sleep would help her recollect her emotions.

CHAPTER SIX

Luck was on Stacy's side. The next day was a repeat of the day before. Mitchell walked, sat at the same booth, and ordered the same meal. Just like the day before, he smiled at her, handed her a $20 before leaving. This went on for two more days. On the third day, when Stacy reached toward the $20, he pulled it back and asked if she had gotten the piece of paper he left with her a few days ago. Stacy's heart raced; she knew this was the moment of truth. Saying yes was simple, but she was not prepared for what came next.

He asked her what she intended to do with that number. Stacy was caught off-guard and just stood there, dumbfounded. Obviously, Stacy thought about calling him the minute she got home, but with her situation at home and Vicky keeping an eye on her at all times, it was impossible. Since it was a Friday, Mitchell said he would give her the weekend to think about it but would be back on Monday for her answer. He got up, smiled at her, handed her the $20 bill, and left. For the rest of the day and the weekend, for that matter, Stacy's only thoughts were about her reply to Mitchell.

On Monday morning, Stacy was a total nervous wreck. She knew if she wanted to live a normal life, she *had* to break free of her parents' shackles. She made up her mind – she was going to be friends with Mitchell and see if it progresses to anything substantial. She knew she lacked the experience to form a meaningful relationship, but she could only hope that there would be something special with Mitchell, that he would treat her as a young adult and just maybe, help her start a new chapter in her life. She was always curious about how it felt to have a boyfriend. Some of her high school friends shared their experiences of having a boyfriend. They described how they had a good time and enjoyed all that young lovers do. Stacy dreamed of being swept off her feet by a knight in shining armor who would free her from the "dungeon" that was her home.

During the weekend, Mitchell also contemplated what Monday would bring, but he had a different agenda. He was accustomed to using his charisma and good looks to get dates, and this time, his eyes were set on Stacy. Even though it had been only a week since he met her, and they hadn't talked in length or even gone on a date, he knew from experience how to win her over. He read through Stacy like she was an open book. She was shy, insecure, looking for love, but reluctant to do so.

His past relationships had only honed his skills further, and he was just waiting for the right opportunity. He wanted a cover for his original plan, and if he could use his wit and charm on Stacy, he planned to launch his business. She would never know what his ultimate goal was, and even if she found out, it would be too late. On Monday morning, Mitchell walked into the restaurant and sat at his regular table. As Stacy walked over with a glass of water, Mitchell noticed that she was shaking from nervousness. He got a sign that he was on the right track. As she put the glass on the table, Mitchell grabbed her hand and held it against the glass. He looked straight into her eyes and asked for an answer. She lowered her head and said in a soft tone that she would call him when she got home. Mitchell let go of her hand and told Stacy he had a better plan. He suggested that, instead of talking for hours on the phone, why not just go on a date instead. Stacy knew this wouldn't be easy with Vicky around. She told Mitchell that she'd think about it and hurried away.

Having walked halfway across the restaurant, she realized that she hadn't even taken his order. Embarrassed, she turned and walked back to his table. But as she approached him, he stood up and told her that he had to report to work early and had only stopped in to get her answer. He promised to come back tomorrow for it, and with that, he left. Even though she was caught off guard with all that transpired, she began to tingle all over with the thought that Mitchell came out of his way only to see her. Now, she was more determined than ever to see this thing through.

Throughout the day, the only thing on Stacy's mind was the opportunity to go on a date with Mitchell. She was not going to let this chance slip away. However, since Stacy had never been on a date before, she didn't quite know what to do. She turned to the one person she could rely on – Christy. It became evident to Christy about the connection Stacy and Mitchell had developed. After Stacy explained all that had gone on between her and Mitchell, Christy came up with a plan. She was going to ask for a switch in the schedule. Stacy would get put on the night shift while someone else covered her day shift. Stacy would pick a night to go out with Mitchell and Christy, even though it meant doing a double shift would cover for her. That way, her parents would think she's at work, whereas she would actually be on a date with Mitchell. Stacy would bring a change of clothes on the day of the date but keep in mind that she would need to change back into her regular clothes when it was time to go home. Stacy was delighted by Christy's plan and couldn't help but hug her in excitement and thanked her. Stacy was quite restless leading up to the big day. She was also extra careful not to upset Vicky in any way, so she won't be grounded.

Stacy knew she would be too nervous to talk to Mitchell, so she wrote a note saying she would go out with him, but he would have to pick her up from the restaurant and have her home before 1 AM – the closing time, which she would explain later. She planned on giving him this note on Tuesday. Tuesday morning arrived, and Stacy spent a little extra time fixing herself up. Like clockwork, Mitchell walked in and sat at his usual table. Stacy approached the table with her heart racing and smiled as best as she could.

After she placed the glass of water on the table, she handed him the note. Upon reading the note, Mitchell smiled and put it in his pocket. He told her that he'd pick her up at 6 PM, on whatever day she sees fit. Stacy knew that it would take time for Christy to adjust the schedule, so she suggested the coming Tuesday – a full week later. Mitchell nodded and placed his order. As she turned around to leave, Mitchell told her to wait. He explained to her that he felt they were drawing too much attention to themselves, and he would now eat breakfast elsewhere. But she would see him next Tuesday, right on time. Stacy walked away, smiling. For her, Tuesday just couldn't get here fast enough.

CHAPTER SEVEN

Christy had managed to switch the schedule. The following Tuesday, Mitchell arrived at 6 PM, right on time - as promised. Stacy was already anticipating his arrival, so she had already changed for the outing. Christy explained to the management what was going on; they had no problem with it; they liked Stacy.

Stacy didn't know where Mitchell was taking her, but she still wore her best clothes and put in a lot of effort doing her makeup and hair. Mitchell didn't come inside the diner. He just honked the horn of his car thrice - Stacy got the message. She gave Christy a big hug and thanked her again, then headed out the door. Once she got in his car, they both exchanged greetings. Stacy noticed that Mitchell was still in his work outfit, but since he didn't bother to explain, Stacy just assumed he was running late and couldn't get dressed appropriately. It didn't matter, though; she was going out on her first official date.

Mitchell took her to the movies at a cinema near the outskirts of town. He bought her some popcorn and soda. Throughout the film, Mitchell was a complete gentleman. He didn't try to kiss her, or put his arms around her, which Stacy appreciated; however, she was still very nervous. After the movie, they went out and strolled down the street talking about anything and everything, trying to get to know each other better. They came up to a hotdog stand, and they stopped to have a bit to eat. They then went back to the car to continue their conversation while Mitchell drove her around - she enjoyed his company. By the time Mitchell dropped her back at the diner, they had already planned their next date. To cover for her missed wages, Stacy began using the money the owner was holding for her and asked him to put it in her next paycheck. When her mother would receive it, it would be the same as usual. The plan was to go out every Tuesday night, and for the next two months, that's exactly what happened.

Nearing the three months of them dating, Stacy began to trust Mitchell and told him about her situation at home. Mitchell realized this was the perfect time to put his plan in effect, so he suggested that they move in together. Stacy was shocked, but the prospect of living *away* from Vicky piqued her interest; besides, she liked Mitchell.

Mitchell convinced Stacy by making her look from a different perspective: Stacy would be free from all of the torment at her home, she could continue to work at her job, and Mitchell would even financially assist her so she could go to college. Stacy was overwhelmed by his offer, she knew they bonded well, but she wasn't prepared for what he proposed. Stacy told him she needed time so she could really think about it and would give him a definitive answer in the coming weeks.

Mitchell's proposal was the only thing that occupied her mind. Stacy knew that if she made this move, she could never come back home. She confided in Christy about the matter, and Christy gave her opinion. As flattered as she was that Stacy came to her at her time of need, Christy told her it was not her place to help her decide - it was a decision Stacy had to take herself. For two more weeks, Stacy thought about Mitchell's proposal. She weighed the pros and cons. Stacy ultimately decided to accept his offer, knowing the situation at home would never change. She knew she was taking a significant risk since this had been her first and only boyfriend. Stacy felt like she needed to experience more outings with other men before making this decision, but she also thought this opportunity was too good to pass up. She felt that Mitchell was a decent and humble man. She knew she didn't love him yet, but because he treated her so kindly, she might grow to love him more and more over time; if not, they would agree to part ways.

Within six months of meeting him, Stacy had left home and moved in with Mitchell in a one-bedroom apartment on the other side of Ft. Wayne. They had agreed not to live anywhere close to her parents. In the months leading up to her moving out, she had taken her belongings little by little to not arouse suspicion from her parents. There were certain things she left on purpose to look "normal."

The fateful day she was going to move out, she told her parents of her arrangements and said she would not be coming back. Vicky unleashed a barrage of verbal assault against her, the likes of which had never been heard before. In fact, Keith had to intervene to keep Vicky from physically attacking Stacy. As a last-ditch effort by Vicky, she continued her verbal onslaught to make sure Stacy left with a broken spirit. Stacy couldn't help but cry briefly - she never understood why her mother hated her so much. The more Vicky yelled at her, the more she realized that she made the right decision. She said goodbye to the rest of her siblings and walked out to begin her new life.

Moving in with Mitchell gave Stacy a new lease on life. Although she didn't know that much about him, she knew he was good at heart and that he treated her with the utmost respect. Mitchell was patient with her on things she needed to learn; he even let her pick out new furniture for their apartment. He provided all the financial support, which allowed Stacy to save the money she earned at work.

The only thing Stacy found odd at the apartment was the fact there was no telephone, but she felt that Mitchell would put one in soon. Stacy already knew how to keep the house clean, but cooking was still a challenge for her. Mitchell knew this and brought cookbooks for her while he patiently waited for her to master those skills. Knowing it would be stressful for her to cook every day, he would often take her out to eat.

Even though things were looking up for Stacy, her mother's emotional trauma could not be easily shaken or forgotten. She was still insecure, somewhat withdrawn, and allowed Mitchell to run things as he saw fit.

Much to her surprise, in April of 2006, Mitchell asked her to marry him. Although she was still apprehensive about a long-term commitment and wasn't really *in love* with him, living with Mitchell was great, and he treated her with the utmost love and respect - even when it came to sex. It was agreed that she would make the first move because he didn't want to pressure her into doing it just because he wanted it. He also insisted that she be on birth control since neither of them was ready for children. Stacy knew if she let this opportunity get away, she might regret it later in life. As attractive as Mitchell was, he would have no problem replacing her.

Stacy accepted his proposal and got married on June 2nd, 2006 - exactly one year after she graduated. Mitchell bought her a new dress and shoes for the occasion. They went to the local courthouse to get married. Christy was one of the witnesses. Stacy was so excited that she couldn't believe it was really happening! She could now be called Mrs. Elkins! The judge found two other witnesses to make the marriage legal. Mitchell had purchased two gold wedding bands and promised Stacy he would buy her a diamond ring when the time was right. The ceremony was short and brief, with each of them writing their own vows. They decided that they would put their honeymoon on hold; Stacy didn't mind that because this was the happiest day of her life.

CHAPTER EIGHT

On her wedding night, Stacy was excited - yet fearful; she was still a virgin, and Mitchell knew of it. Of course, she knew about sex and what it was all about over the years, but hearing about it and *doing* it were two entirely different things. Some girls told of their good experiences, while others had bad ones. Regardless, she trusted Mitchell - hopefully, he knew what he was doing. Throughout their courtship, he didn't try to have sex with her even once; Stacy admired him for that.

The night had been pre-arranged. Mitchell had brought her a red satin negligee outfit, which included a snap-on pair of panties and a three-quarter length matching robe, but no bra. He also got her a black garter belt, with a pair of fishnet stockings and a pair of black, patent leather high heels. To top it off, he even got a special perfume just for the occasion. At around 9 PM, it started. She took great care in her dressing and applied just enough fragrance to not overdo it. She pulled back the covers and replaced the regular, white bulbs with red ones. She began to breathe faster, being nervous but tried her best to control it.

At 9:30 PM, Mitchell entered the room. He was also wearing a three-quarter length skill robe, but his robe was white. He stood for a moment, with a wide grin on his face as he asked Stacy to slowly turn around. She was asked to do this three times. Stacy heard him say, *"My, my, my! What a sight to behold! Absolutely perfect."* He stepped closer, and, with her hands still at her side, he placed his arms around her and gave her a long, passionate kiss. They had kissed before, but never like this. Her passion began to mount. He stepped back and asked her to turn around. He slowly caressed her body and began to remove her robe. He began to gently kiss and nibble her neck and shoulders. The more he did, the hotter she got; Stacy loved it. After a few minutes, he stopped, turned her back around to him, and grabbed both of the negligee's straps, peeling them down until it fell to the floor. He bent forwards and began to gently lick, suck and nibble on her now firm nipples, making sure to give each one equal time. Stacy closed her eyes; she was experiencing a feeling she never knew existed. It was sending torrents of pleasure through her body.

He ravished her breasts for several minutes before stepping back. Her nipples were so hard they began to hurt. Stacy took several minutes to compose herself before opening her eyes. Mitchell knelt down in front of her and unsnapped one side of her panties, then the other one, removing them; they were wet. While staring straight into her eyes, he placed his hand between her legs and began probing. Stacy's legs began to shake involuntarily. As he continued, she began to breathe faster and faster - the pure ecstasy she felt was beyond description. A jolt shot through her body as he inserted his middle finger inside her and just held it there. With her legs still shaking, Mitchell felt as if she might lose her balance, so he slowly removed his finger as she let out a sigh. He gently pushed her back toward the bed and had her sit on the edge of the bed and lay back.

Kneeling down again, he spread her legs and slowly reinserted his finger - keeping it still as he waited for her to get adjusted to it. As he felt her relax, he started moving it, ever so gently, in and out. Although a bit uncomfortable, Stacy liked how it felt until he put another finger in. She could only grunt in pain as her body stiffened. Mitchell waited for her again, so she could get used to it. Once he felt she was comfortable, he began slowly moving his fingers in and out of her. It took longer this time, but she settled down, describing the pain now as pleasurable. It was evident that she was enjoying herself a little more. After several minutes, Mitchell put in another finger; Stacy could only let out a muffled, *"Oh God!"* as she arched her back and gripped the sheets tightly. Mitchell patiently waited until she had relaxed again before continuing to move his fingers in and out.

Stacy's heated passion was beginning to mount higher and higher. He knew she had become adjusted to his fingers; he could hear moaning. When Mitchell removed his fingers, Stacy's body was in complete rebellion. *"No! No! No!"* She said in her head. All she wanted was Mitchell to continue, but he had other plans.

What Mitchell did next sent Stacy reeling. From then on, Stacy would know what the word "cunnilingus" meant. As Mitchell began, she gasped and closed her eyes. The feeling of what he was doing sent shockwaves through her body. She was enjoying it so much that she unknowingly placed her hands around his head, holding him in place. Uncontrollably, she began gyrating her hips as she was thoroughly enjoying Mitchell's tongue.

Wave after wave of pleasure swept over her. The longer he did it, the faster those waves came. The longer he continued, the more intense it got. Building higher and higher until it happened, she had her first orgasm. *"Oh, God, Mitchell!"* She yelled out as the pleasure pulsated throughout her trembling body. Stacy enjoyed her first orgasm. Her eyes were still closed, her hands dropped to her side as she relaxed, and she started breathing easier, but she was still unable to speak. Stacy didn't know how long she lay there, relishing the after effects, realizing that she was now a complete woman. She thought to herself, the girls who said it was always a bad first experience obviously didn't have the right guy - but it wasn't over for Stacy just yet.

Mitchell gently moved her to the center of the bed. She could feel him climb on top of her. *"Wrap your legs around my back and lock your ankles together,"* he instructed. Even though she had very little strength left, she did as she was told. *"Now, wrap your arms around me,"* which she did. After adjusting his position on top of her, and with a gentle shove, he slid halfway inside of her. Stacy could only let out a grunt as she dug her heels into his lower back and clawed her fingernails into his shoulder blades. It hurt, but Mitchell didn't move. Stacy now realized why he used his fingers; he was preparing her for this. It took a minute, but she got accustomed to it. As he began to gently move, in and out, she found her tenseness and pain retreating. She continued to get more relaxed; it felt good, *really* good.

Now sensing that she was ready, Mitchell began to pick up the pace - thrusting deeper and deeper until he was completely inside her. Moving in and out, Mitchell developed a rhythm and kept it up for a long time. Stacy had never felt anything like this before; this was very different than cunnilingus. It was an electrifying feeling, and far more intense than cunnilingus. Her entire body reacted with what was being done to her. Within minutes, she was lost in the heated lust and passion. She didn't know when it started, but her body seemed to take control; it knew what to do. By now, the pain was not an issue. She matched his speed and began thrusting upwards as he was thrusting down. Then, that same feeling returned. She knew she was building toward another orgasm. As Mitchell picked up the speed, she instinctively matched him. In no time at all, it was here. She gripped his back as tight as she could. She screamed several times, then began to moan loudly. It was like waves of pleasure erupted inside of her. It was much more intense than her first orgasm – she didn't want it to end. Mitchell had timed it perfectly and erupted at the same time. Breathing rapidly, she clung tightly onto Mitchell for several minutes until, due to the lack of strength, she finally let go. Stacy was exhausted, her arms and legs became limp, and she fell onto the bed. With her last breath, she let out a *"Damn"* before drifting off to sleep.

CHAPTER NINE

So far, Mitchell had worked his plan to perfection. Now that he had manipulated Stacy into doing his bidding, both emotionally and sexually, he could start his business as an "escort service." Mitchell felt he was too classy to be called a pimp, so being the escort service manager had a more "professional" ring to it.

Sure, he had feelings for Stacy, but he never truly loved her. He just used his charm and wit to bait her into marrying him; he had done his homework. Mitchell was well aware that most pimps were single men. His marriage to Stacy acted as cover for his work. Mitchell didn't want to mix business with pleasure; he wanted someone to take care of him when he wasn't working. Stacy was perfect - she was submissive and had nowhere else to go. Mitchell could now drop his "nice guy" act and do as he pleased. He knew he could use his good looks and charm to lure more young women for his "business."

Mitchell got to know two pimps around town and learned from them. He chose an area right outside of town to call his turf - so he doesn't interfere on someone else's grounds. He knew that part of town had a lot of traffic coming through, and that would bring men who had money to his services. A month after their marriage, Mitchell comes home from work, where Stacy greets him with a warm *"Hi!"* - which he ignores. He showers and put on a suit. A week prior to this, Mitchell had told Stacy to switch back to the day shifts so she could come back home early to prepare dinner and fix herself up. This was just another part of the plan. He insisted that she stayed on the night shifts before this, so he had ample time to "research."

When Stacy tried to start a conversation with him at dinner, he just stared at her and continued eating. She tried again, hoping to get a reply out of Mitchell. It worked, but not in the way she had hoped. Mitchell looked her right in the eyes and said sternly to be quiet. Stacy was shocked; he had never talked nor acted this way toward her before. She was confused and puzzled but thought it would be best to maintain her silence.

She kept trying to think whether she did something or said something wrong, or perhaps he was just having a bad day. At this point, she dare not ask him why he was dressed up or where he was going. When Mitchell finished dinner, he went to the bathroom to tidy up and left without saying goodbye. Stacy's anxiety spiked. She kept trying to think where she messed up for Mitchell to become so cold all of a sudden. She could only hope that upon his return, things would return to normal, but little did she know she was wrong again.

Over the next few weeks, things became progressively worse for Stacy. She began to see less and less of Mitchell. In fact, the only time they saw each other was when Mitchell would come home in the early hours of the morning to sleep. It got to the point where Stacy stopped cooking dinner for him. Even though they continued to make love, it wasn't the same. The sensual kissing, caressing, and foreplay was completely gone; Mitchell used here purely as a sex toy. He didn't care if Stacy enjoyed it or not; as long as he was satisfied, that's all that mattered. When she first brought up her concerns about this one night while having sex, he would put his fingers on her lips to silence her. If she continued to protest, he would squeeze her lips together tightly.

Stacy just couldn't figure out what she had done to deserve this type of treatment. She thought maybe she didn't satisfy him enough, so she became submissive to whatever position that Mitchell demanded. After he satisfied himself, he would push her to the bed's side and go to sleep. Stacy could only turn toward the wall and silently weep; she wouldn't dare confront him at this point.

When she got up the next morning for work, she realized Mitchell was already gone. Stacy found a note attached to the bathroom mirror. It stated that today was the last day she would be working, without any reason or further explanation. At first, she thought it was a joke, but thinking back to his recent behavior and how Mitchell had been treating her, she began to think it was serious. Stacy understood that whatever problem she had with Mitchell, it would be best resolved if they discussed it. So instead of quitting her job, she asked for a week off work for personal reasons. Since Mitchell was now paying all of the bills, Stacy knew, or so she thought, that he couldn't afford to give her money for school. If she did not continue to work, she knew her plan for going to college would be lost. Unfortunately, Stacy never did go back to work.

Stacy was too embarrassed to tell Christy about her situation at home. However, they've been good friends for a long time, and Christy could tell just by looking at her that something was wrong. Christy didn't want to pry into Stacy's personal problems; she's married. What happens at her house is her concern. Regretfully, management gave Stacy the week off, just as she requested. Judging from the way Mitchell was acting, Stacy had a gut feeling that she wouldn't return to work again.

Within a week, Mitchell had taken Stacy's cell phone, shut down the internet, disconnected the landline, and removed the TV - Stacy became a prisoner in her own home.

Mitchell had set aside enough funds to rent out a shabby but furnished one-bedroom apartment. With a little creativity, he managed to turn that apartment into an office. He furnished it with stuff bought from the local Salvation Army store. The office was nothing but a "honey-pot" meant to lure in young women. He would put out ads in the newspaper, which said that his "company" was looking for young women who wanted to get into the acting/modeling business. The number listed on the ad was a burner phone Mitchell had bought specifically for that reason.

CHAPTER TEN

Mitchell made sure his business was running smoothly. He took care of any problems that would arise and often planned ahead. To not arouse suspicion, he set up appointments between 6 PM and 10 PM, Monday to Friday. The reason he gave to the applicants was that, for the most part, he knew most of them probably had a job, and it would be difficult for them to make time to come for an interview. He would schedule each interview at one-hour intervals, so none of the applicants ran into each other. He would ask them to bring a resume, which included a full body picture of them in a bathing suit, which prominently showed their features. There was also a small questionnaire that asked *why* they wanted to get into modeling - he wanted to seem as legitimate as possible. Mitchell knew that, for the most part, the applicants would dress to impress, which would allow him to pick the best amongst them. He would mentally toy with them, telling them how difficult this business was to get into, but the rewards were worth it once you got in.

Mitchell explained to the applicants that before he would pay for them to go to acting or modeling school, he had to be sure that they were dedicated to doing their part. This involved a six month probation period before they could be considered for the role. Most of the applicants that came through had dreams of making it big in Hollywood; they knew nothing of how these agencies *actually* worked. Mitchell told them that sex played a big part in the acting jobs and that it was expected of them should any client request it; since most of his business clients were in the position to bypass the red tape leading to a contract for them.

Mitchell made one rule clear from the start; the girls were never allowed to inquire about their clients' business or personal information; they would be immediately released if they did. The clients would report back to him, and this would be the way of judging whether they had what it takes to be considered for the job. If, at any moment, the applicant would be hesitant or have concerns about the arrangement during the interview, Mitchell would quickly dismiss them. He only wanted those who were willing to do as he said, no questions asked.

He was careful and deliberate, just to make sure that every young woman who applied thought that she was his favorite and that she would be given preferential treatment amongst all of the other applicants. In order to prove this, he would take each one out for a night in the town but made sure it was only once. Mitchell also told all of his "aspiring candidates" that he might even consider them as a business partner if they were loyal and committed to him. However, each of them had to maintain strict confidentiality, especially against the other girls. If he found out that they broke their privacy, they were immediately let go and threatened to have their careers ruined. His plan was coming together nicely.

After Mitchell had secured the promise and dedication of twelve beautiful and sexy young women, he was now ready to move on to phase two of his plan. He placed carefully worded ads in a few selective newspapers and magazines that were targeted toward upscale professionals around his area, who needed "companionship" - who could afford his rates yet be discreet at the same time. Each one of them was given an appointment to meet with Mitchell one-on-one to discuss the arrangements. With every client, Mitchell went over the ground rules, a way to protect his girls. However, he made sure he told every client that his girls were willing to show their appreciation in many ways, but in no way and at no time were they to divulge any information about themselves or any of the girls in his establishment. The clients knew exactly what this meant, and since Mitchell didn't say sex outright, it added to his protection of being an upright businessman.

Each client would be shown three photos of each of the twelve girls Mitchell now had in his service. After the client made his selection, he was then given information about the young lady, including her address, name, and phone number. The client was asked to sign an agreement to keep the meeting and financial arrangements "hush-hush" and to know the rules of what could and could not be done. If they had any disagreements toward this, he would show them the way out. Mitchell meticulously made sure that if, for any reason, things went south, nothing led back to him. Since he had to confirm the clients' details as well, he needed them to sign an agreement, should that be necessary. Each client was charged $500 in cash per date with the woman of his choice. When the arrangements were finalized, and the client had left, Mitchell would call the girl he selected and inform her that she would be receiving a call and gave her enough information about the client so they could recognize him. The girls knew they could not accept a date from any client unless it was cleared by Mitchell first. Within the two months of placing the ads for his clients, each of the girls had at least three dates a week. Mitchell was rolling in money!

On the other hand, Stacy had lost contact with all of her friends and siblings because Mitchell controlled every aspect of her life. Stacy was kept in the dark about Mitchell's business. All he told her was that he had quit his production job and that his new job required him to be away from home much more frequently. Stacy was at home with nothing to do and could not leave the house for any reason. The only time she could was if Mitchell allowed it. The one time she left without telling him, he slapped her so hard she still remembers the pain. It reminds her never to step out of line again. Mitchell didn't want Stacy to discover his business, which she could if she was allowed to leave the house. Mitchell physically assaulted Stacy to keep her in check whenever she tried to challenge his authority. He would be extra careful not to leave any marks on her body, should charges ever be made.

The more his business succeeded, the more submissiveness he demanded from Stacy. Things were a bit different now. He took pleasure in verbally tearing down everything she tried to do, including sex. The only reason he kept her around was that he considered her no more than a servant to him, made to fulfill his needs; he had no regard for her feelings. Stacy became a prisoner in her own home, with nowhere to run and no one to talk to. At one point, Christy stopped by to check on her but, when Mitchell found out about it, Stacy was punished. The years of torment she endured from Vicky came back in the form of Mitchell; she became withdrawn and insecure all over again, with no direction in life. Having lost her job, school, and now her marriage, life as she knew it was ruined. She dreaded the life of solitude and servitude with nothing to look forward to, but she dreaded the times Mitchell was home even more.

The only time Stacy was allowed outside of the house was when she went grocery shopping, but only if Mitchell was glued to her side. Mitchell did not want Stacy to think she could draw another man's attention who might come to her rescue. Even then, she was not permitted to socialize with those around her. If she didn't talk at all, people would realize there's something wrong, so she was allowed to exchange pleasantries; under Mitchell's watchful eye. Mitchell would buy her clothes when he thought she needed some, which was not very often. This wasn't out of concern for her, but rather he wanted her to still look good for him if and when he did come home. It got to the point where she only had seven decent outfits, one for each day of the week. She would have liked to relax in a tee shirt and jeans, which she only had two pairs of each, but she never knew when he would show up.

Stacy wasn't even allowed to get her hair done either, but Mitchell still expected her hair to be well kept from the shampoo and conditioner he got for her. Going to a salon for a manicure or a pedicure was also out of the question. She was told to do what she could at home, with what she had, which was, again, very little since he only bought her two colors of nail polish; red and white. Despite her best efforts, they were in vain. Nothing she did meet his approval. It was like he turned into Vicky.

CHAPTER ELEVEN

Mitchell was determined to keep Stacy under his control and devised another plan for this. Mitchell came to know about one of his neighbors, who was known to be involved in rather questionable affairs by one of his associates. Everybody called him "Nicko." His source of income was purely from hustling. He mostly sold weed but did anything so long as it earned him a quick buck. Nicko knew a handful of petty thieves, who would steal, and he would get it from them under consignment. Whatever he sold those things for, he would split with them; watches, TVs, small appliances, and even tee shirts and socks - anything and everything. He had a live-in girlfriend that worked a part-time job at a local hair salon; she didn't make much.

The only reason she stayed with Nicko was that she got all the weed she could smoke. She was rather dependent on it, and to make sure she had a steady supply, she would do what Nicko asked, no matter what it was. Mitchell and Nicko had an arrangement. Mitchell would pay Nicko to watch his apartment to see if anyone would come over when he was gone or if Stacy left the house. When Nicko wasn't home, he would tell his girlfriend to watch for him. Nicko's apartment was directly across Mitchell's, so they had a clear view, which made it easy to keep track of who came and went. Soon after, Mitchell decided to put his covert watch of Stacy to the test.

Mitchell paid a postal worker to do something for him to "test" Stacy. Nicko was told about this little test so that he could watch everything.

The postal worker was to go to his apartment and knock on the door. He knew Stacy wouldn't answer the door, but he had to convince her to do so. The postal worker would say he has a very important package for Mitchell that had to be signed for. Stacy felt that if she didn't sign for it, Mitchell would be angry with her. She knew that he could have a package delivered anywhere he wanted but, the mere fact it had come at home meant that it must be important. After much thought, she decided to open the door to sign for the package. Once she opened the door, the postal worker looked at the box to check the address and said he had made a mistake. The number of the address was right, but it was a street over.

Nicko reported to Mitchell that Stacy had opened the door for the delivery man. Mitchell got home and told her he knew she opened the door for someone; he had already determined her punishment. Wearing only her bra and panties, he made her stand in a corner, facing the wall, with her hands by her side and her nose touching the wall; she was forbidden to speak. If she needed to go to the bathroom, she was told to hold up her left hand. She stayed in that position for five hours until it was time to go to bed. Mitchell made her sleep on the floor next to his bed without a pillow or any covers. Stacy was relieved that nothing else happened when he left that morning, but she couldn't figure out how Mitchell knew she had opened the door.

A month after this, Mitchell decided to test her again. He hired one of his pimp friend's brother to pose as a friend of Christy's. Here's how they did it: He knocked on her door one morning, several times. Obviously, they didn't get a response from Stacy, despite the fact she was standing right behind the door. Stacy was panicking, just how she always did whenever someone came over when Mitchell wasn't home. After several more knocks, he said, *"Stacy, this is Terrell. I know you don't know me, and I hate to bother you like this, but Christy sent me here; she needs your help."* That immediately caught Stacy's attention. Christy was her only friend; she had not heard from her in a long time; what help could she possibly need? Was she in trouble? She knew that it must be of utmost importance if she couldn't come herself. Stacy was scared and didn't really know what to do. All she could think about was the last time she opened the door without Mitchell's permission - her body was sore for a week.

On the one hand, she would do anything to help her friend. On the other, she knew if Mitchell found out, she would be in big trouble. All this time, Terrell kept knocking on the door, saying Christy really needed her help. Stacy decided that Christy had done so much for her that she would help her friend and just hoped that Mitchell never found out.

Stacy said, *"Just a minute,"* as she mustered the nerve to open the door. She opened a door a few inches to peek through and asked what the problem with Christy was.

Terrell told her that Christy had gotten into a bad accident and that she wanted to see Stacy in case she didn't make it; she sent him since he worked with her. Stacy didn't need to hear anything else. She just knew she had to see her friend. Terrell told her that he had a car and would take her to see Christy. Stacy agreed to go but strictly told him that her husband couldn't find out about this. *"If he knew I left this apartment, I would be in serious trouble,"* Terrell reassured her, saying he had no clue who her husband was. Stacy asked if he could give her a minute so she could gather her things before they left. While she did that, Terrell made a phone call.

They got in his car and drove her to the nearest hospital, explaining the accident along the way. Once they arrived, he parked in the visitor's parking lot and told Stacy to wait while he made a call to confirm the visiting hours. Stacy sat patiently as he finished his conversation, paying no attention as to what was being said. With Stacy completely lost in her thoughts, her door suddenly swung open; it was Mitchell. Stacy froze with fear like a deer in the headlights. Her eyes grew big, and her heart started pounding. She kept rambling, *"Mitchell, I'm sorry. I'm sorry. Please, Mitchell. It will never happen again. I promise. Please, Mitchell. Please."* Mitchell looked toward Terrell and said, *"Terrell, take this piece of trash home. I'll deal with her later."* Terrell smirked as he said, "Sure, boss. Anything you say." Stacy had a panic attack on her way back to the apartment, *"What have you done to me?"* she screamed at Terrell. *"It's not what I did,"* he laughed, *"It's what you did. What can I say? I needed the money."*

Stacy did the best she could to look good for Mitchell, hoping that would distract his attention. It was one thing to open the door, but to get in the car with a stranger and go somewhere? When Mitchell got home, Stacy tried her best to put on a smile, trying to hide her real feelings. Mitchell glared at her and said, *"You're in deep trouble."*

He continued, *"I'm going to take a shower, don't you move from that couch."* He had punished her before on multiple occasions, but this was not her getting out of line - this was very serious. Tears started running down her face as she wrung her hands and couldn't keep still. Her mind became clouded with all the possible things Mitchell would do to her; she knew Mitchell would make sure she paid dearly for her mistake. It didn't take long for Mitchell to come out of the bathroom. He was wearing only a robe. Mitchell looked at her and said, *"You had the audacity to defy MY orders? Perhaps I've been too soft on you - but I won't make that mistake again."* "Mitchell, please-" Stacy whimpered. Before she could add anything else, Mitchell smacked her across the face. He grabbed her by her hair and said, *"Anything else you got to say, woman?"* Stacy knew it was better to stay quiet.

Mitchell yelled at her and said, *"Get yo' black ass up and find me a pair of scissors."* Stacy immediately got up and fetched a pair of scissors from the kitchen drawer and, with a shaking hand, handed it to him. *"Get out of them damn clothes,"* he added; Stacy stripped bare. *"Now kneel down with your back to me,"* he continued - she did as she was told. Mitchell stepped forward and began cutting her hair off in uneven chunks. Stacy screamed internally with anger, but she knew it best to stay silent. Every time he would cut a patch off, he would throw it in front of her to see; Stacy was horrified; some were short, and some were long. Every time the scissors snipped, he would call her a degrading name, like slut and, well, you get the picture. After he was done, he said, *"My masterpiece,"* while looking at her.

Stacy was completely naked, covered with the hair Mitchell chopped off of her head. To degrade her further, he told her to stand up and dance for him while touching herself all over. Stacy had no clue how to do this but did what she thought he wanted to see. He just laughed at her and continued to call her even more degrading names. He told her that wherever he went in the apartment, she had to follow him; while still dancing and feeling herself. Tears began running down her face as she began to sob softly.

After parading Stacy throughout the apartment, stopping several times to look at her, and calling her a name or two, they finally wound up in the bedroom. He told her to get on all fours and crawl around the bedroom floor until he told her to stop. As he sat on the bed, he continued to mock her. She had crawled so much that she started getting carpet burns on her knees. Finally, after what seemed like hours, he told her to stop. *"Now,"* he said, *"Get in bed in the doggie style position, spread your legs and lay your breasts on the mattress."* Stacy was terrified of what was coming next.

Mitchell reached forward and pulled her close to the bed's edge, ordering her to stay in that position. Stacy couldn't see what Mitchell was doing; all she could do was rely on her hearing. She heard the closet door open and him rustling through some stuff, then it closed. The next minute she felt it - Mitchell whipped her with a belt, right across her butt cheek. She couldn't help but let out a scream.

"I'll let you get away with that one, but the next time you scream, I'm going to double your punishment," Mitchell added. Another whack on her other cheek. Stacy clenched her teeth in pain. Another, then another, then another as he relentlessly continued and alternated cheeks. Stacy's tears were forming a puddle around her chin, which was resting on the mattress, due to the sheer pain.

"Have you learned your lesson, stupid woman?" Mitchell shouted. *"Yes,"* Stacy whimpered. Mitchell smacked her with the belt again, *"Have you?"* He continued. *"Yes..."* Stacy cried out—another whack. Mitchell repeated this over and over again for another three minutes. Stacy's butt was on fire, and she wished she would just pass out. Her arms, knees, and shoulders were aching. Finally, Mitchell stopped. Stacy was noticeably crying by now, but Mitchell didn't care; he wasn't done yet. He stood behind her and raped her, forcefully and without mercy, all the while laughing. Mitchell made sure it lasted as long as possible. Stacy broke down in embarrassment, humiliation, and pain, but Mitchell continued until he was satisfied. Once he finished, he told her he was going to take another shower and that she had better stayed in that position until he told her to move, or else.

Stacy had pretty much passed out by the time he returned. She prayed that he was done with her. Upon his return, he took his hand, placed it on her hip, pushing her over onto her side. He said, *"If you think that was bad? Defy me again and see what happens. I'm getting ready to leave now, but you better have yourself together; if or when I get back."*

After fifteen minutes, he was gone. With her joints aching and her butt still on fire, she managed to trudge toward the bathroom. When she looked into the mirror, she screamed. Her beautiful hair, which flowed evenly past her shoulders, was now botched throughout her head, all cut in random lengths and angles. She stood there and stared at her reflection until she covered her face with her hands and started crying uncontrollably.

The door had a full-length mirror attached to the back. Composing herself, she closed the door and turned around to see her butt. It was bruised all over, with several parts of the skin torn open. It hurt her emotionally just as much as it hurt her physically; she felt like an abused animal. She filled the bathtub with cool water and, with great difficulty, gently sat down, twitching and aching as the cold water came into contact with her bruises and cuts. Every ounce of energy left her; she was utterly exhausted. Laying back with the water carrying her weight, she couldn't help but doze off. She must've slept for around 15 minutes before the realization struck that Mitchell expected her to be ready - she needed to be prepared for him - not knowing what type of punishment he'd dish out for disobeying him now. Stacy knew it was best not to waste time. She was trapped. Mitchell had broken her spirit; she saw no future for herself - she was his slave for life. On several occasions, she even thought about suicide. The only thing that preserved some sort of sanity was her Bible that Christy had given her as a wedding present. With nothing to do all day, she started reading the Bible and searched for Scriptures that would bring her some comfort in life. She began to pray in earnest that God would find a way to get her out of this life of misery.

CHAPTER TWELVE

Over time, Stacy's life didn't seem to change in the slightest. She felt like she was stuck in limbo. Her life remained this way for five years; the torment and abuse only increased as time went on. After that night, so many years ago, she knew one thing for sure – never go against Mitchell's wishes. Stacy was his slave and his property. Little did she know, however, God had heard her prayers, but not in the way she imagined.

October 6, 2011, was a day Stacy will never forget. In the early hours of the morning, there was a knock on the door, which by now had become a rare occurrence. In fact, ever since Mitchell had taken control of her life, she couldn't remember the last time someone came to see her. Stacy just assumed it was probably a delivery at the wrong address. However, after a few knocks, she heard the man call out her name, asking if she was home. Stacy vividly remembered what happened the last time she opened the door; she didn't want a repeat. Traumatized by what Mitchell would do to her if he found out, she crouched behind the door, hoping whoever this person was would just go away. The man kept calling out her name, pleading her to come to the door. He was aware she was home because he heard her open the door's peephole.

Seeing how Stacy did not respond, the man made a statement so shocking, Stacy went numb. The man claimed to be a homicide detective. He told Stacy that Mitchell had been shot and was pronounced dead a few hours ago. Stacy stood up straight in sheer disbelief; her heart began to race while having trouble breathing.

Stacy took a closer look at this "detective" from the peephole, who was wearing a shabby suit. *"Is this a joke?"* Stacy voiced out, to which he replied, *"I assure you, Stacy, this is no joke,"* and held up his badge in front of the peephole. Stacy could only pray this wasn't another setup. She realized it would have been just too much trouble for Mitchell to get someone pretending to be a cop with a fake badge to match. She decided to take a chance. She carefully unlocked the deadbolt, removed the chain, and opened the door a few inches, just enough to peek out.

The detective smiled at her and showed her his ID again. He told her his name and reassured her that this was, in fact, official business; he needed her help and cooperation in her husband's case. Stacy knew very well that if Mitchell was alive, and she let this man inside, she would have hell to pay. On the other hand, if whatever the detective was saying was true, she needed to know. *"Are you sure he's dead?"* Stacy asked with her voice, still shaking. *"100% sure,"* he replied. Stacy was hesitant, but she had no other option. She slowly opened the door completely and let the detective inside.

The detective sat on the couch and took out a writing pad and a pen. He reassured her once again that he was, in fact, here to help her. Stacy reluctantly gave the officer information about herself and Mitchell. The more she saw him write, the more confident she felt. *"Is Mitchell really dead?"* she thought to herself. The detective told her that they were still trying to piece together information, but from the preliminary report, it seemed like Mitchell got into a disagreement with another person. According to eyewitness reports at the scene, the two started from a simple conversation, which progressed to yelling, which eventually led to Mitchell punching the man in the face, breaking his nose. However, when Mitchell went in to continue his assault, the man pulled out a

9mm handgun and shot Mitchell six times in the chest. The man got up and ran but was later arrested based on the eyewitness reports.

The police gathered statements from the witnesses who testified against the man who killed Mitchell. The police had some idea as to why this happened, but they hoped Stacy could fill in some blanks for them. Stacy tried to regain her composure as best she could. She took a deep breath and began talking, keeping her head down and avoiding eye contact. Stacy spared no detail and told the detective everything – including how Mitchell treated her. She told him how she barely saw Mitchell on a daily basis. He would either come home very late at night to sleep; only to leave early in the morning, or come home whenever he felt the need to sexually abuse her—staying on occasions. Stacy even told him how Mitchell would set her up. However, she admitted to the detective that she knew nothing about what he did or where he went.

After collecting as much information as possible, the detective thanked Stacy for her help, gave her his card, and told her to contact him if she could remember anything else. Before the detective left, he stated that she would need to come down to the city morgue to identify the body as a formality. Being his wife, she would also have to make the funeral arrangements. After the detective left, Stacy locked up and laid down on the bed. She tried her best to come to terms with this reality. Did this really happen? On the one hand, she relished her opportunity to be free from Mitchell's mental and physical torture. On the other hand, she had been dependent on him for so long; she doubted her ability to survive on her own.

As days went by, Stacy barricaded herself in the apartment, barely eating or sleeping, just trying to make sense of what happened to Mitchell and what her future holds. Three days after the murder, the detective paid her another visit. He was compassionate and understanding of her situation but was stern with his request that she come downtown to view and confirm the body. He even offered to give her a ride to and from the morgue. Stacy knew she had to do this, sooner or later, and asked the detective if he would pick her up the next morning at 9 AM. He agreed immediately and thanked Stacy for her courage – knowing what she's been through.

CHAPTER THIRTEEN

The following day, the detective arrived on time and took her to the morgue. Stacy was overwhelmed by all of this. At the back of her mind, she still couldn't believe it—could Mitchell actually be dead? Eventually, they made their way over to the freezers where they kept the bodies. The attendant slid open one of them, which eliminated any and all doubts Stacy had; Mitchell's pale, lifeless body lie comatose on the cold metal slab. The years of torment done by Mitchell had eliminated any feelings of affections Stacy had toward him. She elicits no response when she saw the body. She identified it was him, filled out some paperwork, and was escorted back home. On her way back, she realized that since she was legally his wife and was responsible for his burial, how would she pay for that?

When Stacy returned back to the apartment, she immediately felt trapped and claustrophobic because she spent a few hours outside – something she hadn't done in a long time. Stacy was uncertain of what the future held, but she knew one thing for sure; she couldn't stay in that apartment, especially since she couldn't afford the rent herself. She gathered all her belongings and decided to leave. Stacy knew that becoming homeless was definitely a possibility. One thing was sure, though. She wouldn't go back home to Vicky.

Although she didn't have much, to begin with, she packed whatever she had neatly into a suitcase. Stacy also took Mitchell's belongings and decided to donate them to the local Salvation Army store. She rummaged through his belongings and eventually found the landlord's contact. She told him about the whole situation and that she was going to move out. The landlord was already informed about the entire situation by the police. He readily agreed to hand her the full $600 security deposit, with the understanding that Stacy would move out within the week. Wasting no time, she went and collected it the very same day.

Stacy also recalled all the money she gave to Christy for safekeeping. Even though it had been over five years, she knew Christy would give it to her. There was just one problem; she had no idea where Christy could be. Stacy also knew she had to find a job. Her first option was to try the diner where she worked all those years ago. To her surprise, not only did the restaurant have the same manager, but he also recognized her right away. He was aware of her husband's death. Stacy asked for the money she made him save separately, which had amounted to nearly $600; he promptly gave it to her. As much as she'd like to work there again, they were working at full capacity and couldn't hire her. Stacy thanked him for all of his kindness, gave him a big hug, then left.

While at home, Stacy prayed every chance she got. She pondered her future and came up with a plan. Stacy searched through the phonebook and found a local church not too far from her. Since Mitchell kept her cut-off from the outside world, she couldn't call as the phone was still disconnected. Stacy decided to ask the Church for help. The next day, she fixed herself up as best she could and made her way to the Church. As if by divine intervention, she happened to find the Pastor in his office. He warmly invited her inside and asked how he could be of service. Stacy bluntly explained her situation to him, about everything that happened between Mitchell and her. She eventually came to the point that she lacked the funds for a proper burial.

The pastor knew she wasn't a member of his Church but felt compassionate toward her for being so straightforward and honest. He asked her how much money she could come up with toward the expense of the burial. Stacy told him that all she had was $1200. The pastor asked Stacy to give him a day to think about the situation and asked her to come back tomorrow around the same time – she agreed. Back at home, she had very little appetite and couldn't focus on anything. Stacy clung to her faith so she would stop feeling so lost and confused; the only comfort she found was in the Bible. Stacy managed to read it from Genesis to Revelation but couldn't understand a lot of things she read. She read the Bible until she dozed off to sleep.

The next morning, Stacy met the pastor in his office, as promised. The pastor had come up with a plan. He asked Stacy to give as much money as she could afford to, and for the remainder, he would appeal to his congregation to cover the rest. After giving it much thought, she gave $1000 to the pastor and kept $200 for herself; not trusting anyone, she kept her money with her at all times.

The local funeral home's owner was a member of his Church and agreed to work with him. The pastor did mention that there would be no wake, no funeral program, or any special amenities, to which Stacy agreed – she just wanted to get it over with as soon as possible. After the pastor took the necessary information for the body to be released, he asked her for an address where he could mail a burial certificate to her. Stacy couldn't help but tear up by this pastor's kindness. He only knew her for a day but was willing to do so much for her. The pastor offered her a word of prayer, gave her a Christian hug, and sent her on her way. Not only would Stacy never see the pastor or set foot in that church ever again, no member of Mitchell's family ever reached out to inquire about what happened to him.

CHAPTER FOURTEEN

The morning after her visit to the Church, Stacy was awakened by a loud and continuous knock on the door. She couldn't imagine who it could be and was hesitant to open the door. The knocking didn't stop, so she got dressed and crept toward the door, gently opening the lid on the peephole to see who it was. To her surprise, it was Christy! Stacy swung the door open and burst into tears; she hugged her tightly, refusing to let go, with streams of joy running down her face.

Stacy pulled her into the apartment, trying her best to collect herself until she could manage to speak. Christy couldn't stop smiling; she was just as happy to see her friend. It was up to Christy to calm her down since Stacy couldn't stop crying. Christy sat her down and told her she knew everything about her situation, and that was why she was here. The only reason she couldn't keep in contact with her was that soon after Stacy quit, she did as well and moved to a small town on the south side of Chicago.

Christy was working for an insurance agency now and took a few days off work to invite Stacy to stay with her. Once again, Stacy's prayers were answered. She was so taken back by her generosity and kindness that the only way she could express it was with a massive hug! Despite her still crying her eyes out, she kept nodding her head, meaning yes. Since Stacy had already packed a suitcase, she only had to gather a few more things and was ready to go. She did one final sweep of the house to see if she missed anything, then got ready to leave with Christy.

On her way out, she took one last look around the apartment, reminiscing how she went from being so happy when she first moved in to how it progressed into all the years of torture and torment. She took a deep sigh and walked outside. Stacy put her suitcase in the trunk of Christy's car and excitedly got into the front seat. She asked Christy for her phone and pulled out a small notebook in which she had written down the landlord's number. Stacy called him and told him that she had moved out and left the keys on the coffee table. She thanked him again for being so understanding of her situation and for returning the deposit.

On the way back to Chicago, Christy told Stacy that she had friends who knew all about Mitchell and his "business." That was how she found out about his death. However, she respected Stacy's privacy as his wife and didn't feel like it was her business to meddle in their affairs. Christy's friends told her how Mitchell accumulated a lot of money in such a short amount of time through the business he ran. Ultimately, no one had any idea where the money could be or if there was any left. At this point, Stacy felt stupid for not knowing any of this, even though it was happening right under her nose. She thought she should have confronted Mitchell, but knowing his temper, perhaps it was best that she didn't know.

As Christy continued to explain, Stacy took it all in, word for word, and was left speechless. After Christy was done, the rest of the drive to Chicago was rather somber for Stacy. She tried to wrap her head around everything Christy had told her. For the life of her, she couldn't understand why Vicky and Mitchell had treated her the way they did, and now this? Why did God allow her to go through this? Christy understood it was best to just stay quiet for now. She turned on the radio so the music would help mellow out the tense atmosphere inside the car. So far, the only thing certain in Stacy's life was that she would never forgive Mitchell and Vicky for everything they put her through.

Christy had rented a two-bedroom apartment on the second floor, in the town of Hyde Park, an area considered the heart of Chicago. Over the next few days, as Stacy got settled in, she began to get more comfortable – her life really was changing, but it would still take time to recover her low self-esteem. Stacy didn't want to be a burden on Christy and wanted to carry her own weight. After around a month of getting settled in Chicago, Christy helped Stacy with a resume, using her address and cell phone as a point of contact. It wasn't much, but they did their best to make it look as professional as possible, even with the lack of work experience.

Stacy's clothes weren't the best; they couldn't be used in a professional setting. With the little money she had, along with the cash Christy was holding on for her all this time, they went to a pre-owned clothes store and spent hours putting together outfits that would be appropriate for work. When she went to pay for her stuff, the bill totaled to an amount she simply could not afford. Stacy apologized to the cashier and thoughtfully began to remove clothes from her trolley, thinking long and hard about each article of clothing before she would set it aside. Fortunately for her, the cashier had observed Stacy when she walked in and couldn't help but notice her kind, soft disposition and character. Wanting to help, the cashier told her she was eligible for a volume discount because of the sheer number of clothes she was buying and brought down the total to the amount of money she saw Stacy carrying in her hand. The cashier's kindness touched Stacy so much that she reached over the counter and gave her a big hug. As it turned out, this would be the last time she would see the cashier. The shop closed a few weeks later, and that's when she realized she never even asked her name.

Stacy soon found out that life in Chicago was of a much faster pace than she was used to. Everyone seemed to be in a hurry to get somewhere. If she wanted to fit in, she had to adapt accordingly. Every morning when Christy would get up for work, Stacy would as well. They would both have breakfast together, get dressed, and head out. Walking from business to business, Stacy dropping her resume at every business she came across. She wore the same outfit every day, saving the others for when she did find a job. Not having a computer of her own to search for employment was a challenge, but Stacy didn't let it stop her. She would only use Christy's computer when absolutely necessary. Even though she lacked confidence and had low self-esteem due to her upbringing and marriage, what she did have going for her was her beauty, determination, and a genuine, soft spirit that others took note of.

After three weeks of pounding the pavement and covering all the local businesses from the area, she didn't get one response, which discouraged her further. Christy kept pushing Stacy so she wouldn't give up; she encouraged her for the best and reassured her that she wasn't a burden to her in any way. Christy was a true friend to Stacy, who only had her best interest at heart and was willing to do whatever it took so she could eventually lead a normal, healthy life. They wound up spending Christmas and the New Year of 2006 together, enjoying each other's company.

CHAPTER FIFTEEN

After three more weeks, Stacy's luck finally began to change for the better. Christy got a call while she was at work; not recognizing the number, she let it go to voicemail. When she checked it during her break, she couldn't wait to get home to let Stacy listen to it. As soon as she got home, she sat Stacy down and said, *"I want you to listen to this!"* She then handed her phone over to her with the voicemail playing. To Stacy's surprise, it was from a bank. The voicemail stated that there was a teller position open and to contact the branch manager if she was still interested.

Stacy was ecstatic! Not only was it from a bank, but it was only three blocks from where she lived; a bank! Never in her wildest dreams did she think she would get a call from a bank. That night, Stacy fell on her knees and thanked God, with a truly grateful heart, for coming to her aide in her time of need. Even though it hadn't crossed her mind in a while, Stacy never forgot that God promised never to leave nor forsake her. She prayed all night that she would get the job so she could finally start a new chapter in her life. Christy left her phone with Stacy the next day, and after calling and stating her interest in the position, her interview was scheduled for 10 AM on the coming Wednesday.

The night before her interview, Stacy could barely sleep. She was up all night, tossing and turning. As nervous and scared as she was, she was just as excited to be going to her first interview after so many years. She got up early and tried her best to make herself look as "professional" as possible. After getting the seal of approval from Christy, and one last scan in front of the mirror, she headed out the door.

She arrived at the bank by 9:45 AM. Upon entering, she told the receptionist that she was there for an interview. The receptionist escorted her to the manager's office, and Stacy was told that she would be there shortly. A little while after, the branch manager came in and greeted her. After the initial introductions were exchanged, the interview began. Stacy was honest and very frank during the entirety of the interview, answering every question truthfully. The branch manager, Mrs. Rene Rogers, was very impressed by her demeanor, but more importantly, her honesty. After about half-an-hour, the interview was over. Mrs. Rogers thanked Stacy for coming and told her that she would make a final decision in a few days. Although Stacy was nervous, she felt she held her own, and, on the way out, she said a small prayer in hopes of landing the job.

On her walk back, Stacy couldn't help but think how better her life would be working at the bank; it would do wonders for her self-esteem and her general outlook toward life. Thursday and Friday came and went, but no word from the bank. Stacy felt that if she didn't hear anything from the bank before the weekend, they would have undoubtedly chosen someone else for the position. The weekend passed with no word from the bank.

Come Monday morning, she went out and bought a newspaper to go through the classifieds. She spent the remainder of the day noting down possible places she could apply for and decided that tomorrow she would go out and hand over her resume at every place she listed. However, God had other plans for her. By 6:30 PM, when Christy got home from work, she excitedly handed over her phone to Stacy with a big grin on her face, *"you have got to listen to this!"* Christy played the voicemail on speaker, which said, *"Hello, Stacy, I'm calling on behalf of the bank to let you know that you have passed your interview and gotten the job! Congratulations! You start on Wednesday... report by 8:30 AM."*

Both Stacy and Christy couldn't control their excitement; they screamed and jumped for joy – it was hard to tell who was happier! Christy took Stacy out to a restaurant nearby to celebrate. Before going to bed that night, Stacy fell on her knees and thanked God for looking after her. Finally, things were beginning to look up for her.

Stacy made sure she was right on time on Wednesday, despite it having snowed a little the night before. When she arrived at the bank, the manager was already there. She took her to her office and told Stacy certain things that reassured Stacy that this job was made possible with the help of God. The manager told her she wasn't really qualified to get the job in the first place. But, she was so impressed by her honesty, integrity, and her looks, she felt she would be a good image for the bank. She also felt that Stacy was a bright young woman who would quickly learn the ropes. Stacy began her training under the supervision of Rose Bryant, who was the teller supervisor.

In the beginning, it was somewhat difficult for Stacy to grasp some of the procedures, but Rose was very patient with her and assisted her whenever she needed it. Stacy felt more confident in herself because she was allowed to handle transactions all by herself after only a month of training. All of the customers seemed to like her, but she felt that most of her coworkers, if not all, didn't really care about her, except for Rose. They were envious of her good looks and her warm attitude toward every customer. It seemed like nearly every male customer who had the luck of having her as their teller had asked her out on a date—even those who were married! Stacy politely declined each one of them; she was not ready for any of that. This, however, did not sit well with her female coworkers, who became jealous. Despite knowing this, Stacy tried her best to get along with them.

There were times when the other tellers would attempt to chastise her for a mistake in front of everyone, but Rose would have none of that; she came to her aid on every occasion. Stacy worked tirelessly, building up her low self-esteem, and it got to the point that she now had some form of confidence in herself. She learned how to communicate with everyone effectively. They accepted her because they worked with her, but that was all. After the 90-day probation period ended for her, she was given a raise. She was thrilled to be making more money now than she had ever before.

CHAPTER SIXTEEN

Stacy and Christy came to an "agreement," which was really more of Christy's plan for Stacy. She refused to accept any money from Stacy and instead gave her the money she was holding on for her. She wanted her to save money so she could improve her wardrobe and work toward buying a car for herself. As much as Stacy tried to help toward the bills and would even sneak in some money in Christy's purse, it seemed like it would always find its way back into her life. Stacy felt as if she was sponging off of Christy but could do little about it. Christy happened to enjoy helping out Stacy; she thought of her as a little sister. Reluctantly, Stacy accepted Christy's plan and opened up a savings account at the bank where she worked.

Bank employees were offered a considerable discount for having their cellphone service provided by a certain carrier through the bank. Stacy reasoned, now that she had a full-time job, a cell phone was necessary for multiple reasons. She went through the necessary procedures, and within a week, she had a phone. It wasn't anything fancy, a simple flipphone, but Stacy didn't mind – she just needed to make and receive calls anyway. These little steps toward independence only made her feel better. Stacy set out certain goals for herself to keep her motivated. With the phone done, the next was improving her wardrobe, and the car followed right after. Eventually, she planned to go to college and get a higher education. Stacy knew this would take time; she needed to be patient.

Gradually, things improved for her. After three years, things seemed to be going her way. All throughout those years, Stacy worked on restoring the emotional damage Mitchell had done to her. She never told Christy about the emotional or physical pain he inflicted on her. Stacy never planned on forgiving Mitchell.

On many occasions, Stacy felt lonely. Often times, the thought of her contacting her family passed her mind, but then she would quickly remember how they treated her, and those feelings would quickly dissolve. With her scars reminding her of her marriage, Stacy was in no hurry to date and kept herself busy in her job, with the housework and studying every chance she got, especially the Bible. There were times when she was able to save nearly her entire paycheck.

After working for a year and a half, Stacy finally convinced Christy that she should pay her share of the rent, food, and utilities. It took some convincing, but Christy reluctantly agreed. Not having to pay for these amenities allowed her to save up a great deal of money, which she did as a Certificate of Deposit. Stacy sent a $10,000 check to the Church that buried Mitchell. As grateful as she was for the pastor's generosity, she felt it necessary to pay back her dues. By now, Stacy felt it essential for her to have her own car; she couldn't rely on Christy all her life and wanted to expand her horizons.

Stacy discussed her intentions of buying a car with Christy. For their convenience, they agreed to only look at cars in the neighborhood. After scouting through Craigslist and various other classifieds, they found a very nice 2000 Chevrolet Camaro convertible, in a beautiful white, glossy finish. They called to make sure it was still available, which it was. They scheduled to see it the next day. The car happened to be a high school graduation gift to the son from his parents. The son had recently graduated from college and was offered a job out of state, which included a new car as a part of his contract.

The Camaro was in immaculate condition. It was never involved in any accidents and had all the service records to prove how well maintained it was. Stacy hadn't been behind the wheel since she got her license in high school. She was nervous about taking her car out for a test drive, but she found the necessary courage with Christy by her side. Surprisingly, neither of the parents accompanied them on the test drive.

Christy faced a lot of trouble with her first car and knew just how vital it was to make sure everything worked before they bought it. She scrutinized every minute detail, inspecting the heat, air conditioning, windows, radio, wipers, and the convertible top as well. To her surprise, everything was immaculate, as if it rolled out the factory just this morning. Both of them knew the $8000 asking price was well below the car's actual value; Stacy could easily afford it. She took the car back to its owner and gave him $500 to hold, saying she would return with the balance via check tomorrow.

Needless to say, Stacy didn't get much sleep that night; she was finally getting her own car! She could now venture out on her own and explore; she wasn't restricted to Christy's schedule, even though she didn't mind. It was now time for her to finally develop some form of independence. By around 11 AM the following morning, Stacy was now the proud owner of her very first car! The car might not have been "new" per se, but it was absolutely perfect for Stacy. Stacy was careful and cautious on her way back home. One thing about Hyde Park was that parking was a premium; you parked where and when you could. This wouldn't stop her, though.

After work on Monday, she went to the local currency exchange to buy plates, stickers and transferred the title of the car to her name. Once that was done, she visited a local car insurance agency and paid for a year of full coverage, premium insurance on her car. After that was done, she went to a mechanic recommended by Christy and left the car there for a day so he could fix anything that could be faulty or broken. Fortunately for Stacy, the repairs that the car needed were minor; an oil change, a new timing belt, brake pads, and rotors. Other than that, the car was a gem that would last Stacy for years to come. The mechanic emphasized how lucky Stacy was to find a car in such great condition. Stacy couldn't help but feel proud – she negotiated and managed to find such a magnificent piece of machinery!

The sense of ownership made Stacy feel proud; finally, she had some control of her life. Despite not being entirely on her own, she took a big step toward it. Thinking about the troubles she faced throughout her life, Stacy couldn't help but sob the entire drive back home. The next day, still beaming with excitement, she decided to drive her car to work to show her coworkers. Even though she knew that most of them would become even more envious of her, she could only hope that a few of them would be happy for her, and maybe, just maybe, having her own mode of transportation would lead to her being invited to some of the company events.

CHAPTER SEVENTEEN

Stacy arrived at work early the next morning, making sure she was the first one there so that everyone else would see her car parked in the front of the lot. However, she wasn't the first to arrive. The other car in the lot belonged to the security guard, who was standing in front of it. She hadn't seen that car before, which meant this was a new guard. As she parked a few spaces over, he smiled, knotted, and watched. Although he was a more mature man, he seemed to be friendly enough and was still rather handsome, in her opinion.

According to the bank's procedures, one employee would open the bank; escorted by a guard, and shut down the overnight security system. The other bank employee, which was Stacy in this case, waited in her car till the guard did a complete sweep of the premises. Usually, the guard would signal from the doors to indicate it was all-clear. However, this guard did something different, something no other guard had done before. When he guaranteed that the bank was secure, he actually walked up to her car to escort her inside. His small gesture of chivalry made Stacy feel special. The guard introduced himself; his name was Stan Wallace.

There were two sets of doors to enter the bank. Stan opened both of them for her with a smile. No one had respected or treated Stacy with such caring and subtle gestures before. For a complete stranger to be doing this was something she took note of. Outside of exchanging pleasantries, they had no further conversation. Stacy hoped this would be the beginning of a good day. Unfortunately, that wasn't the case.

Since all of the other employees knew each other's cars, they assumed the new car in the lot was Stacy's. When they asked her to confirm their suspicions, they decided to slyly berate her rather than be happy for her. The remarks ranged from, *"So, I guess now you think you're better than us."* To *"Why do YOU need a car? You don't even go anywhere."* To even, *"If you're trying to impress us, don't bother; it ain't working."*

Stacy didn't try to defend herself; what was she supposed to say anyway? They already made up their minds. Their remarks echoed in her mind throughout the day and bothered her so much that she actually went to the restroom a few times to compose herself so she didn't burst into tears in front of them. Stacy couldn't understand why it was so difficult for them to accept her. All her efforts were in vain.

There were times when she'd bring in donuts for everyone or buy thoughtful cards for special occasions like birthdays and anniversaries. Stacy understood she was envied for her intelligence and looks, but this was something she couldn't change.

As she left work that day, Stan escorted her to the car once again. As he opened the car for her to get in, Stan spoke out, *"Stacy, from the look on your face, it seems like you're rather upset. I've heard things; don't let their problems become yours. You have a wonderful car – if that makes you happy, then that's all that matters."* Stacy couldn't help but smile at his thoughtful words. As he closed her door, he continued, *"By the way, in case you didn't know, most people address me as Officer Wallace, but you can call me Stan. Enjoy the rest of your day."* Stan went back and stood at the bank's door and waited until Stacy left before he went inside. This made her feel a little better.

As time went on, Stacy tried to cope with the situation as best she could. She continued to seek God for answers. She and Christy would have many discussions concerning her problem. However, Christy would tell her the same thing as Stan did; basically, sometimes, *"life is not fair."* There are situations in life that you must deal with in order to build a positive character. It is vital not to confront everything on an emotional level. Christy further explained that if she allowed others to dictate her emotions and kept herself occupied by trying to figure out 'why,' she would never be able to live her own life.

Stacy took Christy's advice to heart; she was her best friend; she knew she would never steer her in the wrong direction. Stacy found peace and comfort in many of the Bible's verses, which she began to read every day before work. On the days where her coworkers would treat her unfairly, she recalled the Bible verses she read, which brought her solace. Apart from the Bible, she did experience a new source of strength; Stan.

Stan was a tall, light-skinned brother who was about twelve years older than Stacy. He was a handsome and lean-built gentleman with the intelligence to match. He kept in shape and had an air of confidence in his stride, which made heads turn.

Stan's professional demeanor was due to the fact he was once a successful businessman himself. Unfortunately, his partner scammed him and took off with the money. He was able to recover from that financial blow and resume an earnest living, but he was no longer willing to put in the time to make it what it once was. Stan married his childhood sweetheart shortly after graduating from high school. He somehow felt that, with the time he spent building and maintaining his business, he inadvertently contributed to the loss of his marriage.

Through the divorce, he acquires sole custody of his two children, who had, by now, both graduated from high school and moved on with their lives. They were attending college in California and were temporarily staying with their mother. Shortly after they moved out, Stan sold the house and moved into a comfortable apartment. Stan sold his house to not only help finance his children's education, but he planned on putting the additional income, from his job in security, toward his invention—which he planned to sell online. He received many positively reinforcing compliments from his peers, which only encouraged him to pursue it.

He took an interest in Stacy and helped her out by giving her advice whenever possible. However, he had to be very careful in the way he interacted with the employees due to company policy – but he did the best he could (whenever he could) when it came to Stacy.

CHAPTER EIGHTEEN

Although Stacy had days where things worked out relatively normal, she never quite knew what the next day would bring. For Stacy, work was much more bearable thanks to Stan. He seemed to genuinely care about her feelings and had come to her aid, in a professional manner, on several occasions when Stacy's workmates belittled her. On the first day of work, Stacy was told that fraternizing with the employees, including security, was strictly forbidden. The security guard was to never get involved with bank employees in any way whatsoever.

What impressed Stacy the most was that Stan seemed to ignore these rules when it came to doing the right thing; that always came first. The bank management respected him, and this allowed him to get away with several things other guards couldn't. This was due to his keen attention to detail, his professional approach to his work, and most importantly, he managed to point out several administrative and security flaws that the bank improved on, helping them in their daily procedures.

Stan was very tactful in his approach, so he didn't cause confusion nor draw attention to himself or others. Stacy couldn't quite put her finger on when, or how, it happened, but she began to look at Stan as something more than the bank's security guard. As much as she tried to contain her emotions, she began to look at him as more than a protector. Although strictly forbidden, there had been times where Stan would sneak in a compliment, whether it be her dress, her smile, or her new hairstyle. Stan was the sole reason Stacy's job was much more toler-able. Of course, Christy knew all about him.

On Thursday afternoon, Stan's training would be put to the test. A young man came in and stopped at the customer service desk, which had a few pens, deposit and withdrawal slips. The man stood there for a moment, scanning the premises. He immediately caught Stan's atten-tion because he wasn't a regular customer. Without filling out any form, he went proceeded through the line and waited for the next available teller. Eventually, he approached Stacy's counter. She asked her how she could help, to which he pulled out a check from his back pocket and handed it to her.

During this time, Stan had slowly worked his way toward the counter to be able to hear what was going on but kept far enough to not make the customer uncomfortable.

Stacy took the check and asked him if he was a client of the bank, to which he stated that he wasn't. She advised him that, in order to cash the check, he would need two pieces of identification. The young man pulled out his wallet and handed her only a driver's license. When she asked for a second form of ID, the license was all he had. Stacy in-formed him that bank policy would prevent her from cashing his check without two forms of proper ID. That did not sit well with the young man. He began to create a scene. He loudly called the bank's policy into question, demanding his rights as a black man, and started questioning Stacy's ability as a competent teller or a woman in general. He insisted that the bank find a way to cash his check because he desperately needed the money.

When Stacy told him again that it could not be cashed without proper ID, his demeanor and character worsened, becoming audible to the entire bank. Stan approached the young man and politely said, *"Sir, I can understand your frustration, but the teller doesn't make the rules.*

However, your actions are not only disrespectful to the teller, but you are creating a disturbance within the bank. Since you cannot produce a second ID to get your check cashed, I believe your business in the bank has been concluded." Stan walked over to Stacy's station and asked her for the check the man gave her, which she returned. Stan handed it back to the man and stated, *"We have two exits, Sir. One to your left and the other to your right. Have a nice day."* After that, Stan stepped back a few feet.

The young man was still furious. Without saying a word, he took a bold step toward Stan. Immediately Stan took a step back while his right hand went to the top of his holster as he said, *"Sir, you don't want to do what you think you want to do; you will lose, and you will regret it. I suggest you exit the bank."* A brief stare down began. Stan stood firm as he breathed normally and stared into the young man's eyes with unflinching conviction. The young man realized Stan was serious and that he had made a grave mistake. His continence changed from anger to concern for his safety. He looked around. Everyone was staring at him. He felt embarrassed but tried his best not to show it. He mumbled an apology as he slowly headed for the back door.

Stan followed him at a safe distance, his hand still on the holster. Stan watched the young man get in his car and drive off. When Stan came back in, the whole bank was talking about what had just happened. Stan calmly walked over to his podium and began writing out an incident report after calling in for a case number. The branch manager walked over to Stan and thanked him for his professionalism in defusing a potentially explosive situation. Stan simply smiled, nodded, and said, *"You're welcome."* He turned to Stacy, gave a smile and a wink, and continued writing his report. Stacy smiled and thought, *"My hero."*

CHAPTER NINETEEN

A week after this incident, as Stacy made her way to work, it began to snow lightly, which kept piling on the entire day. By the time she finished her shift, there was around 3 to 4 inches of snow. She didn't look forward to removing the snow off her buried car, but, then again, she had no other choice. On her way out the door, Stan was right behind her. This wasn't anything new, since he walked all the employees to their car. However, this time it was different. As they walked toward Stacy's car, he asked her if she had a brush for the snow and a scraper to remove the ice. When she told him she did, he politely asked her to hand them to him and suggested she get in the car and start it up so she could get warm. This simple, caring gesture touched Stacy. She couldn't help but swoon over him.

Although it took a few minutes, he managed to clear out all of the snow and ice from her car and windows. When he was done, she opened the door, and he placed her brush and scraper on the backseat floor. Stacy sincerely thanked him for his help. Stan took his time to meticulously remove every bit of snow and ice from her car. Stan, being the gentleman that he was, simply replied that it wasn't a big deal and was glad to do it for her. He wished her a good night, close the door, and walked back to the bank, looking behind him all the while to make sure she got out of the parking lot safely.

While Stacy was getting ready for work the next day, she spent a lot of time thinking about the special treatment given to her the day before by Stan. She wondered if Stan had done the same for her coworkers. It didn't take her long to find out. When she got to work, the first thing she heard from several of her coworkers was that Stan had taken the time out to clear the snow and ice off of only two cars, hers and the branch manager. Throughout the day, they would make snide remarks about what went on the day before, but this time something was different.

No matter what they said, her thoughts circled back to why Stan had chosen to clean off only two cars. For the most part, it wasn't hard to understand why he would clean off the branch manager's car. Even though the security service paid Stan, he felt the bank's safety was as important as protecting his family. He made sure to make the branch manager's job as easy as possible and would help above and beyond his line of duty. Even though she and Stan would speak on occasions throughout the day, as he did with the others, she felt special to be the only one, other than the branch manager, to have her car cleaned. Stacy made a mental note to thank him again before the day was complete.

Toward the end of the day, Stacy found Stan posted at the end of one of the teller counters. Since there were no customers in the bank at that time, now was her chance. She slowly walked up to him and, hesitantly, lightly tapped him on the shoulder. When he turned around, she thanked him again for what he had done the day before. Stan couldn't help but smile, wink, and said it was no problem. Stacy had all intentions of walking away and leaving it at that, but for some strange reason, as if some spiritual force had taken control of her mind and body, she could not stop asking if there was something she could do to repay him. She stood frozen in her tracks. Stacy couldn't believe she actually said that. Her heart was now pounding in her chest, and she was very nervous.

She stood there, staring at Stan for what seemed like an eternity. She wished she could just up and walk away, but her feet refused to cooperate. By now, something else dawned on her. This was possibly a breach of company policy. All these thoughts flooded her mind for what seemed like forever, which was just a few seconds in reality.

As he stared right into her eyes, he gave a slight smile and asked if he could think about it. Stacy smiled, nodded in agreement as Stan walked away; she was still frozen in place. Finally, composing herself as she walked away, she looked around to see if anyone had noticed what she did; fortunately, she was safe.

When her day was done, Stan escorted her to her car, opened the door for her, wished her a good night, and said he would see her tomorrow. That entire evening Stacy wondered what made her ask Stan that. She thought about confiding in Christy what had happened earlier with Stan but chose, for now, to keep it to herself. She kept tossing and turning in bed that night, replaying the encounter in her head over and over again. She was proud of herself but, at the same time, scared. She reached the conclusion that the ship had sailed; there was nothing she could do about it now. The following morning, as Stacy was getting ready for work, she had an epiphany; what exactly did Stan think when she said, "Repay him?" That word could imply a lot of things. Stan seemed like a nice enough guy, but how would he take it? Had she opened up an invitation that she might not be capable of or ready to fulfill? If he did suggest something and she said no, where would that leave them? All she knew was that she couldn't take back what she had said. She said a little prayer that whatever the request was, it would be something she was able to do.

Throughout the workday, Stacy was expecting Stan to approach her at any time with his request, but it never happened. He was his usual professional self and, even though they spoke a couple of times throughout the day, he never once indicated he was ready to give her a reply. Stacy couldn't help thinking, *"My God did he look good in that uniform."*

Even though her coworkers continued to take shots at her that day, she was on cloud nine, trying to anticipate what his answer would be. The day passed without a reply, and, as usual, as Stacy left the bank, she was escorted to her car by Stan. After he had opened her door and she was seated, he handed her a small envelope. After she had taken the envelope, he wished her a good night, closed the door, and walked back to the bank, keeping an eye out, as usual, to make sure she left the parking lot safely.

Stacy was too nervous about opening the envelope, so she stuffed it in her purse, buckled up, waved to Stan, and took off. Her entire drive home was focused on what could possibly be inside that envelope. When she got home, she went straight to her room, closed the door, pulled out the envelope, sat on her bed, and just stared at it. Her heart was going to jump out of her chest. She didn't know what to do. Finally, she decided to open the envelope just before she went to bed and sleep on whatever it said. After she had eaten, talked with Christy for a little while, Stacy got ready for bed. She sat down and, with mixed emotions, she slowly began to open the envelope. Inside was the branch manager's business card. On the back of the card, it simply *said, "will you have dinner with me?"* Stacy breathed out a sigh of relief. A big smile crossed her face as she answered, "yes" out loud. This was something she could do and would look forward to doing. She put the card back in the envelope and put it under her pillow. She fell asleep, wearing a huge smile across her face.

CHAPTER TWENTY

The following morning on her way to work, Stacy wondered what would be the best way to answer Stan's note. She could either wait for the opportunity and say yes or write yes on the card and hand it to him. Either way, she wanted to make sure she answered him as soon as possible. After much thought, she decided it would be best to answer him by writing it on the card, handing it back to him as he did for her. She also felt this was the best way to keep others from eavesdropping on her.

Stacy's working hours had changed, so by the time she came in, Stan would already be at his post. She was confident that the opportunity to slip him the card would arise during the course of the day. As subtle as Stacy was trying to be, what she *really* wanted to do was shout *"YES!"* across the bank to him; sadly, for her, this was not reality. Stacy could only hope her simple gesture would also bring forth her enthusiasm along with it.

Stacy kept the small envelope with the card in her pocket, so she would be ready when the time was right. The opportunity arrived at lunch break. As she headed toward the lunchroom, Stan happened to be close by and opened the door for her. Stacy assessed the situation and thought this would be the ideal time to hand him the card. She quickly reached inside her pocket, pulled out the small envelope, and gave it to him with a smile. Stan smiled, nodded, and closed the door; but kept himself reserved. Stacy knew Stan wouldn't elicit much of a response because of how tactful and professional he was. She knew he would find a way for the two of them to communicate to plan for the dinner. Stacy couldn't help but feel giddy for the remainder of the day; she wasn't going to let anyone ruin that no matter what.

Stacy suspected that Stan would most likely answer her in the same way; she was right. Just like he always did, Stan escorted her to her car after work. He opened the door for her and closed it once she was seated. As Stacy put the keys in the ignition, he tapped on the window. She rolled the windows down, and he handed her an envelope, wished her a good night, and walked away, wearing a smile on his face. Stacy was overjoyed that he gave a response on the same day. As curious as she was about what Stan had written, she decided to open it at home.

After what seemed like an eternity, Stacy was finally done with her bedtime routine and sat on the edge of the bed, holding the envelope in anticipation. She gently opened it and, just like before, the note was written on the back of the manager's card, *"I have made reservations at the Signature Room for Saturday night at eight o'clock. I hope that works for you. I will pick you up at 7:15; need your address..."* Stacy couldn't help but shriek in joy, which made Christy rush into her room, panicked. Stacy assured her she was ok but felt it was high time she told her about Stan. She told Christy all about him, but not about the arranged date.

It had been a very long time since Stacy had been on a date. She had three days to decide what she was going to wear. However, before she could make that decision, she needed to know what type of place the Signature Room was, so she asked Christy. Christy looked it up online and found out it was a Michelin star restaurant located at the top of the John Hancock building. Christy had a solid hunch about why Stacy would randomly ask her about a fine dining restaurant but thought it best not to pry. She felt if Stacy was ready to tell her, she would.

Stacy started mentally picking out an outfit for her date night, thinking about all her clothes and what combination of them would look best. She couldn't help but wonder, *"What type of outfit would Stan like? Would he like something more reserved? Or something sexy? Would he like pants or a dress? Would he prefer bright colors or dark? Heels or boots? So many options!"* Stacy couldn't help but overthink the situation to the point that she even considered making a list for him to choose from; fortunately, she changed her mind. Stacy knew he was a professional and straightforward person; her first impression counted.

Not wanting to disappoint Stan, Stacy decided to tell Christy about the date and that she needed her help deciding what to wear. She handed Christy the note Stan gave her to read. As she read through it, her eyes widened, and she wore a massive grin on her face. Then, she proceeded to shriek in joy, matching Stacy's outburst. Christy couldn't help but hug Stacy; she was in sheer joy. Christy was truly happy for her friend.

From what Stacy told about Stan, Christy felt as if he was a good man and would treat her right. However, she couldn't help but think about Stacy's past and her whole debacle with Mitchell. Christy couldn't help but feel proud of Stacy for moving on with her life – everyone needs a chance to love, and she was glad Stacy had come out of her shell; she couldn't be happier for her best friend.

Going through her wardrobe, Christy suggested three different outfits for Stacy to choose from. She helped pick them out but wouldn't pick the one to wear – that decision was left to Stacy. Stacy felt that the three outfits were absolutely fantastic, but she was just indecisive and couldn't make up her mind. After repeatedly looking over each outfit, she picked the one that caught her attention the most. She finalized her choice, said a small prayer of gratitude, and went to bed.

The next day at work, Stacy found an opportunity to give Stan an envelope, which contained a note with her address. The rest of the day at work was fairly routine, with nothing out of the ordinary. Stacy was afraid she couldn't hold in her excitement at work, and her coworkers would guess something was up; however, she somehow managed to maintain her composure.

The three days passed in no time at all – it was finally Saturday. Stacy had already booked an appointment at a salon and got her hair done. She decided to keep her hairstyle the same since it was what Stan was used to seeing her in. After her salon appointment, Stacy used a spa coupon Christy gave her and visited a local spa, where she got a facial, manicure, and pedicure. After she got home at around 5:00 PM, she took a shower and began to get ready; putting on her make-up carefully.

Finally, the time came for her to get dressed. She chose a black and gold, somewhat snug, dress for the occasion. It was around knee-length and matched her calf-length, black boots perfectly. Stacy had even bought herself an elegant winter trench coat for this special occasion. The closer the clock got to 7:15 PM, the more nervous she became.

Right on time, the doorbell rang at 7:15. Christy met Stan at the door, and they both introduced themselves while exchanging pleasantries. Christy took his coat and asked him to take a seat while she went and got Stacy. After a few minutes, Christy came back with Stacy right behind her, looking absolutely stunning. Stan stood up and was grinning ear to ear – admiring her beauty. Neither said a word.

Stacy couldn't help but notice Stan also, who looked dapper in his black, double-breasted suit. He didn't wear the conventional shirt and tie with it but was wearing a gold turtleneck. By pure coincidence, they wore matching colors!

Stacy couldn't help but think this was going to be a splendid evening. As she reached for her coat, Stan walked up to her, put his hand on the coat, and simply asked, *"May I?"* Stacy took a step back and nodded;

with that, he took her coat and stepped behind her as he helped her put it on. As Stan walked back to the coat rack to get his own coat, Stacy shot a quick look at Christy, who smiled and gave her a thumbs-up while mouthing, *"Have fun!"*

CHAPTER TWENTY-ONE

As Stacy and Stan walked toward the car lot, Stacy noticed she couldn't see his car anywhere. Stan clicked the remote, and a car started beeping a few feet away from them. It was a beautiful, gold-colored 2008 STS Cadillac. As he opened the door for her to get in, she noticed it had a striking black interior; it was evident that the car was very well kept. Stan explained he only used this car on special occasions; Stacy couldn't help but blush. She was trying her best to compose herself as best as possible, not to show her excitement. On their drive to the restaurant, they made some small talk, but the only thing Stacy could think of was to be careful not to say too much to give her excitement away.

It seemed like both of them were once married; the only difference was that Stan was divorced – not widowed. He apologized for the loss of her husband. Stacy was grateful for his sentiment but did not let on about his past. As they pulled up to the restaurant, he didn't let her get out, despite the valet opening the door for her. He exited the car and walked toward her side, extending his hand as he helped Stacy out of the car – like a true gentleman.

Stan had already made reservations, a table for two by the window, which overlooked downtown Chicago. From the time they entered the building till the time they were seated at the table, Stan opened every door for her. Stan complimented her on several occasions regarding her beauty and outfit. Stacy couldn't help but smile and blush while she thanked him. As the night continued, Stacy slowly became more comfortable with him. Stacy felt a connection with him; she thought if anything substantial was to come out of this, she needed to be honest with him from the get-go. She told him a lot about her past and most of the things that happened to her.

To her surprise, regardless of what she told him, he took it all in stride, maintaining his calm composure, all the while being very understanding and compassionate. Stan was grateful that Stacy trusted him enough and was comfortable with him to share details about her life like that. Appreciating what she had done, Stan laid out the history of his life in a nutshell for her. He had seen his share of ups and downs but learned from each experience, which ultimately made him a better man.

Stan was smooth, professional, and definitely a ladies' man. Stacy felt like he could probably have any woman he wanted – yet here she was, sitting across from him on a date. After their meal was finished and the date was coming to a close, Stan signaled the waiter for the check. Although Stacy insisted on splitting the bill, Stan simply did not listen. Stan paid via credit card.

When the waiter returned with the receipt, he brought a red rose along with him and handed it to Stacy. She was caught off-guard and asked who it was from. The waiter simply tilted his head toward Stan and smiled as he left. She looked at Stan wearing this huge smile. Stacy couldn't help but feel her heart flutter; she had never felt this way in her life before – even with Mitchell. There wasn't much conversation on their drive back home. Stan could sense her excitement and thought it would be best to give her some quiet time. Arriving home, he helped her out of the car, escorted her to her apartment, and made sure she was safely inside. As she turned around, Stan reached for her hand, raised it to his lips, and gave it a kiss – all the while letting her know he had a wonderful time. With that, he gave her a wink, bid her good night, handed her the rose as he walked back to his car; Stacy watched as he drove off. As she went inside, she just stood still – she was on cloud nine. Before she went to bed, she picked out an encyclopedia from the bookshelf and put the rose in the middle to preserve it.

Try as she might, Stacy simply could not fall asleep that night. She kept replaying the evening over and over again. In spite of her insecurities and her past, Stan made her feel special. She felt cared for and began to contemplate what a relationship with Stan might bring, even though it was just their first date – Stacy craved to be loved. She wanted a man who would hold her hand in public, respect her feelings, help her grow into the type of woman she wanted to be, kiss her with passion from his soul and support her desire to better her career.

She knew she was asking for a lot but only hoped that Stan was capable of fulfilling most, if not all, of her dreams. Stacy couldn't help but wonder just how he felt about her at this point. Stacy's mind began to race with all kinds of thoughts. *"Would he accept her family if they ever met? Where would they live? Does he want children? Would he want her to continue working? Would he allow her to continue her education?"* Besides all of these thoughts, there was one that she tried to avoid thinking about; how was Stan in bed? She had to admit to herself that she was sexually attracted to Stan, although she had been inactive since leaving Fort Wayne. From her experience with her ex-husband, she felt sure that those emotions and feelings were dead.

Although she couldn't quite put her finger on it, Stan had somehow managed to awaken her womanhood and passion. Due to the trauma Mitchell caused her, she never thought about sex, nor was she sexually active. Stacy was never a promiscuous woman and would not allow a man to take advantage of her again. Because of the way Mitchell treated her in bed, she really didn't know if she could satisfy a man anymore.

However, in spite of all those negative thoughts, her body couldn't help but respond to the idea of Stan making love to her. As if controlled by another force, Stacy suddenly realized her hands were caressing her body, and she was squirming in bed. Suddenly realizing what she was doing, she sat straight up and thought, *"Stop it, Stacy! What are you doing?!"* She decided to take a nice, cold shower to get herself back in control. Once she got back to bed, she kept her mind occupied by reading the Bible until she drifted off to sleep.

The next day, Christy and Stacy spent all day talking about her date. Christy noticed that Stacy had a certain glow about herself. She knew Stacy quite well, and this was the first time she saw that look in her eyes and noticed the tone in her voice. Christy could tell by the way she talked about Stan that he was quite special to her. No matter how much Christy tried to change the subject, Stacy found one way or another to get back to talking about her date—about Stan. Christy was well aware that Stacy had not known Stan very long. She could only hope she was not getting ahead of herself – to be eventually let down and hurt. However, it seemed the more she tried to make Stacy cautious about her feelings, the more Stacy defended them.

Christy was truly happy for Stacy and hoped she had found her knight in shining armor. She wished she was as fortunate as Stacy. Christy had been hurt in several relationships and wasn't keen on dating any time soon; she concentrated on her work.

Stacy did need help from Christy for one thing: How to approach Stan and carry herself at work the next day. Christy did her best to give her some pointers, which was pretty much general advice. Nevertheless, the best advice she gave Stacy was to be herself and let Stan make the first move. Again she warned Stacy not to get her hopes up; some men move slower than others in contemplating a relationship if, indeed, he even wanted one. Stacy hoped that Stan felt the same way about her. She wasn't considering anything serious, like a marriage, but she wanted to develop a mutual relationship where they would often see each other. She could only wonder what Monday would bring. Again,

Sunday night brought about the same restlessness as Saturday. By the time the alarm went off for Stacy to get up and get ready for work, she might have slept a mere two hours. Nonetheless, she took great care, preparing herself to look good for Stan.

CHAPTER TWENTY-TWO

Monday happened to be Stacy's turn to close the bank. When she arrived at work, Stan was assisting Brinks with their drop-off and pickup of the currency. Consequently, he didn't see her come to work. Right from the time Stacy woke up, she had butterflies in her stomach, wondering how the first encounter with him would be. She tried to think back to their date; if there was anything she had done that might have caused him to be disappointed in her. After much thought, Stacy came to the conclusion that things had gone as well as could be expected. As nervous as she was, she couldn't wait for them to continue where they left off. About 20 minutes into her workday, she noticed Stan approaching her station.

She tried to maintain her composure, but the closer Stan got, the harder it felt for Stacy to remain calm. Without her realizing it, she was already smiling. As expected, being the professional that he was, Stan casually walked up to her station. They exchanged subtle pleasantries. He asked how she was doing, to which Stacy replied, *"I'm fine."* Stan's response to that was, *"I know that you're fine; finer than most women I've come across – sexy and beautiful. But young lady, I was asking how are you emotionally?"*

That response caught Stacy completely off-guard. Her heart began to race, and she could feel herself blushing as she stared straight ahead. She was speechless, yet impressed at Stan's confidence to flirt with her at their workplace. Her eyes widened as she grinned; it was obvious she was beaming with joy. Stan continued, *"Well, judging from the look of things, you're doing alright."* with that, he smiled, winked, and walked away. They both knew that, since she was closing, they would get to see each other on the way out. During the course of the day, Stan kept his distance from Stacy, occasionally smiling toward her. He was smart. He knew that Stacy had trouble containing her excitement every time they spoke, and he didn't want others in the bank to catch on to that. It would raise suspicion and cause others to ask questions, which he wanted to avoid.

After the bank was secure and the final door was locked, Stan escorted Stacy to her car. To Stan, she was the vision of an angel, and from the little time he had spent with her, he knew she had a heart of gold. Stan sensed that Stacy was compassionate and full of love but, at the same time, was a bit insecure—no, not a bit, a lot.

Judging from her reaction during the day, Stan felt that Stacy had developed some type of feelings for him. Even though he had not known her very long, for some strange reason, he couldn't help but feel drawn to her also. Stan knew what type of woman suited him best and felt, at least at this time, Stacy had what he called "it".

After opening her car door, he positioned himself so that they had to stand face to face. As they looked into each other's eyes, Stan put his hands on her arms, pulled her closer to him, and gave her a warm kiss on her forehead. Stacy's eyes closed as she went limp for a moment but quickly regained her composure – her heart was racing. She felt like she was having a panic attack.

Stan stepped aside, allowing Stacy to enter the car before he closed her door; she heard him say, *"Goodnight, little princess."* Although she heard it loud and clear, she was still in a daze. By the time she regained focus, he was gone. She watched him as he walked to his car. The only thing Stacy could do was to take a deep breath and let out a long sigh.

Stacy wanted to just sit there and take in what had just happened, but she knew that Stan would not leave the parking lot until all employees' cars were gone.

She started her car and headed home—her mind still clouded by what just happened. She was amazed that she got home in one piece since the only thing she could concentrate on was what had just taken place in the parking lot. She even touched her forehead to make sure the kiss was still there. When she got home, however, something took her mind off of Stan. Christy was all bubbly and excited and asked her to sit down because she had some news that she couldn't wait to share with her.

Christy had been offered a junior executive position with a big-time insurance firm in California. She explained that not only would her salary exponentially increase, they would also pay for all the moving expenses. They were going to fly her out on the coming Wednesday, for a week to look over the position and for her to see if the town is to her liking. If she accepted, they would locate her in an apartment with the help of the HR department. The company was willing to pay the security deposit and the first three months' rent. She had the option of either driving her car to California or, for a month, they would provide her transportation until she was able to buy another car under their discount plan – Christy chose the latter.

Christy had already made up her mind on accepting the position; she just wanted to know if Stacy wanted to go with her or not.

Stacy was awestruck and was at a loss for words. Finally, after everything finally sank in, Stacy reached out and hugged Christy with all she had. After a long embrace, Stacy congratulated Christy on her new position and felt this was an opportunity of a lifetime. She explained to Christy that she was honored by her invitation to join her, but she would like to sleep and pray on it before giving her a definitive answer. Stacy promised to give Christy her answer the next day.

That night, Stacy viewed the opportunity from all angles. Stacy even made a "pros and cons" list. This was a life-changing decision for Christy, and if she was going to go with her, it would be a huge leap of faith. However, after giving it much thought, she decided she would stay back in Chicago for three main reasons. Firstly, it would look bad on her work record if she upped and quit. Secondly, it was time for her to establish her independence. And thirdly, Stan.

She knew in the back of her mind that if things didn't work out in the bank or with Stan, she could always join Christy in California, but a possible relationship with someone like Stan wouldn't come around very often, so she was willing to take the chance. Stacy was just happy to have Christy as her safety net.

On Tuesday morning, she told Christy her decision. Christy was understanding of her situation. Regardless of Stacy's decision, Christy was immensely happy for her. She informed Stacy that she would be flying out around noon on Wednesday, returning the following Wednesday in the afternoon.

To celebrate, they went out and spent a night on the town with dinner and a movie. Before they headed back home, Christy took Stacy to one of the local lounges to meet some of her friends. Every time Christy did this, Stacy felt somewhat out of place. She didn't drink, smoke or dance, but that was about to change. One of Christy's friend, Keith, asked Stacy for a dance. She politely declined, but that didn't stop Keith from being persistent. Christy kept motioning to her to join her on the dance floor. Stacy finally confided in him that she didn't know how to dance. Keith smiled and offered to teach her and, after pleading with her to trust him, Stacy caved; besides, Christy was there to protect her should Keith get out of line.

She started off a little clumsy, but, before long, she got the hang of it. She was seemingly dancing to nearly every song. Before she left, she had learned how to step and even slow dance, all thanks to Keith's patience. Little did she know, Christy had warned Keith that Stacy was off-limits – from any advances from him and any of his friends.

Stacy was glad Keith didn't act on impulse, and she had a genuinely fun time. She had now learned something new. Stacy was proud of herself.

CHAPTER TWENTY-THREE

Arriving at work on Tuesday morning, Stacy noticed Stan's car wasn't in the parking lot. Stacy casually asked the replacement guard about Stan, to which she was informed that he had been assigned to one of their other branches for the rest of the week. Stacy's heart sank like a rock in a river. How was she going to get through this week without talking to or seeing him? To make matters worse, a simple fact dawned on her, which made things worse.

Despite all of their interactions, they had never exchanged phone numbers. This was not good. Just the thought of not being able to see Stan for a week was very distressing for Stacy. She began to overthink, jumping to conclusions; *"What if they never send him back?!"* Stacy decided it would be best not to think about it too much – spending her time praying about it throughout the course of the day. She was convinced this was a test of faith and her independence.

As the days went by, she survived the best way she could, knowing that it was a mere week before she would see Stan again – he had to come back; he just had to. Unfortunately for her, that expectation was short-lived. When Stacy asked about Stan again on Friday, she was informed that Stan would be posted at the other branch for another week. Needless to say, Stacy was devastated. No, Stan, and, by tomorrow, No Christy. Stacy reassured herself; she told herself that she was a big girl now – suck it up; stay positive. She used that mindset to push herself through the following days.

Once Christy came back home and settled down, she anxiously waited for Stacy to get home. Later that afternoon, when Stacy got back, they hugged and jumped for joy like they hadn't seen each other for years. After exchanging some pleasantries, Christy informed Stacy that not only had she accepted the position, she also found a wonderful, furnished, two-bedroom apartment that was just perfect for her. Christy had returned to pack the rest of her belongings and had worked out with management to have Stacy sublease the apartment.

The following day, after signing the lease and putting all the utilities in Stacy's name, Stacy helped Christy pack all of her belongings. Most of the things she kept, a few of her clothes she either donated or gave to Stacy. Christy ended up giving her car to one of her nieces. They decided to go out for the night to celebrate. The two of them went to an expensive restaurant for dinner, knowing it was going to be a while until they saw each other again.

Stacy's mind couldn't help but linger to the thought of the loneliness she felt after Mitchell's murder, realizing now that both Stan and Christy would be gone. However, she knew that there was not much she could do about her loneliness. On Friday morning, while both of them were getting ready, they knew words could never express the love they had for each other, so they ended up hugging each other tightly. Stacy knew that Christy would be gone by the time she got home – this time for good. But a smile crossed her face knowing that she hoped to see Stan again in a few days, and that thought helped her get through the weekend.

Sunday morning. Stacy had planned to eat a nice, hearty breakfast and tend to some pending errands. Stan was due back the next day, and she couldn't wait to see him. While Stacy was eating breakfast, her phone rang; it was Christy. After she told Stacy that she arrived safe and sound and that everything was alright, she told her that she had received a voicemail for Stacy on her phone on Friday, asking if Stacy would be interested in a position. This was rather odd; it had been over three years since Stacy gave out Christy's number for contact. Christy gave Stacy the woman's name and number and said it wouldn't hurt to give her a call. After contemplating it for a few minutes, Stacy agreed to call.

To her surprise, the next day, Stan was not there. She was vehemently disappointed. Stacy now felt very alone, more so with Christy gone. Stacy silently prayed for Stan, hoping he was well. During her lunch break, Stacy made the call to Ms. Rogers, the woman who had left the voicemail on Christy's phone, about the opening they were looking to fill.

A woman picked up the phone and introduced herself as Ms. René Rogers, the human relations supervisor for a large advertising agency downtown. Once Stacy introduced herself, Ms. Rogers immediately remembered leaving a message for her to call. She explained that they were holding interviews to fill a position that had just become available; an administrative assistant. Stacy couldn't remember whether she even sent them her resume. However, her question was soon answered when Ms. Rogers stated that someone had recommended her for that position. Stacy couldn't think of anyone who would have done so. Ms. Rogers asked Stacy if she was currently working or still looking for employment. Stacy informed her that she was currently employed but would not mind being interviewed for the position available. Stacy knew that working for the bank was a starting point in her life. If she wanted to advance her career, she would have to consider other options when they presented themselves.

Ms. Rogers went on to say that the company offered a tuition reimbursement program for all its employees. That sentence immediately grabbed Stacy's attention. Her plans in the future were to go to college and get her degree. Ms. Rogers apologized to Stacy for giving her such short notice but explained the interviews were being held tomorrow only. Stacy had to work the following day, so she asked her if the interview could be conducted in the afternoon. She agreed, and Stacy was given a 3:00 PM appointment at the corporate building downtown. Stacy confirmed she would be there, thanked Ms. Rogers, and hung up.

Stacy was excited. She couldn't wait for her workday to be over. Since Stacy didn't really have many friends at work, to begin with, it wouldn't be a problem to quit. But not seeing Stan? She didn't know how she was going to solve that dilemma; that was a huge concern. However, realizing that her work schedule would conflict with her appointment, she decided to request a personal day off – which was granted.

March 23, 2015. Stacy selected a business casual outfit for the interview. Since Ms. Rogers didn't mention she had her resume, she felt it best to take an updated one along with a notepad and pen to jot down any information she would need to remember. Stacy felt this approach might impress Ms. Rogers and add to her chances. Before leaving the apartment, after saying a little prayer, she checked herself several times to make sure she looked alright, grabbed her folder, and headed out the door. Throughout her drive to the interview, she tried to think of possible answers to any question Ms. Rogers may ask. She knew that she was not the only candidate for the job and wanted to be as professional as possible.

She started her car and headed to the interview, giving herself plenty of time to get there early and find a parking space. She had only been downtown a handful of times with Christy and knew downtown could be congested with traffic. She would take Lake Shore Drive and get off on Randolph Street. Fortunately, there wasn't a lot of traffic, and it took her no time at all to reach Randolph Street. She turned on her right turn signal. Spotting a clearing, she began to move right. That's when it happened – from out of nowhere, she was violently rear-ended.

The hit sent her car veering into the left lane horizontally. The initial shock had caused her to go into a state of panic. As if in slow motion, she watches the truck ram into her broadside. A life-ending jolt, a bright flash, and a sharp pain surged throughout her face and eyes. The sound of tires screeching and people yelling, the smell of gasoline and burnt rubber all faded out as Stacy lost consciousness.

Her car was pushed three car lengths, into another vehicle, before coming to a complete stop. Before help arrived, she regained consciousness. Her frantic heartbeat begins to slow down. She tried to breathe normally. Her body ached terribly; her head felt like it's in a vice. Something warm was running down her face – her eyes. Her eyes were on fire. Searing pain like she had never felt before. Her shoulders and chest were in excruciating pain. No matter how much she tried to move – she couldn't. As she fought in and out of consciousness, the faint sound of sirens and people screaming begins to fade. Her body couldn't handle the pain, and she slumps into unconsciousness once again.

CHAPTER TWENTY-FOUR

Though still very groggy, she hears her name being called from a distance, over and over again, until she regained enough consciousness to realize someone is standing next to her. That's when she became aware of her pain. Her eyes felt like they are on fire. She had a terrible headache, her left shoulder hurt, and her chest was in unbearable pain. Stacy can't feel her legs. She tried her best to move but couldn't. Stacy can finally comprehend what that faint voice was saying, *"Hi, Stacy. Squeeze my hand if you can hear me."* With all her might, Stacy managed to squeeze her hand.

"I'm Margaret Nelson, your nurse. I doubt you'd remember, but you were involved in a terrible car accident yesterday and were brought here at St. Luke's Hospital. You suffered a concussion and a dislocated left shoulder. The shoulder has been put back into place, and we recently administered a painkiller to help with your discomfort, which should also help your headache. You have a bruise and some abrasions across your chest due to the seatbelt, which is causing you discomfort, but that should go away in a few weeks. Your spinal cord took a hard hit. It affected some of your nerves, which is why you can't feel your legs, but don't worry! Nothing is broken or out of place. You should recover nicely from all of these."

Stacy tried her best to move but felt like she was tied up. The nurse continued, *"As you probably realized by now, we felt it necessary to put you in temporary restraints to keep you as stable as possible."* The nurse gently grasped Stacy's hand as her voice softened. She added, *"I want you to brace yourself for what I'm about to say; you see, during the collision, slivers of glass penetrated and damaged the cornea and iris in both of your eyes. An eye surgeon was called in, and he performed emergency ocular surgery on both eyes to remove the glass fragments. However, there are some complications".*

Even though partially sedated, Stacy's first reflex was to reach for her face as the panic set in. She made feeble attempts to try and free herself from her restraints while repeatedly muttering, *"No, no, no!"* over and over again. The nurse, full of compassion, didn't leave her side; she gave Stacy all the time she needed to gain composure. After several minutes, Stacy's strength began to leave her. Although her struggles subsided, her disbelief of the news didn't – her voice faded as she drifted out of consciousness once more.

After a few hours, Stacy awakes as the pain she felt everywhere had somewhat subsided. A nurse told her that she was administered fentanyl for pain because of the severity of her injuries. As she was slowly coming to terms with what had happened, she remembered what the nurse had told her about her eyes. Stacy tries to lift her hands and touch her eyes, but her restraints wouldn't let her. Stacy now feels a pair of hands gently holding her down.

"Mrs. Elkins, this is Nurse Nelson. Can you hear me?" She asked. *"I can hear you,"* Stacy replied softly. *"But please, call me Stacy."* Stacy despised being called by her married name after what Mitchell had put her through. As long as it wasn't necessary, she would not even tell people her last name. From then on, she requested everyone to just call her Stacy. *"Alright, Stacy, it is."* Nurse Nelson responded. *"I have Dr. Browdy, the eye surgeon, here to answer any questions you have concerning your eyes."*

Fighting the urge to scream, Stacey calmed herself by repeating, *"Jesus, help me"* over and over again in her mind. The doctor waited for her questions patiently. After a long pause, Stacy spoke up. *"Doc, in simple English, are my eyes okay?"*

"Hi, Stacy. Again, my name is Dr. Browdy, and I'm an ophthalmologist. Stacy, during the accident, glass shards impacted the cornea and retina of both of your eyes. The cornea is the clear tissue that forms and covers the front of your eye. The iris is the color part of the eye. The impact damaged them to the point that not even light can penetrate into the eye to reach the light-sensitive retina, which is necessary for vision to take place." The doctor took a short pause, then continued, *"I realize this will be very difficult to accept, but, unfortunately, you are left without sight in both of your eyes. Regrettably, this, in all likelihood, is permanent. I am so sorry to have to tell you that. We have restrained you to prevent you from rubbing your eyes."*

Stacy listened contently, then asked, *"Will further surgery help? If not, what are my alternatives?"* Dr. Browdy replied, *"If it was only the cornea, then we might have been able to do something about it. There is a procedure called Corneal Transplantation. We remove the damaged cornea and sew a new one in its place using a very fine thread. The thread stays in for several months or even a year, depending on how long it takes to heal. Sadly, science hasn't come up with a way to repair the retina once it's damaged, so there is, unfortunately, no way to restore sight to your eyes."* Stacy slowly began to lose her composure, *"So, what you're saying, doc... is that I'm blind without a chance to see again?"* *"Yes, I'm afraid so,"* the doctor replied solemnly.

This revelation was nothing less than life-changing for Stacy. Just yesterday, she had perfect vision; she couldn't imagine living her life blind. Her career, social life, and dream of being happily married one day came to a grinding halt. Stacy feels her life is gone, over

Stacy tried to free herself from her restraints once again, shouting, *"No! No! NO!"* Along with the help of Dr. Browdy, the nurse held her down as she was administered another sedative. In a matter of minutes, the sedatives put her to sleep.

Throughout the night, Stacy couldn't help but replay the flashbacks of her accident in her mind. The nurse had to go check on her constantly during the night because she was shouting in her sleep. She woke up the next morning, hoping it was all a dream. Stacy took a deep breath and tried to raise her hands, hoping she could touch her face – the restraints stopped her; it wasn't a dream.

Throughout the day, Nurse Nelson, along with various hospital staff, try their best to make her feel as comfortable as possible. Nothing relieved her self-pity. Nurse Nelson informed her that all of her belongings from the crash scene were placed in a drawer next to her bed. She also took the liberty of looking in her phone for contact information and found the bank's number along with another number. The nurse assumed that the bank might be her place of employment, and she was right when she called. She got hold of the branch manager and gave her details about Stacy's accident and condition.

Although still quite upset, Stacy thanked her for her help. Some of the patients on the floor stopped in to see her and asked about her well-being. They happened to hear her screams the night before and reassured her that some of life's setbacks do not end life itself. Although Stacy appreciated all the love she was being shown, her heart was still in despair; how would she get by now that she had lost her vision? Her independence?

All those things she took for granted now became massive obstacles for her to overcome. Something she never even put into consideration, like walking, will now become a daunting task. She couldn't walk without bumping into things; she couldn't cook because she couldn't see what she was doing. She couldn't get dressed because she wouldn't know what she was wearing – how would she accomplish anything!?

Throughout the day, all these questions kept running through her head. The more she thought about it, the more depressed she became. She managed to get through the first two days with the nurses' help, who fed, washed, and clothed her – which was very embarrassing for her; having to be escorted to the bathroom was degrading. On the third day, however, Nurse Nelson and Stacy had a long discussion about the restraints and the further use of sedatives. Stacy agreed to calm herself and to not touch her eyes, eliminating the need for additional sedatives. She was taken off the heavy painkillers and was now on codeine. Still, Stacy lay awake most of the night. She fought to find a reason for why this had happened to her. Not finding an answer, she started questioning God and his wisdom. Nothing was right about this, nothing! Eventually, she drifted off to sleep.

CHAPTER TWENTY-FIVE

As much as Stacy didn't want it to be, the fourth day felt like yet another repeat of her stay; that was, until lunchtime. Nurse Nelson read Stacy the menu and, after jotting down what she wanted to eat, told her she would return in about twenty minutes with her meal. Just as she left, Dr. Browdy walked in. After exchanging pleasantries, he informed her that he would do a routine examination of her eyes to see how they were coming along and would be changing her bandages. For a brief moment, the bandages were removed, and Stacy prayed that she would be able to see something – even if it was just light; unfortunately, her eyesight was completely gone. From his inspection, Dr. Browdy found no signs of an infection.

After the examination was done, he asked her to lay down with her head tilted back so he could administer some eye drops, which were likely to sting. To both their surprise, it did more than just sting. Stacy clenched her teeth, inhaled with a hiss, and held her breath as an immediate reaction to the intense burning sensation the eye drops caused. She froze this way while she waited for the burning to subside, only to realize the pain had now shifted to her hands because of how tightly they were gripping the railings on the bed. Dr. Browdy had to hold on to Stacy's arms to ensure that she did not reach for her eyes. Once he knew she was ok, he placed a fresh, sterilized gauze pad on each eye, then rewrapped her head to keep the gauze in place. As much as she detested it, everything was pitch black for Stacy; whether her eyes were open or not.

The doctor noted his findings on a clipboard and said, *"Stacy, you are recovering at a fairly decent pace, and if there are no setbacks, I believe you should be well enough to be discharged in a few days; that is, of course, if your other injuries have sufficiently healed. I will talk to nurse Brown and your primary physician, who will give you more information regarding our discharge policy in these matters."*

Not too long after Dr. Browdy left, Nurse Nelson came in with her lunch. As usual, a nurse's aide assisted in feeding her. After lunch, the nurse informed Stacy that Ms. April Willis, from the hospital's Social Service department, would be paying her a visit before dinner. Regardless of how kind everyone was treating Stacy, she still spared none of her grievances against God; whenever Stacy was alone with her thoughts, she continued to question God, asking Him how He expected her to survive in her condition. She understood how this happened to other people, but she wasn't exactly *other people.*

Stacy took the few hours of solace she had before dinner to contemplate these things. About three hours later, Ms. Willis came in to talk to her. She informed her that she was from the hospital's Social Service staff and her job was to provide information in situations such as hers. With decades of experience under her belt, she reassured Stacy to the best of her ability, motivating her to adjust to her newfound lifestyle. Despite the life Stacy had known, which was now drastically changed, Ms. Willis told Stacy that she had to power on through, finding courage from whatever she could. Her best bet was to push through life under any circumstances. Ms. Willis continued, stating that she worked in conjunction with the Illinois Department of Human Services, and inside that department is the Department of Rehabilitation Service.

She also informed Stacy of another organization in Chicago, called Second Sense, which also helped individuals that had similar cases to her. Both would help with the transition of being able to live at home independently. She gave Stacy some material to hold on to about both services and what they provide. She also provided her with Dr. Browdy's information and suggested she make an appointment to see him within a few days of her release. Having been given permission by Stacy, Ms. Willis packed up all of her personal belongings and put them in a bag next to her bed. She told Stacy she would keep her in her prayers and if there was anything else she could do for her, just let her know.

After another week in the hospital, Stacy's physical injuries had substantially healed, and on that basis, she was released. Unsurprisingly, none of her colleagues from the bank had bothered to pay her a visit while she was hospitalized. Stacy, knowing how they felt about her, was rather unfazed by their treatment. However, she was somewhat disappointed that neither Rose nor Rene had stopped by.

Besides providing transportation home, Ms. Willis also arranged for a volunteer, Sharon Williams, from one of the local church organizations, to stay with Stacy until she was in bed for the night; since Stacy had no one staying with her. It was arranged that Sharon would come at 9:00 AM and leave at 5:00 PM every day, Monday through Friday, until Stacy secured other means of self-support or didn't require any further service from her. Additionally, she would also come over on weekends if absolutely necessary. Amongst other things, Sharon was responsible for preparing Stacy's meals, doing the dishes, laundry, and layout the clothes she was going to wear, among other daily requirements.

Stacy sat quietly and waited until Sharon showed up. After the initial small talk, Sharon told Stacy a little about herself; she was from the New Jordan River Church. She helped Stacy into her wheelchair and wheeled her to the exit, parking the wheelchair in the vestibule while she got her car. After assisting her into the car, Sharon asked for her address and took her back home. During the ride home, Sharon gave Stacy some additional information about herself. Despite the fact Stacy was still quite angry about her situation, Sharon was pleasant and easy to talk to. The minute Stacy got home, she remembered Christy. *"I'm sure she had been trying to contact me."* Stacy thought to herself.

Stacy asked Sharon to dial her number for her. When Sharon looked at her phone, she was shocked to see that Stacy had twenty-five missed calls and twelve voicemails. Stacy knew it was either Christy, the bank, or the missed appointment – it was all of them.

Once the phone started ringing, Sharon handed the phone to Stacy. When Christy answered, she was terribly upset with Stacy for not replying to her text messages and voicemails. With a deep sigh, Stacy began to explain what happened. After learning about all that had transpired, Christy profusely apologized and began to cry. Without missing a beat, Christy tried her best to persuade Stacy to come to live with her, but Stacy declined. Christy had done enough for her; Stacy did not want to burden her any further. After an hour-long conversation and several promises to talk daily, they ended the call. Once that was done, Sharon helped Stacy clean up, get dressed for bed, and made sure she took her medication, which was a mild pain reliever and a low-dose sedative. Seeing how the only person that truly mattered to Stacy was Christy, she never did reply to those other messages. The only people that had any concern for her well-being was Christy and Stan. For someone of her age to only have two friends was something she considered pathetic.

Sharon wanted to know if Stacy could find her way safely to the door to let her in tomorrow or would she allow her to have her door key. Stacy elected not to give her the key since she did not want to be caught off-guard should she come in. But really, this was a desperate attempt to retain some sort of independence for herself, so the least she could do was get up and open the door. Stacy listened to everything Sharon had to say, albeit rather half-heartedly. Like a broken record, the only thing that kept running through her head was, *"I'm blind! Blind! I can't be blind. I refuse to be blind. Just wait and see. I'll be fine."*

Stacy was convinced; she didn't need anyone's prayers. Even though she was still upset with Him, God had seen her through other situations, and this one was no exception. He would give her back her sight, and no one would be able to tell her any differently. On the bright side, it was finally good to be back home and sleep in her own bed. Throughout the night, Stacy rubbed the dial-pad of the flip-phone so she got accustomed to the protruding rubber keys, knowing she would at least be able to make any calls if necessary. With the medication taking effect. She lay down and fell asleep.

CHAPTER TWENTY-SIX

Right on time, the doorbell rang at 9:00 am – waking Stacy up from her sleep. Surviving a restless night's sleep, she was groggy but sat up in bed, coming to her new life. She thought for a second about who it could be. Then it hit her – Sharon. After yelling, *"Just a minute!"* she put her robe and house shoes on, which were laid out for her on a chair next to the bed the night before by Sharon. Stacy had a pretty good idea about her apartment and made her way to the door. She opened the door to be greeted by Sharon, who smiled as she said, *"Good morning, Stacy."* After exchanging pleasantries, Sharon continued, *"Here, give me your hand and let me see what I can do for you. First of all, how are you feeling?"*

Although Stacy was still very upset about her condition, she explained that she still had a slight headache, eye, and back pain, but it wasn't unbearable. Her shoulder had a dull ache and was still a little stiff. Although she still had the bruises, the pain in her chest and legs had greatly subsided. Stacy asked Sharon for the date, to which she replied it was April 1st. *"April Fool's, that's what it feels like."* Stacy thought to herself. Was she a fool for thinking she would be able to see again? According to Dr. Browdy, she was. Nothing about her situation helped her depression in any way.

Apart from her eyes watering often, Stacy was recovering rather nicely. *"Well,"* said Sharon. *"It seems like you are well on your way back to some form of recovery."* Sharon began to explain to Stacy that there was an agency in Chicago, Illinois Department of Human Services, that provided home care for clients with her condition. Ms. Willis had taken the liberty of contacting them for Stacy, and they would be coming to see her at noon. Dr. Browdy had only given her enough pain and sedative medication to last a week but advised her not to take them unless it was absolutely necessary. Sharon had also brought over some eye drop medication given to her by Dr. Browdy. Stacy was instructed to administer these drops three times a day, which Sharon showed her how to do.

Sharon asked Stacy if she had any questions for her, to which she just shook her head. With that, Sharon jumped up exclaimed cheerfully, *"OK, young lady. Let's start!"* She got Stacy cleaned up, dressed, and cooked her breakfast, all the while having Stacy assist her with some little things she could do. The rest of the morning, Sharon spent trying to engage in conversation with Stacy as a means to distract her. It must have worked because around that time, the doorbell rang, *"It must be Ms. Riley from the agency. I'll let her in."* said Sharon. As she was let in, they exchanged greetings.

Ms. Riley was the perfect combination of professional and personal traits. She had worked for the department for nearly 20 years and knew her duties quite well. Although she was a bit stern, she was fair. Who could blame her? Her job was in no way easy, having to deal with emotions that could switch in a matter of seconds. But she was prepared for anything.

"You must be Stacy. Good afternoon. My name is Malinda Riley, but most people just call me Malinda. I'm from the Illinois Department of Human Services. Our Rehabilitation Service division has several agencies under this division. I happen to be with the Bureau of Blind service." She explained.

At this point, Sharon asked Stacy if there was anything else she needed her to do. Stacy thanked her, saying she would be fine since she had laid out everything she would need for the remainder of the day. With that, Sharon bid each of them a good day and was out the door. After Stacy and Malinda sat on the couch, Malinda explained to Stacy about all the programs that were available to her through the agency.

She was appointed to help Stacy with understanding and, possibly, implementation of the programs. Depending on the programs Stacy selected, Malinda would turn it over to those who had the skills to teach those programs. Again, although Stacy heard every word Malinda spoke, she still vehemently denied the fact that she would remain blind. Malinda knew very well what Stacy was going through. She could hear it in her voice and see it on her face.

There are seven emotional degrees a person who is suddenly struck blind goes through. They are Trauma, Shock & Denial, Mourning and Withdrawal, Reassessment and Reaffirmation, Coping & Mobilization, and finally, Self-Acceptance & Self-Esteem. The same also applies to cancer patients.

Stacy had somewhat gotten through the trauma stage and was now in the denial stage. Not everyone goes through each stage, and the time they stay in each stage varies from person to person. Malinda knew that when Stacy finally realized her condition was permanent, withdrawal and depression were sure to follow, but she was ready. She planned to give Stacy two days to think about what she had laid out for her. But, after that, she hoped that, at the very least, Stacy would give the programs a try and work on improving her situation. The rest of the time was spent in small talk and trying to lift Stacy's spirit. Having done all that she could do, Malinda left around 5:30 PM. She told Stacy that she would be back in a couple of days for an update about her plans. After eating dinner, Stacy took her meds, applied the eye drops, and listened to some TV. A couple of hours passed when she decided to call it a day. Getting undressed and putting on her nightclothes, she climbed into bed and fell asleep shortly after.

The next morning, shortly after Sharon arrived, the doorbell rang. When Sharon opened the door, the gentleman at the door introduced himself as Mr. Stewart from Staten Insurance, which was Stacy's auto insurance company. Sharon invited him in, asked him to have a seat while she informed Stacy. Sharon told Stacy that she would be busy fixing breakfast while they talked. When Stacy came into the room, he rose and introduced himself. She said, *"Hello,"* and sat down. Mr. Stewart explained that he was an attorney working for Staten Insurance and was covering her case. He started off by giving his condolences for her situation but was there to hopefully help brighten up her day.

He had secured all the necessary information and documents from the police, including detailed eye-witness testimonies as to what happened. He informed her that her car was totaled but had replacement value. His company was going after not only the trucking company of the driver who broadsided her but the vehicle that rear-ended her and caused the accident. It would take some time to settle the case due to all of the medical bills and lost wages that had to be submitted to determine the appropriate settlement payment. Mr. Stewart reassured Stacy, telling her that he would handle all the paperwork and the only thing he would require from her was her signature when the time came.

Speaking of lost wages, the health insurance provided by her employer included a side policy, similar to AFLAC, that should provide her with enough money to pay her rent, electrical and phone bill, food, and other expenses she may have. If, for any reason, she had to come out of pocket for anything, she was to keep a record and would, most likely, be reimbursed at a later date.

Ms. Willis had taken the liberty of contacting Stacy's employer to explain what had happened to her. It was strange, but Stacy had to admit that, in her state, not once did she consider how she would pay her bills. Although still bitter, she welcomed the good news. Mr. Stewart informed her that he had stopped by her employer and had filled out and even mailed the necessary papers, so she should expect her first check soon. He asked if Stacy had any questions, to which she had none at that time.

As he got up, he said, *"Thanks for your time Stacy. I left my card on the table. If you think of any questions, please let me know. I will be giving you an update as things progress. Good day, Ms. Riley. It was a pleasure meeting you."* Malinda showed him the way out and shut the door. It had been a minute, but Stacy said a small prayer, thanking God for continuing to looking out for her but wanted him to finish the job and restore her sight; denial would not go quietly.

CHAPTER TWENTY-SEVEN

The next day Stacy had an appointment to see Dr. Browdy for her eyes and Dr. Brown for her other injuries. Except for cooking breakfast, Sharon had, somewhat, taught Stacy to wash up and dress. Sharon picked up Stacy at 10:00 AM, and by 10:30 AM, they reached the hospital and waited their turn.

Dr. Brown called for her first. He examined her thoroughly and had her do some stretches to determine her pain threshold and range of motion. Other than a hitch here and there, Stacy had significantly improved and did fine. He advised her to get off all the medications she was taking and do some daily exercises to further aid the healing process. He had contemplated sending her to physical therapy but determined that was not necessary since her body was recovering well without it.

However, other than exercises for her current injuries, Stacy wanted to keep her figure; working and walking did that for her, but now, that wasn't possible. Stacy asked Dr. Brown if he could give her some exercises that she could do at home that would help her maintain her weight and figure. Dr. Brown was delighted to see Stacy was still concerned about her physical wellbeing. He asked her to wait as he stepped out of the room to gather some useful material for her. After a few minutes, he returned with several copies of exercises that he said Sharon could read out to her and show her how to perform them. Sharon added that she would even do them with her if she had the time. Besides maintaining her physique, this also gave Stacy something to do since she was confined at home. After having completed a full assessment, Dr. Brown gave Stacy a full release. However, he stated that she was more than welcome to visit him if she experienced any setback. She thanked him and, accompanied by Sharon, went back to the waiting area for Dr. Browdy to call her in. After about fifteen minutes, she was called in. As Stacy walked toward the room, she started praying, asking God that, through Dr. Browdy, she would hear some good news about her eyesight. After carefully removing her wrapping and bandages, he did a thorough eye exam.

Stacy immediately knew that he was raising them to get a better look into her eye when he touched her eyelids. When there was not even the slightest sliver of light, she became depressed; God had let her down. After Dr. Browdy concluded the eye exam, he begrudgingly confirmed Stacy's greatest fear – she was blind. Whatever little hope Stacy kept had dissipated, and she fell into despair. She sat there, in silence, shaking her head slowly as tears streamed down her face.

Sharon stepped forward and hugged Stacy without saying a word – she understood. Sharon had been through these situations many times before. Dr. Browdy had a seat and quietly waited; he knew this was the type of thing you could not rush. After several minutes, Stacy composed herself. She apologized to Dr. Brown for breaking down and thanked Sharon for her support. Dr. Browdy reaffirmed her and offered his help in any way he could. He told Stacy that the bandages were no longer needed and left them off. Sharon, always prepared, handed Stacy a pair of sunglasses; she put them on without a thought.

After they left the office, Sharon knew that Stacy did not take that news lightly, and she needed something to distract her. Sharon stopped by a Baskin-Robbins on their drive back home, and they both got a double scoop. When the employee asked for their flavor of choice, both spoke out, *"Double chocolate!"* Sharon got hers in a cone but Stacy, not wanting to waste it on herself without knowing, got hers in a cup. As they sat in the car enjoying the treat, Sharon did her best to take Stacy's mind off of her situation by talking to her about her life, marriage, kids, and work, which she continued on the drive back. By the time she had finished, they were back at the apartment.

No sooner had they got back in the house and settled, the doorbell rang. Stacy had found her way to the room while Sharon got the door. Stacy's mind was so preoccupied with the disheartening news she received at the doctor's office that she didn't hear the door shut or anyone come in. Finding her way back to the living room, she asked Sharon who was at the door. Sharon replied, telling her that one of her co-workers had stopped in to see her. Stacy was overwhelmed; *"Finally. Someone finally came to visit!"* She thought. Stacy walked in, saying, *"Hello!"* thinking it was probably one of the tellers or possibly the branch manager. *"Hello, Stacy."* came the reply. It hit her like a bolt of lightning; she felt weak in her knees, and her legs almost gave out. *"Oh, God! No!"* She cried out as her hands covered her mouth. It was Stan.

"Please go! Please go!" she managed to snivel as she turned around and began to cry. She was embarrassed to have him see her this way; Stacy wished she could just disappear. *"Sharon, please tell him to leave,"* she pleaded. *"Stacy,"* she said, *"This gentleman has gone out of his way to visit you. It wouldn't be proper for either of us to treat him as an unwelcome guest."* Of all the people to see her like this, why Stan!?

As she attempted to walk back into her room, she felt a pair of hands touch her shoulders, slide their way down to her elbow, and then back up again. His touch sent shivers through her soul. For a moment, she forgot all about her life-changing problem and was focused entirely on his touch – his gentle touch. She had been touched before, but not like this; the warmth and passion she felt from that small gesture sent chills through her entire body.

It took a minute for her to compose herself and snap back into reality. He turned her around slowly and placed his hands on her arms, *"Stacy, the bank filled me in on everything. Although I can't feel what you feel, I can only imagine what you're going through and the thoughts going through your mind. I can understand why you wouldn't want me to see you this way; I truly do. But I want you to think about something; I was with you when things were good, and I'm here now that things aren't so good. What does that tell you?"* Stacy's mind was swirling; she wanted to speak, but her mouth wouldn't open. Then, it happened. Stan stepped forward and hugged her. She instinctively tried to pull back, but he held on to her. He pulled her to his chest and held her there. *"Don't lose hope,"* he said, *"Have faith."* Stacy took a deep breath and melted into his arms – there was no point in resisting the person she longed for. She lay her head on his chest and, as if being controlled by another force, wrapped her arms around his waist. He was warm and strong, and, if it were possible, she would have stayed, just like that, for the rest of her life.

She lost track of time and didn't know how long she had been in that position. In a brief moment of clarity, she realized that Sharon was still there. Like being awakened from sleep, she removed her arms from around his waist as she lifted her head from his chest. Stan, getting the unspoken signal, removed his arms from around her as well and stepped back. Helping in "breaking the moment," Sharon invited Stan to stay for dinner.

Stan thanked her for the invitation but said he would take a rain check. After exchanging goodbye pleasantries with Sharon, he walked over to Stacy. *"Young lady, would it be too much to ask for your phone number?"* Stacy was overwhelmed with joy – she thought he'd never ask. Her phone was in her pocket, so she pulled it out and handed it over to him. He dialed his number and saved his name in her contact list. He now had her number, and she had his.

He dropped the phone into her pocket. But, before he left, he gently held her head in his hands, kissed her on the forehead, and said, *"See ya' later, cutie. I'll call you."* And with that, Sharon escorted him to the door. Meanwhile, Stacy just stood there. Her mind drifted into another realm – completely oblivious to what was happening. All she could feel was Stan's kiss on her forehead. He kissed her; for the second time, he kissed her. She vowed never to wash her forehead again. Sharon had witnessed the whole thing. *"Stacy,"* she said, *"It's none of my concern, but I feel as if there's a special bond between you two; unless I'm missing something. I'm only asking this because I need to know if he's going to be a frequent visitor or not."* Stacy didn't know how she could answer that. Finally, she said, *"Well, I don't know how much of a bond we have, but I certainly hope that he does visit regularly."* Sharon knew there was more to it than Stacy was admitting to, but she left it at that.

Stan had taken that day off for personal reasons. Earlier, he had decided to stop in at the bank to greet the staff and see how his replacement was holding up since he was still assigned to another bank. While there, after inquiring about Stacy, the branch manager pulled him to the side and told him everything she knew about the accident and that Stacy had recently been released from the hospital. Stan was taken aback but still maintained his composure. Of course, he has heard of and witnessed accidents before, but knowing the condition Stacy was in was devastating. Realizing the fact that they had only known each other for a relatively short amount of time, he was having trouble coming to terms with why he felt for her the way he did. She was very beautiful, smart, shy, and neat, had good morals, great shape, no kids, independent, worked, and got along with him nicely. Hey, wait a minute! Duh! Those were all the things he looked for in a woman!

Now, being realistic, there were other things he did not know and had to know about her before going any further. However, judging from everything that he did know, she fit his expectations, so far, to a tee. One thing he knew for sure, without question, was that Stacy had developed feelings for him, judging by the way she acted around him. However, he struggled with the idea of stopping by to see her, especially unannounced, and now with the added dilemma of her situation. Would she be comfortable seeing him in her condition? Would he do more harm than good by seeing her? Would she even answer the door? Ultimately, he decided to stop by and see her and that, by doing so, she at least knew he was thinking about her.

Not knowing her emotional makeup, he chose not to bring her anything if she refused or rejected it. Putting all that to the side, one reason he needed to stop by was to get her phone number, which he was pretty confident she would give him. That way, she wouldn't think he came over to feel sorry for her. To him, it wasn't feeling sorry as much as it was caring. So he decided to pay her a visit on his way home.

The next morning, Stacy was already up when the doorbell rang. Expecting Sharon, she opened the door only to be greeted by another woman who said, *"Good morning. Are you Stacy?" "Yes,"* she replied. *"I'm Hattie Bailey. Malinda was called out of town on a family emergency, so I'm filling in for her,"* she stated. *"Please come in, Ms. Bailey,"* Stacy replied politely. *"Oh! Please, just call me Hattie!"* she exclaimed as Stacy let her inside. Sharon came in shortly after Ms. Bailey arrived, introduced herself, and continued on with her duties. Hattie tried her best to explain the different programs available to Stacy. Despite being a professional, she was not Malinda. Malinda had a more interpersonal connection with Stacy, which Hattie lacked. Hattie spoke well, but it wasn't with feelings; rather, it seemed that she was just reading a script. It seemed to Stacy that, to Hattie, it was just a job. Stacy needed someone more akin to a big sister to relate to. If Hattie was a representative of the type of person she could expect to work with, she preferred to compare them against someone else's organization. Stacy didn't imply Hattie was incompetent. She simply wanted someone with who she could connect on a more personal level. Knowing that Malinda may be gone for more than a few days, Stacy remembered the other service that Mrs. Willis recommended. She thanked Hattie for coming over and said she would give the agency a call when she made up her mind. Sharon escorted Hattie out. It took a few minutes of searching but, eventually, Stacy found the information on Second Sense. Ms. Willis had placed raised numbers on a card for Stacy to recognize their phone number.

CHAPTER TWENTY-EIGHT

The next day, Stacy called Second Sense and explained her situation to them. A meeting was scheduled for the following day with one of their client reps, Ms. Charmaine Roberts, who would pay Stacy a visit around 10:00 AM. Stacy didn't want to go through this; she wanted to be the same, independent woman she strived so hard to be. She didn't want to have to rely on other people to help her as if she were helpless – she knew she would feel embarrassed. But, every time she would start feeling this way, she had to think of something to get her mind back on track. And, of course, you know what that was – Stan.

The next morning, at exactly 10:00 AM, there was a knock on the door. Sharon was busy prepping breakfast, so Stacy decided to answer the door. Upon opening the door, Stacy heard, *"Well, hello there! You must be Stacy. I'm Charmaine Roberts from Second Sense." "Hi, Ms. Roberts. Will you come in?"* Stacy replied. Just from that short introduction, Stacy knew she had Malinda's character. It was important for Stacy to bond with someone who would be in her life for a few months. Honestly, she was looking for someone like Christy. She knew she wouldn't find anyone who could hold a candle to her, but someone close would do. She started to see certain similarities in Malinda and now hoped that Charmaine would pick up that torch and continue that race with her. Once settled on the couch, Ms. Roberts said, *"Please, call me Charmaine."* Charmaine began to explain about her organization and the programs they had to offer her.

Second Sense was established in 1947 as a non-profit organization. Since their advent, they have been developing unique programs for the visually impaired. All their staff is professionally trained and certified to provide the highest quality service. Along with the staff, there is an entire community of volunteers, clients, and partners to deliver their program. Their mission is to inspire the visually impaired to move beyond their disability and to believe in their abilities. Charmaine further elaborated on how Second Sense works individually with each of their clients since no two clients are the same. Best of all, all the services they offer are free of charge and are available to anyone with vision impairment. Stacy was surprised to know that, at last count, 238,692 people in Chicago were blind or visually impaired. Stacy was shocked to hear that figure. She had, on occasion, bumped into others who were blind or had some form of vision impairment but to know there were that many? Knowing that piece of information, Stacy became a little less depressed about her situation by the day's end. Now, she didn't feel so alone.

Charmaine further elaborated on the services offered by Second Sense. There were three primary areas of training: Orientation & Mobility, Independent Living Skills, and Assistive Technology. Orientation & Mobility focused on safe travel techniques, navigation, and traveling with a mobility device such as a white cane. Independent Living Skills focused on daily living skills such as cooking, reading, Braille, and so on. Assistive Technology focused on adaptive technology that assists in the use of computers and cell phones. Each client is assigned a personal instructor for the specific program they are receiving. Their training is customized to their needs, learning style, and ability. There is no timetable; each client learns at their own pace. Each function has its own techniques and skills, which can be lengthened or shortened based on the individuals' comprehension and adaptability. There are a variety of different tools and equipment used in certain programs. Charmaine gave her a sample list of products available.

Audio Items: Audio Message Recorder – plays, records, and deletes messages. It has 12-hours of recording time.

Daily Living Aids:

Coin Wallet: pocket-size while each coin has its individual slot.

Sock Sorters: keeps socks together even during washing.

Kitchen Aids:

Liquid Level Indicator: lets you know when the glass is full by the beeps that gradually keep increasing as the liquid reaches the top. Palm Peeler: lets you peel vegetables while keeping your fingers safe.

Labeling Accessories:
Braille Labeler: A label machine that prints words such as commonly used contractions, punctuation marks, and numbers in Braille that is transferred to tape, which can be applied to objects for easy identification. Bump Dots: Loc-Dots have raised dots that help mark oven controls, keys, telephone, keyboards, and more.

Talking Products:

Electronic Calculator – eight-digit talking calculator with auto shut off switch when not in use.
Talking watch – announces the time in a clear voice with the push of a button.

Charmaine would also teach her the folding currency system, which is: $1 bills are not folded; $5 bills are folded in half crosswise; $10 bills are folded in half twice; $20 bills are folded in thirds.

As Charmaine went through the list of services and devices, Stacy realized a crucial thing; she was not the only one involved in improving her situation. If it were left up to her, she would sit in the middle of the floor and just wither away. But, she couldn't shake the words of encouragement Stan gave her. Was it going to be a challenge for her? No doubt about it. Would it be worth it? If it meant the companionship of Stan? Darn skippy it would. Stan did not seem to mind her condition. But, if there was a chance to possibly form a relationship with him, she would have to hold up her part of the relationship. She knew she couldn't do everything a sighted person could, but if she applied herself and obtained all the things that would make life easier for Stan, she would go that far and prove to him she was willing to do all that she could to create independence; it surely couldn't hurt. She made up in her mind to take the courses offered that would best suit her circumstances.

Charmaine further explained to Stacy that training could take place either at home or at the office. Although they did not provide transportation for clients, many clients use paratransit transportation services for their traveling purposes. She also suggested that Stacy talk to a Certified Vision Rehabilitation Therapist to answer any questions she may have and also work out a plan or schedule of what steps to take first. She knew that Stacy's world had come crashing down overnight and that a therapist could give her some emotional support and encouragement. At the very least, therapy would help guide her in the right direction.

Those individuals who become gradually blind are not as emotionally traumatized as those who lose sight unexpectedly. Stacy thought it was at least worth a try, so Charmaine made an appointment for her to see one. After thinking it over, Stacy decided to start her training in-house. That way, she could learn to get used to her immediate surroundings and not be clumsy when Stan came over.

[OK! Let's take a break. Before I move on with my story, I want to give my readers some valuable insight. What if, one day, you went blind? Does it matter whether you went blind gradually or overnight? What about your age? Would you rather be blind from your youth, which gives you many years to master your independent living skills? Or, would you rather go blind, in your old age with, at least, having seen things most of your life? What about if you're young and single looking for a companion. Does your blindness affect the ability to land a girlfriend, boyfriend, or spouse? Do people see you as half a person? OK. Let's say you're middle-aged and become blind, for whatever reason. Are you going to be able to retain your job? How are you going to support yourself when the bills just keep stacking up? Most people never think of these questions when they have sight. But lose it and see (no pun intended) what happens.

Tell you what. Do something for me. Before the day is over, close your eyes or blindfold yourself for 30 minutes and go about your normal activities. Knowing that you will be doing this at home makes it easier since you are already familiar with your surroundings. You pretty much know where each piece of furniture is. You already know how to operate the stove, microwave, and the layout of things in the refrigerator, and you pretty much know how to even operate the TV remote control. And if you did do this little experiment, be honest and tell me how many times did you bump into something? One, two, six, twelve? Now, let's spice it up a bit. Do the same thing but go outside and walk around your property.

Go ahead. I'll wait...

Did you do it? How did it feel? Bump or step into anything? If you actually did it, were you nervous, apprehensive, and a bit (if not a lot) scared? Nothing to be ashamed of. Now, let's go one step further. Take or find something that would resemble a white cane. If you remember, the height should come up to your armpit.

Now go outside, have someone blindfold you and have them walk with you for safety. Take your stick and walk a block... straight. You can't peek or ask the person you're with how you're doing. They are only there to keep you out of danger. After completion, how many times did you have to be corrected? Did you feel anxiety? Wondered where you were? You were able to take your blindfold off after a block to see where you were. The blind can't do that. Most of the blind know that feeling. You also have a good idea of your neighborhood and beyond. You could probably tell me where everything is within, let's say, a five or ten-mile radius. And that's good. However, if I were to say, "Hey, let's take a trip to, Oh! I don't know, Denmark." And once we got there, I left you. Now how would you feel? Face it; you would be, for lack of a better word, lost. No friends. No familiar surroundings. You don't know which direction to turn first. Well, those who are completely blind have to tackle such a situation in their lives on a near-daily basis. Somehow, they have to sum up the courage to live a normal life as much as possible.

Fortunately, technology, being what it is, has come a long way in assisting the visually impaired. However, nothing can take the place of rearranging the physical and emotional changes that take place when losing your vision completely. Ever wonder what a blind person sees? There is no set pattern. Each person may have different experiences. Some describe seeing complete darkness, like being in a cave. Some see sparks. Some see vivid visual hallucinations that form recognizable and unrecognizable shapes, colors, or flashes of light. The darkness is somewhat expected. But what about the shapes, colors, and flashes? Want to go through that show for the rest of your life? Believe it or not, the person who is blind learns to accept their circumstances through training and with time. What they can't do anything about is alter how others view them. If a blind person is walking down the street toward you, what's the first thing you notice? How tall or short they are? What's their race? What type of outfit they're wearing? None of those, I bet. The first things you see or that crosses most people's minds are, looking at the cane and saying to themselves, "They are blind." It's just human nature.

A blind person is just like any other person. Blindness doesn't change who they are – basically speaking. They have to deal with issues just like us; only, they have a specific challenge. Due to blindness, some don't want to leave their home or apartment. Some are embarrassed to be seen in public. Some fight the use of a cane so as not to draw attention to themselves. Some choose to hang on to another person rather than try to become independent. However, in the end, they are still just plain people inside, but with an issue that they have to deal with. It's not going away. Ever heard it said that a blind person's other senses become heightened? Is that true or not? The brains of those born blind make new connections in the absence of visual information, resulting in enhanced abilities such as hearing, smell, touch, and cognitive functions like memory and language. So, yes, it's true, they do. Hey, just like one of your superheroes! Just ask Daredevil!

There is a lot more I could add, but why am I telling you all this? So that you don't think you are any better or any worse than those who have impaired vision or total loss of vision or, for that matter, anyone who has a handicap in any form. So, other than getting in their pathway when they are walking, give them the same respect as you would a friend. Yes, there is a lot of stereotypes surrounding a blind person by the general public, but it's the public who "can" see that comes up with these conditions that hardly apply to a blind person. I was fortunate. God gave me favor. But these are rare instances. And, as you continue to read, the training process is quite involved. It takes a certain resolve to be willing to be taught to operate your life in darkness. They shouldn't be pitied; they should be praised. It's like, taking all those courses to land this particular job, then throwing them all away to learn another occupation. But, before I let you go, so you can continue reading, nothing, and I mean nothing, could have been accomplished by me without God's help. I'm not referring to being cured. I'm referring to the journey that leads me up to that point. Had it not been for my faith, I would have just given up and just existed, day by day, until my time to be called home. But there is more to life than sight. You may not understand that logic but, then again, you have never been blind (not referring to those who are and can read this book). So, yes, have compassion for the blind but treat them as you would anyone else. You will gain a friend. OK! Enough of that – back to the story!]

CHAPTER TWENTY-NINE

Two days later, Stacy had an appointment with the therapist. Accompanied by Charmaine, they went to visit him; his name was Dr. Edward Calhoun. He engaged in an hour-long session with Stacy, in which he was surprised at how upbeat and positive Stacy was for someone who had recently lost her sight. He had seen patients who experienced a depressive episode for several months after a sudden loss of vision. Even the patients who had gradually lost their vision had bouts of depression in one form or another.

Curious, he asked Stacy how she could be so positive and cheerful at a time like this, to which she simply replied, *"Oh! I have my reasons."* She wanted to tell Dr. Calhoun that the real reason for her happiness was Stan. However, she did not want any personal information to be divulged, which wasn't pertinent to the real reason she was there. After going back and forth and thoroughly discussing the pros and cons, Stacy and Dr. Calhoun came to an agreement that she would go with the O&M program first, followed by the Independent Living Skills and finally, if necessary, Assistive Technology.

Stacy and Dr. Calhoun reasoned that, since she was taking her training at home, it would be more beneficial for her to get additionally acquainted with the layout of her apartment. She did not want to cause injury to herself while learning to be independent through the programs. Stacy wasn't big on computers at that time, so she decided to take the last program if she felt up to it after she finished the other two.

Dr. Calhoun asked Charmaine to come into his office, and he explained Stacy's decision to her, asking if she had any feedback on Stacy's decision. Charmaine stated that she thought Stacy's choice, along with Dr. Calhoun's suggestions and observations, was in line with her own.

Arriving back home, Sharon had prepared lunch for Stacy and Charmaine, which they ate in silence. The remainder of their time was spent with Charmaine teaching Stacy some simple procedures involved in the O&M program. Before she left, Charmaine informed them she would be back tomorrow morning. Soon after she left, Stacy called Christy to give her an update on everything that had taken place.

As usual, Christy encouraged her to keep at it every day until she felt comfortable living on her own. She reiterated how the invitation for her to move to California was still available, and she would welcome her with open arms; they made one heck of a BFF pair. The rest of the day went on as usual. At night, while lying in bed, Stacy couldn't help but think how proud Stan would be of her having overcome a large portion of her depression so quickly. The last time he saw her, she had completely broken down. She started reminiscing about how it felt being wrapped in his arms – she felt peace with the world. She hoped that was the start of many more to come. Before long, she fell asleep with Stan on her mind.

The next day, Charmaine came over to give Stacy an update on her training program. She pointed out that each program required a different instructor. Since she had wished to take the O&M program first, the administration staff put her training into the hands of Marie Coleman. She gave Stacy the following information. Marie had been with the organization for five years. She was one of the best O&M instructors they currently had on their staff. Every person she had trained praised her not only for her teaching ethics but also for her caring nature. She treated everyone like family.

Marie was patient with her clients and moved forward with their training only when they were ready. She was a cheerful woman who smiled a lot; with her witty sense of humor, she made sure her patients smiled just as much – if not more. Marie truly loved her work. She often kept in touch with her clients even after their training was completed. Stacy said, *"Charmaine, if Marie is half as nice as you are, I'm sure we will get along just fine."*

Charmaine thanked her for that compliment and assured her that Marie was the perfect match for her. She had arranged for Marie to stop by at 10:00 am the next morning. After a few more minutes of conversation, Charmaine stated that she had another appointment to get to and bid Stacy and Sharon goodbye. After she left, Stacy sat down for a late breakfast.

In the process of helping Sharon clean up, her cellphone rang, *"Hello?"* she answered. *"Hello, young lady, this is Stan. How you holdin' up?"* Stacy was immediately caught off guard; she almost dropped her phone as a smile crept across her face. Stacy was so mesmerized by his voice that she didn't say a word, prompting Stan to ask, *"Stacy, you there?"* *"Oh! I'm sorry. Ugh, what did you ask me?"* she replied. Stacy heard nothing else once he said his name; shame on her for acting that way – like a schoolgirl who got noticed by the school's handsome star quarterback! Stan continued, *"I asked how are you holding up?"* Composing herself, she said, *"I'm fine. I'm fine. I was just surprised to hear from you."*

"Well, I was on break and can't talk long, but I was thinking about you and thought I'd give you a call to make sure you were alright," he said. *"That was so nice of you. I really do appreciate that."* Stacy replied, still wearing this huge smile. Stacy filled him in on her decision to take advantage of the programs offered to her by Second Sense and that she would be starting the very next day. She thanked him for being a big

part of her getting over most of her depression and for motivating her to move forward with her life.

Stan was overjoyed to hear about her progress and assured her that she had made the right decision. He reminded her that she was young and that her whole life was ahead of her with many things she was going to accomplish. Overwhelmed with joy as is, Stacy was recollecting herself with all of the positive reaffirmations Stan was so generously providing her with. Out of everything he said, it was the last statement that made her heart skip a beat. He said, *"And, no matter what, you can always count on me to be there to give you support whenever you need it."* *"Really?"* She asked, *"You mean that?"* *"Yep, I do, young lady. Wouldn't have said it if I didn't mean it. Got to run. I'll be checking in. Take care. Bye."* *"Bye, take care, Stan."* She replied as she hung up. Her entire outlook on life had changed because of Stan. She was determined to see things through yet, was still apprehensive about her ability to catch on to her training and adjust to her new life.

The next morning, Stacy got up, cleaned up, and got dressed while Sharon was preparing breakfast. Stacy didn't know what she would do without Sharon. She seemed almost like a sister to her. Not as close as Christy, but quite close nonetheless. Sharon was always positive. She never complained about anything she had to do for her. When Stacy was feeling sick, depressed, or just upset about something, Sharon was always there to nurse her back to health or a normal state of mind.

Stacy never thought about it before, but being a volunteer wasn't easy. All work and no pay for it – you have got to have a genuine love for people and love what you are doing to be able to do that. There were several instances where Stacy tried to give Sharon a little something for all she did for her, but she would always politely refuse. Sharon stated that her reward was seeing a smile on her face and leaving knowing she had brought a little happiness to her life, no matter how small that may be.

Sharon was married and had a family of her own, but this is what she did. She would always say this is what God called her to do. Stacy couldn't help but think how fortunate her kids must be to have a mom like her and for her husband to agree to have her work, for several hours, outside the home with no financial compensation. Sharon vowed not to leave Stacy until she was completely independent and could manage everything on her own – she was truly blessed to have Sharon.

CHAPTER THIRTY

Like clockwork, at 10:00 am, there was a knock on the door. Sharon opened the door and let her in, knowing Stacy was expecting her. Shortly after, Stacy arrived. Marie introduced herself, *"Good morning. My name is Marie. I'm from Second Sense. You must be Stacy."* To which Stacy replied, *"I am, and I'm glad to meet you. Please come in and have a seat."* Sharon and Marie exchanged some pleasantries, then Sharon excused herself to get back to her duties.

Marie gave Stacy detailed information about herself and the O&M program. She was a Certified Orientation and Mobility Specialist (COMS) who had a master's degree in O&M training. They learned how a person's loss of sight affects their ability to accomplish daily living tasks and travel independently. In fact, Marie had spent many hours blindfolded, learning the cane techniques and orientation strategies they teach. She spent 350 hours of discipline-specific practice and had to pass a certification exam. Stacy had no idea that O&M training was so involved. She had to admire anyone who would put that much time, money, and effort into helping others.

Marie went on to say that O&M is the art of teaching a person with vision loss to travel safely, efficiently, and independently. This, in most circumstances, involved the use of a cane. This would aid in the self-protection of Stacy—not hurting herself when moving around in and outdoors. Stacy would be taught how to use verbal and non-verbal cues to use when she depends on someone else to escort her to various places.

She would also be taught the proper use of a cane to detect information such as any obstacles in her path, stairs, benches, and potholes, or change of surfaces. Stacy would be taught non-visual skills, using various elements like sound, textures, timing, and forming a mental map that would aid her in traveling. Additionally, she would be trained to use sound to help in her travels to know where she is or how close she is to her destination.

There was a device that she could purchase that provided her with audio GPS information. All of this was becoming cumbersome for Stacy – so much to soak in all at once! However, Marie assured her that everything would fall into place once she got into the program. After reading off a list of products that were available for purchase from their product line, Marie asked Stacy what products would she be interested in for her personal use.

Stacy already knew what products she wanted, as she had gone over the catalog with Charmaine and Sharon and had already written out a list. She ordered an audio message recorder, liquid level indicator, bump dots, a big number talking calculator, a money/currency identifier, a talking wrist-watch, and a foldable white cane. Marie took down Stacy's request and said she would find out the total cost and bring that with her tomorrow. Marie left but assured Stacy that she would return at the same time tomorrow.

As promised, Marie came back the next day with the total cost of the items. Stacy asked Sharon to write her out a check, which she did. However, Marie had brought over the folding cane she ordered so they could get started with the program. Marie explained to Stacy that there are various lengths of the cane, and the ideal one, with the tip on the ground, should reach around the height of her armpit. After showing Stacy how to open and close the cane, she let her practice on it until she got the hang of it. Marie then continued her instructions.

Generally, a right-handed person would hold the cane in their left hand and vice versa. The person should hold the grip firmly but loosely. It should be held belly button high but slightly off to one side; stand erect but relaxed when in use. When walking, Stacy needed to alternate her swing with each step. As she stepped right, the cane moved left and vice versa.

The tip needed to contact the surface at all times, but some choose to lift it slightly as they swing it from side to side. The swing should be approximately shoulder width. Marie taught Stacy how to go down the stairs, aided by the cane. She needed to let the tip of the cane fall to the next step and not swing, in case there are other people on the stairs. She would push the cane slightly forward to find the next two steps and to know when there were no more steps left.

To go up the stairs, she needed to grab the cane in a vertical position, lifted up by about two feet, and let it down as it hit the step pushing slightly forward to find the base of the next step or know when there are no more steps. By repeating this, one step at a time, and by paying attention to the sounds, it would give Stacy a general bearing of the environment around her. With that, Marie concluded her lesson.

"Yeah, right! Easy for her to say," Stacy thought. Nevertheless, it was time for her to begin her training. Marie took Stacy through all the steps she had explained to her within her apartment, for starters. Even though Stacy pretty much knew her apartment, she was surprised to find out how quickly she could walk with the cane, letting her know what's in front of her. Before she used the cane, she would walk cautiously, with both arms straight out in front of her, swinging from side to side or stretching them out wide and back together again. Stacy admitted using the cane was easier, but the right foot, left foot thing was something she would have to get used to. As she walked, Marie stayed close by her side, occasionally making sounds by clanking objects together to test Stacy's hearing perception on distance and sound identification.

Marie was very patient with her and encouraged her with every little progress she made. If Stacy did make a mistake, Marie would just laugh it off and let her know everyone made those same mistakes. In a way, Marie did possess a rather large chunk of Christy's character in her – in the way she would always radiate positivity. Marie had Stacy perform the tasks repeatedly throughout the day.

They would take breaks, talk for a while, and then be back at it. By the end of the day, Stacy had gotten the hang of it. By the time Marie left, she was proud of Stacy's progress, as was Sharon. She had heard all the instructions and witnessed them in action. She offered to help Stacy if need be, but, from that day forward, Sharon was not going to assist her in where she walked – Stacy agreed.

The next day, right on time, Marie was at her door. Once inside, she asked Stacy how she thought yesterday's lesson went. Stacy told her that it was a repetitive process, but she finally got the hang of it. Marie was very glad and hugged her; it caught Stacy off guard, but she didn't mind.

Marie continued, *"Now that you've completed inside training, it's time to go outside putting the information and what you learned to the test. It's a little nippy out there, so you might want to grab a jacket."* Sharon was there, so she would watch the apartment in her absence. Stacy grabbed a light jacket, put it on, and headed out the door with Marie by her side. As they went along, Marie would, at first, tell Stacy what was coming up and to listen. Certain sounds could tell her where she was.

With some help from Marie, Stacy stabilized her swing and walking pattern so she could generally walk in a straight line. She tutored Stacy on how to pay attention to the sound of house or business doors opening, the sliding fabric sound of revolving doors, and the sound of car doors opening and closing to judge what portion of the sideway she was walking on. They went inside a building with stairs.

This was a little difficult for Stacy. She would either push the cane too far or not enough – but Marie was there to adjust and correct her every move. They must have stayed in that building for hours going up and down those stairs. But, eventually, it became easier for Stacy. She knew she had to practice more to feel confident with doing it. Marie praised her accomplishments and suggested they call it a day. Stacy agreed – she had had enough for one day. Tomorrow, they would try crossing the street.

As usual, the next day, Marie showed up on time, carrying all the items that Stacy had ordered. Marie took her time and let Stacy handle each product to get a feel for it. Sharon recited the directions of each product to Stacy for her to know how each one operates. All of the items were rather simple to use. They went over each one, step by step, until Stacy had a good idea of how each one functioned. Going through all of the items took up most of the day. Finally, Marie said, *"OK. Now that that's done, it's on to phase two of our outdoor assignment. Today, we're going to learn how to cross the street."*

The thought of having to cross a street that had traffic struck fear in Stacy and brought flashbacks of the accident. Sharon and Marie immediately noticed a change in Stacy's demeanor. Stacy was fine walking on the sidewalks and going inside buildings to practice going on stairs, but there was no way she was going to venture onto the streets. *"Stacy, what's wrong?"* Marie asked. *"I'm sorry, Marie, but there is no way I'm going to attempt to cross a street when there is traffic around,"* Stacy answered, visibly shaken.

Both Marie and Sharon knew about Stacy's accident, and they did understand her hesitancy about being around cars, especially fast-moving ones. But, as they both knew, they had to somehow convince her that it was in her best interest to face her fears. Stacy listened to all of the reasons they brought up, but none of them were convincing enough for her to give her consent. Marie explained to Stacy everything that was involved in the training and assured her she could do it, but Stacy did not budge. They both felt that resuming the discussion would prove fruitless, so Marie opted to let Stacy dwell on the reasons she had given her.

Shortly after arriving back home, it was time for Marie to leave. She told Stacy that she would be back in two days to teach her more things. Stacy thanked her for her time and was grateful that she understood her situation. Sharon's time was up also, so they both bid goodbye to Stacy and left together.

After eating dinner, Stacy got ready for bed but just sat on the couch to think. The more she thought about it, the more she felt she just couldn't do it. As she was deep in thought, her concentration broke when the phone rang, *"Hello."* she said as she answered. *"Hello, good looking."* came the reply – it was Stan. Stacy immediately perked up and forgot all of her worries.

"Hey, Stan! How you doing?" she asked. *"I'm hanging in there, young lady. They say, working as a security guard or a police officer, the objective is to always return home in one piece, taking it one day at a time. So here I am; God saw me through. What's new in your world?"* Stacy told him about Second Sense, the products she had purchased, and the first time she went out practicing with a walking cane.

"Hey, that's great! I know it's not an easy thing to learn, but you're a smart cookie. You'll get the hang of it. If you don't mind me asking, what was the hardest thing for you to do?" He asked. *"Well. Ahhh. Hmm..."* was all that she could muster – Stan had caught her off guard. *"OK, young lady, something is bothering you. Take a moment but tell me what it is. Maybe I can help you?"* he said.

After taking several deep breaths, Stacy mustered the strength and told him about her fear of crossing the streets with traffic. She felt foolish and rather childish for telling him, but he asked, and she was not about to lie to him. *"Aw, honey!"* He said, *"This is just another step in getting you back whole. Sometimes, the hardest thing to do is face your greatest fears. Everyone, at one time or another, has faced those fears. Those who go on to live a normal life are those who overcome their fears. And you, young lady, are strong, trust in God, and have a good supply of faith. So, what good is having faith if you're not going to use it?"*

Stan had made a lot of sense – he usually did. While she was still contemplating her answer for him, he said, *"Tell you what. How about if I come over and accompany you on your training regarding street crossing?"* Talk about turning from sad to glad! Stacy jumped out of her seat, *"Stan! Really? You would do that for me? Seriously?"* *"Yes, I would,"* Stan replied. *"But, you will have to promise me that you will give it everything you've got and will not give up until you have mastered the skill! I will help you for the first day but, after that, you have to promise me that you will stick with it and not create a problem for your trainer."* Stacy was grinning from ear to ear. *"Oh, Stan! You are just wonderful. I'll do it. My lesson is on the day after tomorrow at 10:00 AM."* Stan said, OK! *"I'll let dispatch know, and I'll take a personal day off. Let's do lunch, and feel free to invite Sharon and your trainer. You can decide where you want to go."* Stacy's happiness increased tenfold. Not only was he going to accompany her on the lesson, but lunch too? She would do practically anything for Stan.

Stacy wished she had told Marie to come back tomorrow, but that would be too soon for Stan to take off work. She now had to patiently wait a day and a half to see him – something she found very difficult! The next day, Stacy told Sharon all about her talk with Stan the night before. Sharon was truly happy for her; she knew that they had a special bond for each other and that Stan's suggestion was just what Stacy needed to go through with her training. Stacy wanted to look good for

Stan, so Sharon made arrangements for Stacy at the beauty salon to get her hair done and the spa for a manicure and pedicure. Once back home, Sharon picked out a special outfit for Stacy to wear. By the time that was done, Sharon's day was complete. After she left, Stacy ate dinner and relaxed, still excited about seeing Stan in two days. She managed to fall asleep that night with Stan on her mind.

CHAPTER THIRTY-ONE

The following morning, Stacy had gotten up early and ate the break-fast Sharon had laid out for her the day before. As usual, Sharon arrived first – followed by Marie and lastly Stan. It had been over two weeks since Stan had seen Stacy. Stacy introduced Stan to Marie and explained why Stan was there. Marie was delighted to hear that. Anything that would help Stacy face her fear was definitely worth a try.

Marie had been trained to address these situations, but now, she didn't have to; Stan had done the work for her. They sat down and exchanged pleasantries for nearly an hour before deciding to begin training. Sharon stated she had chores to do around the apartment and would not be joining them. Stacy grabbed a light jacket, and they headed out the door. Once she was outside, Stan momentarily stopped Stacy. He grabbed Stacy by her arms, pulled her close to him, and gently kissed her forehead. As always, Stan had that magic that completely enthralled Stacy; the world didn't matter to her at this point – all she could think about was his touch and his kiss.

Stacy came back to reality when Stan said, *"Young lady, I have to say. You are one magnificent creation. The way you dress and care for yourself, you are going to make some lucky man very happy one of these days."*

He leaned forward and gave her another kiss, this time on her nose. Stan winked at Sharon, who was watching the two from the doorway. She gave a slight nod, closed the door as they started their walk. All the while, Stacy kept yelling in her head, *"Please! Let that lucky man be you! Stacy, Stop! Geez, get a grip, girl! You act like you expect the man to propose to you. He's given you no signs of wanting a relationship with you. You're reading way more into this than you should. But, his touch! His kisses! Girl, Stop! For crying out loud! Concentrate on what you're doing!"*

Here is what Marie had explained to Stacy during her street crossing training. Acoustic traffic or Accessible Pedestrian signals are the same things. These are push-button devices placed on traffic poles that communicate information about the walk and don't walk through audible tones at different intervals. The problem for Stacy was that Chicago has less than a dozen spread throughout the city. There are curbs or slopes of a ramp leading to an intersection. On certain corners, there is what's known as tactile paving – pavement that can be felt. On them are raised bumps, also known as Braille paving, to help the visually impaired detect when they are about to leave the sidewalk and enter the streets.

When attempting to cross the street, Stacy was instructed to hear traffic flow to determine which direction it's moving. She had to make sure that the traffic flowed perpendicular to her before she crossed. Till Stacy got familiar with the intersection, she had to wait for at least two cycles of lights to be sure of traffic flow before crossing. Stacy was advised to make a "mental map" before she left home to keep track of where she was; by counting blocks or streets. If it is a busy intersection, you can gauge, by the flow of people traffic, when you should cross. If there are other people waiting to cross, many times, someone will assist you in crossing.

Stacy walked in front of Stan and Marie. Naturally, she walked at a much slower pace since she wasn't used to it. Stan and Marie did not assist her in the slightest, apart from the occasional, *"You're not walking in a straight line, Stacy,"* from Marie. When Stacy came close to approaching an intersection, Marie hurried to her side and said, *"Stacy, stop. Now, listen; tell me what you hear."* Stacy concentrated on her surroundings.

She could hear people talking, walking, car horns, and the sound of traffic. She described what she heard to Marie. *"Great!"* Marie replied.

"Now, tell me, based on what you hear, how close do you think you are to an intersection?" Stacy shrugged and said, *"About fifteen feet?"* Marie replied, *"Actually, you are about eight feet from the street."* Stacy got startled and took a few steps backward. She was starting to get quite nervous. Stan picked up on that and took action. He positioned himself right behind Stacy so that, the next step she took backward, she would bump into him. *"Stacy,"* He said. *"You can do this; I'm right here. I'm not going to let anything happen to you. But, I'm not going to be with you all the time. This is something you have to do on your own. If I asked you to meet me somewhere, and it was several blocks away, would you?"*

Stan's supportive words brought Stacy back to reality. She thought, *"Of course I would! Even if it meant... crossing the street."* Stan had left her no choice; knowing him, he might even ask her to do that one day just to test her resolve. *"OK,"* she said. *"I'm ready; tell me what to do."* Marie looked at her and said, *"Try to remember what I taught you. Take a minute to think about it and proceed. I'll be right here in case you get it wrong."* Stacy stood for a minute, retracing all of her instructions.

Finally, Stacy slowly moved forward, swinging her cane from side to side, then, she felt the sloping of the pavement. *"Is this the slope?"* She asked. *"Do you think it's the slope?"* Marie replied. To which Stacy said, *"I think so."* Stacy moved to where the slope began and, feeling it slope down, took a step forward and stopped. The people around her knew she might be training, judging from Stan and Marie assisting her, so they gave her room to do so.

Stacy waited for two cycles of lights but didn't hear any audible sounds that could have helped her cross the intersection. Listening to the flow of traffic, she waited until she heard the traffic begin to flow perpendicular to her. Knowing that Stan and Marie were close by, she took a deep breath and proceeded to cross the street. This time, she started walking a little faster to get across the intersection as fast as possible. In her haste, she started veering off-course. Marie called out to her and said, *"Stacy! Slow down! You need to walk more to the left."* This got Stacy right back on course.

Within a relatively short amount of time, she felt the incline slope from the other side. She hurried up the slope and stopped. She could still hear the traffic flowing in the same direction. Her heart was pounding so fast and hard that she thought it would jump right out of her chest. Then, for all of her efforts, came her remedy.

Stan walked up to her from behind and hugged her around her waist. Stan said, *"Now, that's what I'm talking about!"* Stacy took a deep breath and couldn't help but push herself up against him. As soon as he let go, Marie went around and gave her a big hug as well. Stacy couldn't hold back her tears of joy – she did it! They walked all morning, then stopped for lunch; Stan's treat. After lunch, they walked all afternoon, with Stacy crossing as many streets as possible. Heading back home, Stacy thought, *"Now, if Stan asks me to meet him somewhere, just watch me."*

It had been over a month since the accident; Stacy had come a long way. Overcoming this difficulty was beginning to have a positive impact on her low self-esteem, and with the continued help of Sharon, Marie, and especially Stan, things were beginning to look up. But, there were still times when Stacy would get bouts of depression when she would realize she was blind for life. Marie continued to work with her for three more months. It got to the point that Stacy could cross the street with relative ease. Another phase of Stacy's training was Route Planning.

Stacy would learn how to get information about her destination and how to use prior knowledge and utilize different resources before and during the travel. This included: Making sure she was comfortable going to both familiar places she couldn't see anymore and unfamiliar places she's never been before. To implement her training, Marie encouraged Stacy to plan on going shopping at Hyde Park Produce the next day. Stacy had been there before but wasn't recent.

On the way to the store, Marie encouraged Stacy to listen and smell along the way. Stacy remembered there was a Dunkin Donuts a block or two from the store. As they walked that way, she came across the smell of donuts; Stacy used this as a cue and knew she was close to her destination. That's what Marie meant by using different resources.

Marie taught her how to maneuver around the crowded grocery stores and how to shop using her sense of touch, sound, and smell with produce. Next, Marie took Stacy downtown via public transportation. For this, the trip had to be planned. Stacy had to know where the bus stops were, what direction they were headed, and which bus to take.

Fortunately, she had a recording device. Sharon recorded specific instructions on how to get from the apartment to Willis Tower. She even told her how much it would cost and when to buy a transfer, if needed. All Marie did was follow closely behind Stacy with words of encouragement and advice – or corrections if necessary. It took her a minute to catch on to all of this, but she managed.

With technology advancing as it did, Stacy wondered if there was a device that would guide her to the places she wanted to go. Marie looked into it and did indeed find a device; it was called the Trekker Breeze Plus – a handheld, talking GPS. It could record where she wanted to go and give her step-by-step audio direction along the way. Stacy wanted one of those. Second Sense did not have such a device in the product line, so Sharon ordered it for her. *"This would definitely make traveling a lot easier,"* Stacy thought. At this point, Marie indicated that her O&M training was complete. It was now time to move on to another program. Since Stacy wished to take the ILS next, Marie would arrange for a new trainer to visit her tomorrow. Stacy became emotional and hated to see

Marie go. She had become just like a sister to her. But she knew she had other clients who needed her help. They hugged, and before she left, she promised to keep in touch.

CHAPTER THIRTY-TWO

The next morning, the doorbell rang. Stacy was in her room and heard Sharon shout, *"I'll get it!"* As Stacy stepped into the living room to meet the guest, Sharon said, *"Stacy, this is Valerie. Valerie, Stacy."* *"Hi, Stacy,"* Valerie spoke out. *"Hi, Valerie,"* she replied. After settling on the couch, Valerie indicated that she was her Independent Living Skills instructor. Valerie was a certified CVRT vision rehabilitation therapist. Her job was to instruct people with vision impairments in the use of compensatory skills and assistive technology that will enable them to live safe, productive, and interdependent lives. The skills she would teach Stacy would enhance vocational opportunities for her, as well as provide independent living and educational development for Stacy.

Marie had given her rave reviews about Stacy's ability to apply herself. Valerie's job would be to train Stacy to do the following: Use smartphones/tablets and speakers to increase her independence. Take notes which she can read or record. Cook, clean, do laundry, amongst other household chores. Organize personal space – from Stacy's purse to her closet and kitchen cabinets. Use devices with buttons like remotes, microwaves, and push-button phones. Learn how to keep her private financial transactions, well, private. Read Braille, create Braille labels, and read Braille on elevation panels. She would even teach Stacy hobbies to keep her occupied, such as gardening or playing an instrument.

Stacy had to admit, all of it was a lot to learn. But, she had also kept into consideration that she didn't have to learn everything at once; it was one at a time. What Valerie wanted to know was which subject Stacy wanted to take first. After discussing what was involved in each one, Stacy decided to learn Braille first. While she would eventually do each one, Sharon was there to help in the other subjects, so it was not necessary to learn them yet. However, Stacy knew she couldn't teach herself Braille; she wanted to learn it as soon as possible because she wanted to get back to reading the Bible.

Sharon had already done some research and found a company called Braille Bible International. Since 1957, they gave Braille bibles, free of charge, to anyone who was visually impaired – even though it cost about $400 to produce each set. She was glad to know it was the KJV. The 1611 Authorized Version contained eighteen Braille volumes and required sixty inches of shelf space, twelve inches high to store them all. Now that she was going to begin reading Braille, she had Sharon order a set but sent a $100 donation along with it. Sharon rearranged Stacy's shelf-space to accommodate the eighteen volumes.

Now, it would take too much time to go over each one of these subjects Stacy had learned. Naturally, some are more important than others, such as Braille. Stacy had known what it was but was clueless as to how it worked. Braille is a tactile reading and writing system for blind persons in which the raised dots represent letters of the alphabet, to put it simply. It also contains equivalents for punctuation marks and provides symbols for letter groupings.

Valerie gave Stacy a basic introductory lesson on Braille, *"It's read by placing your finger along the line of dots moving from left to right. Braille consists of a row of dots, two across and three deep. Think of it like how the number six is represented on a pair of dice, which is called a cell except, instead of being counter-sunk, it's raised. They are small enough to fit under the tips of your finger, and from the different arrangements of those six dots, you get the entire alphabet. Amazing, right? So, if you only feel two dots across the top, you have the letter "c." Let's say you only feel two dots stacked on top of each other in the left row; you now have the letter "b." Now, let's say you feel five dots and the one missing is on the lower right side that would be a "q." Believe it or not, the letters A through J only use the top four dots –ingenious!"*

One of the difficult parts Stacy faced was trying to remember which set of dots represented which alphabet. There isn't a lot of space between sentences, which makes it more troublesome. In case you are wondering, Louis Braille, who was also blind, at the age of fifteen, started teaching this code to his classmates at a school for the blind in France in 1824. There are two types of Braille systems today. Uncontracted Braille, known as Grade 1 Braille, or Contracted Braille, is known as Grade 2 Braille. The training process in reading Braille required Stacy to use all of her fingers, but, in reality, only one finger is reading. The others are sort of "searching" for punctuations, capitalizations, numbers, or the end of a sentence. However, some only use one finger on one hand to read. There are also Braille codes for math, as well as music. *"Now, you might be wondering,"* Valerie stated. *"Why not just emboss the alphabet on paper? That was done. But embossed books were very expensive and hard to find. They were too big to be carried around or held comfortably on a lap. When embossed, a page contained only a few sentences."*

A slate and stylus are the tools used to write Braille. A slate is a metal or plastic guide that opens up with a hinge on one end – like two rulers riveted together on one end. It has various sizes depending on the paper used. On the other hand, a stylus is a small tool about three inches long, with a metal point at one end and a wooden knob or plastic handle at the other end – like a three-inch nail protruding out of a golf ball. A card stock paper is used for the slate since the regular paper is just too thin. The card stock is inserted into the slate at the top.

The stylus is used to punch holes in the stock. The holes that are punched are the raised dots that will be read by touch. It's interesting to note that you must write the cells in reverse when you write Braille, and you must write letters from right to left, unlike from left to right for English. So, when you remove the paper from the slate and flip it over to read the raised dots, the cells will be in the correct orientation and order to properly read them – not easy to learn at all; it's like learning another language.

[I hope you have developed a new appreciation for those who took the time to learn Braille. Each person learns at their own pace. Some catch on faster than others. I caught on easier by reading the bible in Braille since I already remembered verses and knew what words would be next. In my case, it took a good four months of constant practice before I became comfortable]

After learning Braille, the next thing that Stacy needed to do was to "reclaim" her kitchen. She already knew how to cook, but now, she had to organize things and cook without injuring herself. Valerie taught her to pour drinks or prepare items over or on a large tray to catch spills for easy cleanup. Utilizing the corners of the tray is even more beneficial. On one corner, Stacy would keep a small bowl to place all of the food scraps.

On another corner, she would place small items like measuring spoons, lids, and small ingredients like garlic cloves, salt, and pepper shaker. Buy food that comes in different shapes and sizes for easy recognition. Stacy was taught to utilize an easy identification system using rubber bands to identify items; for example, two rubber bands around a container indicate that it's salt. Apart from that, placing Braille labels or remove the wrappers from certain cans or jars works well.

Stacy was instructed to only buy what would fit in the pantry comfortably. By designating a certain place for each item in the cabinet or drawer, it became easier to know exactly where everything was – the same principle applies to the fridge. Using bins to store similar groups of items was also efficient. Stacy was taught to be extra cautious with knives and to place all knives in a holding block. Once a knife is no longer used, it was to be placed behind the kitchen faucet, blade down, and handle to the right. After Valerie went over a few more things, Sharon, having been there to observe everything, took over to make sure Stacy was doing it correctly. Apart from learning Braille, cooking in a safe way was very difficult. As a general rule of thumb, Stacy was instructed to lay out everything she would use whilst cooking, including spices, utensils, timer, oven mitts, and the preparation board. Additionally, she was told to always wear short-sleeved clothes whilst cooking so she wouldn't catch her clothes on fire.

After a considerable amount of time training, Stacy, with only the observance from Sharon and Valerie, put her knowledge to the test by preparing a meal – a steak, baked potatoes, asparagus, and a salad on the side; with lemonade to drink. With Valerie and Sharon's previous help, the bump-dots Stacy had bought at the beginning of her training were strategically placed on the appliances in the kitchen.

Things like the start and stop button of the microwave, another on the timer, and the knobs on the stove. Stacy already had a mental picture of what everything looked like, where they were in the kitchen and where the controls were located since she had actually seen them. If you were new to this, you would have to spend time feeling each item as someone explained to you where each control was and its function.

Having laid everything out for the meal, it was a "simple" task to retrieve each required item. Stacy began with the steak. After rinsing it off, she laid it on a paper plate and placed it at the bottom of the tray. The potato and the asparagus were placed at the top of the tray on opposite corners, along with the spices at the top-middle section. The tray Stacy used was quite large, measuring twenty-four inches left to right and twenty inches top to bottom. Taking a paper towel, Stacy dabbed the steak on both sides, removing as must water as possible. She seasoned it well on both sides and let it sit for a minute. Stacy chose a large, heavy skillet with a round handle to prepare the steak. Since the stove's electrical coils were cold, she placed her hand on the burner she wanted to use. Stacy turned the knob to the desired temperature and removed her hand when she felt the heat from the selected burner.

Holding her hand a safe distance above the heat, Stacy placed the skillet directly under her hand. Of course, using a gas stove, the procedure would be a little different. She took a wooden spoon and went around the outside of the skillet, feeling for strategically placed dots to make sure it was centered on the burner. After waiting for a few minutes for the pan to heat up, the steak was ready for searing. Using a long handle pair of tongs, wearing the oven mitts, and finding the handle, she placed the steak in the middle of the pan.

Having set the timer, Stacy turned the steak about every minute, even after the searing, because she wanted it to cook through evenly. Just by pressing a steak, you can tell if it's rare, medium, or well-done by the resistance. The more well-done a steak is, the firmer it will feel. Stacy enjoyed a medium-well steak, so that's what she was going for. Once it got close to where she wanted it to be, she could either turn the burner off or to a very low setting and just leave it there for a minute. Now, it was time for the baked potato. Having already washed it thoroughly, Stacy would, ordinarily, wrap it in aluminum foil and bake it. But, since it was only one potato, that would be a waste of electricity, so she decided to microwave it. Using a fork, she punched a few holes evenly around it, so it didn't explode with all the pressure that builds inside it as it cooks. She put it in the microwave for five minutes, then, once done and using a mitt, turned it over for another five minutes. While it's baking, Stacy moved the skillet with the steak to a cold burner. Turning the heat back on medium, following previous procedures, she placed another skillet on the burner.

Having already washed the asparagus and grabbing three at a time with her hands, she grabbed them with a pair of tongs and placed them in the skillet, whole, horizontally. For directions, she would use the ends of the asparagus to find the edge of the skillet. Stacy, using her finger to gauge the amount, sprinkled several teaspoons of chopped up garlic from a jar on the asparagus. Next, having pre-measured, she poured in her special, thick vinaigrette/teriyaki sauce and covered it for a few minutes.

By this time, the potato was done. She took a plate, went back to the stove, and removed the steak from the skillet – placing it on the plate, she moved it to one side of the large tray and stopped once it touched her finger she used for a guide at the edge. Stacy, going back for the asparagus and carefully searching for the handle as a guide, removed the cover and, using the tongs, carefully flipped the asparagus in the opposite direction. To replace the cover, while holding the pan's handle, she pointed that thumb in a horizontal position toward the pan. She moved the cover around until it touched her thumb.

From there, push it forward a couple of inches, and she should be close to the center of the skillet. Wearing a mitt, she removed the potato from the microwave, placed it on a small plate, then, using her fingers as a guide, carefully cut it in half, in one direction, then in half in the other direction and let it fall open. She sprinkled some salt, a few patties of butter, and a scoop of sour cream before placing it on the large tray.

By this time, the asparagus was done, so she grabbed another plate. Again, searching for the handle as a guide, still wearing her mitts, she removed the cover, and feeling around with the tongs, managed to scoop up all of the asparagus in three tries. Using her finger as a guide, she searched for the middle of the plate and placed the asparagus there. Stacy set the plate on the large tray. She then retrieved the lemonade from the refrigerator and grabbed a glass. Just like Valerie taught her, she placed the second joint of her index finger on the rim of the glass and bent it straight down. This helped her keep the glass steady and to know when the glass was getting full. Once she felt the liquid touch her finger, she would stop pouring.

As a general rule of thumb, Stacy only bought liquids in small containers, never in a gallon, since they're quite difficult to maneuver. However, for a full container, she would place the glass rim just below the opening of the container, keeping it there while slowly tilting the container down. One hand on the container while the other is on the glass with her index finger inside the glass as a gauge. This way, avoiding any spills when she would start pouring.

The salad was the simplest of all. Taylor Farms make salads that are good to go. Some already contain the dressings in a variety of flavors. She would shake the bag until there was empty space at the top. Holding the top with her fingers, she would cut several inches below them. Next, just pour in a bowl, and add the dressing... *et voila!* You now have a meal fit for a king. Having prepared everything in advance, Stacy was done in about half an hour. [Think you can do this, blindfolded?]

By now, Stacy thought, "*If Stan did happen to take me out on a date, I best know what I'm doing.*" So, Valerie taught her Dining with Confidence. Here are some of the things that comprise it. To reach for her drink, Stacy would have to slide her fingers across the table with her fingertips until she touched the glass. By lifting the empty fork and spoon, she could judge when there's food on it. Knife handles are flat on the top but curved on the bottom, where the blade is. The fork needs to be used to gently probe where food is on the plate. Use a piece of bread or a knife to push the food unto the fork – no fingers! Cutting close to the edge of your food will ensure small bite-size pieces. When it's time to eat, it's always best to lean over the plate when she needed to take a bite to eat. In other words, "come to the food." Using her spoon, whenever possible, prevents most foods from sliding or rolling off. The last bit of advice Valerie gave Stacy was whenever she would order soup, order it in a cup; it prevents a lot of embarrassing spills.

CHAPTER THIRTY-THREE

Valerie was nothing short of an angel. She was very patient with Stacy even when she got upset about something that she just couldn't seem to do or understand. No matter how many times Stacy would ask, she was always calm and professional, giving her the answer even if it was for the thousandth time. Valerie covered home safety procedures like using Velcro on the throw rugs' ends so they could not curl up and trip her. Sharon had pretty much taken care of the rest. Valerie also covered Human Guide Techniques. That's just another way of saying how to walk safely with another person on your arm.

Like Marie, Stacy was sad to see her go, but she had other clients that needed her attention. Stacy completed her course in December of 2015. She really didn't want to take the Technology Solutions and Training course because she was not big on computers or any electronic device for that matter. However, Stacy knew that to be completely independent and, one day, find a job, she had to know some computer skills.

Christy showed her things like email, typing letters, and searching for information, but how was she going to do that blind? The program was free, so she decided to suck it up and take the final step. Besides, if Stacy was lucky enough that Stan wanted a relationship with her, it would be best to help out financially. She told Valerie to give her a day to think about it, and she would give her an answer, which she did. They would be sending someone in two days.

As promised, two days later, the doorbell rang. Stacy went to the door and asked who was there. *"Hi. My name is David Reid from Second Sense. I'm looking for Stacy."* He said. She opened the door and said, *"Hi, I'm Stacy. Please, come in."* David came in and, after some brief formalities, explained to Stacy who he was. David was from the Technology Solutions and Training department and had a CATIS certification. CATIS stands for Certified Assistive Technology Instructional Specialist. They are highly trained experts who specialize in working with blind, visually impaired individuals or who have functional visual limitations. They empower them to achieve their life goals for education, employment, recreation, and independence through the use of assistive technology. The Technology Solutions and Training department were broken down into three sub-departments.

Individual Technology Training

They teach you how to use a computer, from turning it on to being job-ready. The client sets the goals for training, and an instructor will work with the person to determine the skills needed to reach that goal. Stacy would meet with an instructor for one-to-one and a half hours one day each week.

Individual Technology Tutor

They could also help with technology needs but in a different field. The volunteer tutors could help with (in Stacy's case) Microsoft Word and Excel, navigating the internet, setting up web-based emails, basic gestures for iPhone and iPad, how to download audiobooks, and how to troubleshoot hardware issues.

Half-Day Classes and Workshops

They offer a wide range of classes on the latest tools and technology. The classes are held in their computer training classroom with ten workstations, each equipped with the latest technology. Stacy could take classes on software such as Advanced Word, Excel Spreadsheets, and PowerPoint. Apple iPhones, Apps, and Settings. Adaptive Technology Software, online shopping, and social media.

Stacy already knew how to operate a computer with Christy's help. Although they offered a lot of technology, she wanted to know which programs would give her the best chance to land a job. Things like social media, iPhone, iPad, and shopping online would be useful to know but won't help her get a job. So, David asked her what she had in mind as far as a career or occupation was concerned. Stacy had never really thought about that. She was doing well at the bank and had another opportunity downtown, but, unfortunately, she had to face the here and now. So, Stacy had a long talk with David, and both weighed the pros and cons.

Since Stacy liked the office environment, David suggested she take up office programs like Word, Excel, and PowerPoint to start with. Stacy already knew how to search the web and download information. So now, Stacy had to choose which sub-department she would prefer. She chose the Half Day Classes and Workshop for two reasons. Firstly, it would get her out of the house, and she could practice her traveling skills. Second, the Technology Tutor was only given on Tuesdays and Thursdays. Half-Day Classes were on weekdays and Saturdays. Talking it over with David, they both agreed the Half-Day Classes was the way to go.

OK. Before we continue, I want to explain some things to you. The ability to work on a computer by a blind person is done through voiceover software that permits the computer to talk to you. However, you must have a good idea of how to type using a computer keyboard. Not just the numbers and alphabets but other essential keys such as tab, ctrl, alt, caps, enter, etc. But, if you don't know this, they will teach you. If you don't know anything about Word, Excel, or PowerPoint, they can teach you, but you will have a lot to learn in order to become proficient at qualifying for working in that field. I will give you a small sample of what I mean by a voiceover by taking you through the procedures of sending an email.

I purchased a used 2009 MacBook Pro laptop. It has a thirteen-inch screen but, at this point in my life, since I can't see, who cares if the screen is six feet or one-inch long. As stated earlier, there is an option that will read the contents for you called voiceover. Here's how to do that. Having been taught how to do the following, you would go to System Preferences then click Accessibility. A window or box will open up. Inside the box is a title: Enable Voiceover. Check the box. A voice will then tell you it is activated. So, let's say I want to send an email to Christy. You would go to Documents, scroll down to finder, and continue scrolling until the voiceover says "mail." Hit the space bar to open. To start, hit "command N" It will then indicate "new message window." That is asking who you want the email to be sent to—type in the sender's email address. Don't forget; it repeats everything you type, so you will know if it's the correct address. You will drop down one line by hitting the tab, which is the "cc" line. Tab one more time will take you to the subject line and will say "subject, edit text," After that, tab down one more time to type in your message. Once you are done composing your email, you are now ready to send it. Hold down command and shift at the same time and the "D" and you're done. It's not very hard as long as you know the buttons on your keyboard.

Now, before I continue any further, you're probably wondering about Christy and Stan and what they've been up to all this time. Well, Christy and I would talk about three times a week. She had found someone that interested her, but, at this time, they were only friends. I really did wish Christy would find the right person. She would make an excellent companion for the right guy but, Christy was picky and, knowing the hurt her past relationships caused her, I didn't blame her. She was happy now, so I hoped it would keep getting better and better each day.

As for Stan... Well, that wonderful man called me about every other day to check up on me. He would give me advice on whatever I asked, on something I may not understand or did not want to do during the course of my training. Stan was like my rock. Even though those things I found difficult or didn't want to do, he put it all in perspective and, by the time he was done talking, it was all good. Stan was there for my birthday, he was there for Fourth of July, Memorial Day, Easter, Christmas, you name it, and he was there.

He even remembered the day we first met. His company was done bouncing him around, and he was permanently posted at a bank not too far away. He would come over and spend time with me, helping me with my training before and sometimes after dinner. He did not assist me in anything unless I asked but, even then, he made sure it was something I really couldn't do. That kept me on the path of being independent.

Excel and PowerPoint were taught the same way. At this point, it had been almost a year from the time of Stacy's accident. The staff at Second Sense said I was one of the fastest learners they had come across. *"Wisdom from above."* Stacy would always reply. Although there was a lot more for her to do to master all the programs that she needed, Stacy could now consider herself eighty-percent independent. But, something interrupted her training. This had nothing to do with Stacy; this was utterly divine intervention – something she did not see coming. By now, Stacy was fully prepared to continue all the courses they had available to land a good job. She wanted to hold up her side of the relationship, should Stan want to form one with her. But, if not, Stacy still had to make a living.

Here's the revelation. Stacy thought about how she would come into contact with a blind person from time to time but never considered how they felt in their state or how they felt about what we felt about them. Perhaps the biggest thing she [and us] never, ever considered was what it took for them to be standing in front of her at that time. [Think about it! What would it take for you to do that?]

The time had come, which turned into a very emotional event. Stacy had now learned to be self-supporting to the degree that she no longer needed Sharon's help. No, that wasn't entirely true. She still needed Sharon's emotional support when those times of feeling down and a little depressed came. Sharon was like her big sister and would be considered part of her family. But Stacy knew she had a family of her own and had volunteered her time for over a year. It was time to let go. Stacy and Sharon celebrated by Stacy taking Sharon out for pizza at Beggars Pizza then went to play miniature golf in one of the towns close to where Stan lived. It was really difficult for them to part ways. Stacy always kept Sharon in her prayers.

CHAPTER THIRTY-FOUR

It was time for Stacy to see Dr. Browdy for her routine eye check-up. She didn't know why she kept doing this; it was the same diagnosis every time. It was tough for her to keep hearing that her eyes were normal except for the already known damage. What's normal about no sight? Sounds like an oxymoron. She called for her ride, which showed up in five minutes.

Arriving at his office, as usual, she had to wait after checking in. Of course, she could hear others in the room waiting to see Dr. Browdy, but she often wondered what their condition was. Were they blind as well? Did Dr. Browdy have the ability to correct what might be wrong with them? Were they born this way or, like her, did something happen to them? *"Stacy, the doctor will see you now,"* was the next thing she heard.

The assistant escorted her to one of the room and said the doctor would be right in. A few minutes later, he walked in. *"Hello, Stacy. It's that time again, huh?"* He said. *"Hi, Doc. Yeah, it's that time again,"* was her reply. *"Well, swing around and lay on the bed, and let's take a look at you."* Every time she did this, in her deep subconsciousness, she wondered if she would ever be able to see the light from his ophthalmoscope. Wait for it. Wait for it... and... NO! NOTHING! *"Hmm."* She heard Dr. Browdy say out loud, breaking the silence in the room. *"Hmm?"* Stacy thought. *"What did that mean?"* He repeated his "hmm" several times, pausing between each one.

Now, she was really curious. Why does he keep saying that? *"Stacy,"* he began. *"I don't quite know how to tell you this, and I can't explain it. Now, don't get too excited when I tell you this because it might not be anything, but it seems that both irises show signs of repairing themselves. The damage the shards left behind could be compared to scars. But, somehow, oddly enough, they are disappearing. In all my years of practice and medical knowledge, I can't explain that."*

Stacy was confused, *"You say my eyes are repairing themselves, but I can't see. Really? That makes no sense. Doc, I don't understand. What are you trying to say?"* Dr. Browdy replied, *"Well... before I go any further, I want to give you an exam with what we call a slit lamp. It allows me to get a better picture of your cornea, iris, and pupil. We'll schedule that test for your next visit. Stop by the desk and make another appointment in two weeks. See you then."* And with that, he was gone.

Stacy thought, *"OK! What just happened? He can't explain what? What the heck is a what lamp? Scars?"* All she knew was something happened, and the only person who had the answer was Dr. Browdy, and he was gone. It started to tax her brain, trying to put all the pieces together, then, abruptly, stopped. She was not about to drive herself crazy, trying to answer questions she couldn't possibly answer. So she said a little prayer and asked the Lord to take care of it. Just when she was finishing, the door opened, and the nurse came in to walk her out.

The next day Stan called in to check on her. He asked how she was doing and wanted to know if there was anything she needed. Ever since Dr. Browdy said what he said, all she thought was whether or not to tell Stan. Maybe she should just tell him what was said and take it from there? But then, like her, questions would be asked which she couldn't answer. Maybe she should get more information before telling him? After all, she didn't have anything conclusive to say. But then he might get upset that she hadn't told him sooner? Now that he was on the phone, a decision had to be made. She decided to tell him; they had always been honest with each other, so this should be no exception.

"Hey, Stan. I'm doing as well as possible. And no, I don't need anything. I'm good," was her reply. *"But, there is something I need your thoughts on."* Stan inquired, *"What's up, hon?"* Stacy explained the entire visit to the eye doctor and tried to tell Stan, word for word, what the doctor had said. *"Hmm,"* he said, *"Now that is interesting. It sounds like there is something there, but the doctor doesn't want to commit before he can do additional tests."*

He was very analytical and reasonable and didn't start peppering her with questions. Just another reason she felt the way she did for him. "So," Stan asked, *"What do you think it means? I know we're just guessing at this point, but what does your gut tell you?"* *"Well, I know I shouldn't get my hopes up too high, but, on the other hand, from what he said, it sort of gives me hope. But I don't know what I'm hoping for?"* Stacy replied hesitantly. *"That's understandable,"* he said, *"But I'm sure you will find out more in two weeks. In the meantime, remember something, babe. From the time this accident happened, you have asked God to intervene. Could this be His answer? Maybe, or maybe not. But you have always had faith and hope. But, no matter how we look at it, Dr. Browdy saw something. The Lord is going to do whatever He pleases. Either way, regardless of the outcome, God is always in control."*

That's exactly what she needed to hear. Not that she didn't know that, but she just needed reaffirmation. Instead of praising God for the good news, even though not knowing where this would lead, she started with all these questions. *"Stan,"* she said, *"How many times are you going to lift me up?"* *"As many times as it takes,"* He said. *"Now that we have some inspiring news, we should celebrate. Two scoops of double chocolate should do the trick, don't you think?"* *"Perfect for the occasion,"* Stacy replied cheerfully. *"I've got a couple of things to do, but I should be there in about 40 minutes. See you then, cutie,"* he said. *"I'll be ready. See ya then,"* She replied.

After disconnecting, she thought to herself, *"Where would I be without Stan?"* She had to admit, Stan was basically her only spiritual support and that, even if he wasn't, she was being drawn to him more and more each day. In her eyes, no pun intended, everything about him was perfect even down to the way he walked. She found it difficult trying to understand why Stan would stick around knowing her situation when he could, pretty much, have any woman he wanted? Could it be he might have feelings for her that went beyond friendship?

If he ever approached her, wanting a relationship, what would she say? *"Hell Yeah!!"* she said out loud – she would be crazy not to. But, coming back to earth, she was jumping the gun. She knew he knew what he wanted. If she were fortunate enough to be that special person in Stan's life, she would relish the chance. If not, and they just remained friends, Stacy would accept that too. Either way, having him would make her content. *"Wait, what time is it?"* She thought. *"He's coming over!?"* She had gotten lost in her thoughts and nearly forgot! Stacy made haste, preparing herself for his arrival. As always, she wanted to look good for him.

CHAPTER THIRTY-FIVE

Two weeks couldn't get here fast enough. Although Stacy was still very apprehensive, her appointment was in a couple of hours. She had replayed everything the doctor said to her during her last visit. She said it over and over again in her head, for two weeks. Stacy was hoping there was something she missed during the conversation, which would give her some new information; that didn't happen.

Every time she went down this path, she would wind up at the same conclusion, and that was, Stan was right – it was out of her hands. God knew, and He was going to do what he does. Whichever way it turned out, she would accept it as His will even though she really wanted to have our sight back. The time had come for her to leave. Her phone rang. It was the driver letting her know he had arrived.

Arriving at the doctor's office, she checked in and sat down, awaiting her turn. After about fifteen minutes, she heard her name called. She was placed in the first room, but as soon as she sat down, Dr. Browdy walked in. *"Hello, Stacy,"* He said. Stacy returned his greetings, and he continued, *"We spoke about giving you a more thorough test on your eyes on your last visit. So, let's do that. The examination room is down the hall so let's take a walk."* Once in the room, Stacy sat down in what felt like a dentist chair. To prepare for the exam, the assistant placed drops in both eyes, containing a dye called Fluorescein, to basically wash the eye. After a few minutes, additional drops were put in, allowing her pupils to dilate. Once that took effect, she adjusted the chair to the proper height. *"Stacy,"* Dr. Browdy said, *"I want you to lean forward slowly until I tell you to stop."* Stacy complied and started leaning forward. *"That's it. OK... a little more... and... stop."* Stacy felt him place her chin in a plastic cup and tilted her head forward until her forehead rested against a plastic bar. "Try not to blink," he said.

It took a minute or two to adjust the machine and conduct the test. After several minutes he said she could sit back and relax. *"Young lady,"* He said, *"I'm sure you remember the last conversation we had regarding your irises. Well, it seems that Mother Nature is doing something that no man has yet to do and probably will never do. The damage the shards did to your irises, and I can't medically explain it, are repairing themselves. During the last two weeks, I have spoken to other ophthalmologists about your case and none of them, in all their professional years, has heard or seen a situation like yours."* Stacy was baffled, *"OK, doc. You have me on the brink of an anxiety attack. For heaven's sake, please, in plain English, what are you getting at?"* Dr. Browdy continued, *"Well, if indeed the healing process continues and completes itself to the degree it's headed, there is an outside chance that you may regain sight. Now, hold on. Because we haven't seen this before, I can't say how much of your sight you will regain. It could range from 1 to 100. However, putting all that aside, your irises have to heal completely before we consider the next step, which presently they're not."*

Stacy wanted to shout for joy but restrained herself. Even if there was a 1% chance, it was better than none. Her thought was interrupted by Dr. Browdy, *"We'll see you in another two weeks. Any questions?"* *"No,"* she replied, *"I'll see you in two weeks."*

Stacy was escorted to the waiting area to wait on her ride. Then it hit her, something Stan had reminded her of. She immediately dropped her head and thanked God in a special way. Stacy had maintained her faith in Him to work a miracle with her sight. She was trying to live right by Him. He said come to Him like a child, and He will hear. She felt that not only did He hear, but He also acted. She was so deep in prayer that someone had to come over and shake her to let her know her ride was here – Her spirits were indeed lifted.

Stacy couldn't wait to get home to contact Stan and tell him all that Dr. Browdy had said. On the way home, she spent the time in prayer and telling the driver, in her excitement, about what just took place. The driver was very happy for her and, being a Christian, reminded her that God is always in control. Once back home and settled, she called Stan. She knew he was at work and wouldn't answer his phone, so she was going to leave him a voicemail. To her surprise, he picked up the phone. *"What's up, little princess?"* *"Hi, Stan,"* She said. *"I was going to leave you a voicemail since I know you're at work. Do you have time to talk?"* *"I've got a few minutes,"* He said. He could tell, from the sound of her voice, she was excited about something.

Starting from the beginning, she told him all that took place at the doctor's office. *"Hon, that is great news. Let's celebrate. When I get off of work, I will pick up dinner. What are you in the mood for?"* *"How about Chinese. Haven't had that in a while,"* She said. *"Sounds good to me,"* He replied, *"What's on the menu?"* Stacy thought for a few seconds and said she would like chicken fried rice and vegetable egg foo young. "And don't forget the extra sweet and sour sauce." She said. *"Got it. See you at 6:00 PM. Ciao!"*

As soon as Stan hung up, her mind immediately went to what to wear. She knew Stan was a dress and heels man. Should it be a short dress or a long one? Should she leave her hair down or pin it up? And what color dress? Every time Stan was around her, she wanted to look good for him no matter the occasion. There was an outfit she had not worn before. It was a knee-length pink and black sleeveless dress. She knew it was form-fitting and didn't want to send the wrong message, but she also knew Stan liked her figure. She decided to wear that dress with black heels. She was going to shave her legs so she could skip the stockings.

Shortly after 6 PM, the doorbell rang. *"Hey, babe." "Hey, Stan."* After he was in, she closed the door. *"Ms. Thang,"* He said. *"You are a vision of beauty. Next to the word sexy and beautiful in the dictionary, they have your picture. You are every man's desire."* Stacy had this grin from ear to ear. *"I'm starving, Hon. You ready to eat?" "I haven't eaten much all day waiting for this, so let's do it,"* She said. Stacy had already laid out the plates and utensils. Stan asked Stacy to have a seat and that he would serve her. She gladly obliged. They didn't say much during dinner. Stan didn't ask any questions since he wanted to give her his full attention when she told him. Likewise, Stacy wanted to tell him all about it without being interrupted.

After clean up, they went to the living room and sat next to each other. *"I can't wait to tell you this,"* she said and told him all about her doctor's visit and even told him about her ride back home. When she was done, she inquired, *"So, what do you think? Am I too optimistic?"* Stan replied, *"Honey, although nothing has been confirmed, it sounds like you have good reason to be excited. In my opinion, this is not something man did nor, for that matter, anything in your control. Now, I might be wrong, but I think this is an answer to your prayers. Like the doctor stated, no one knows how much vision you will have and to what degree. Having said all that, I am so happy for you."* He leaned forward and kissed her on her nose.

Stacy knew he was right. She didn't want to get her hopes up too high then be disappointed. She would continue in prayer and take it one day at a time.

CHAPTER THIRTY-SIX

"Hey, we forgot something," Stan said. *"We forgot to open our fortune cookies; be right back."* He got up, went to the kitchen, and came back within a few seconds. Stan said there were three fortune cookies. Stacy would open two, and he would read it to her, then open his and read it. She opened the first one and handed it to Stan. It said something about success in business. Next, Stan opened his, and it said a long-lost friend would visit him. It's what happened next that Stacy was unprepared for. Instead of a fortune cookie, Stan placed a small box in Stacy's hand.

"It's not a fortune cookie, but it's still something that has to be opened," he said. Stacy was perplexed as to what it could be. Maneuvering it around in her hand, she was finally able to figure it out. She held the bottom of the small box and pulled the lid up, which was the box's full depth, off. *"OK, now what?"* Stacy asked. *"Like the fortune cookies, you need to find out what's inside,"* he said. Reaching inside, within seconds, she froze, her mouth dropped open, and her heart started racing. It was a ring.

Stacy screamed, *"Oh my God! Stan! What is this? What are you saying? What does this mean? I don't understand!?"* Stan reached out and held both of her hands. *"Honey,"* he said, *"We haven't known each other that long, but I do think we have a connection that's undeniable to both of us. During the time we have known each other, I can tell, unless I'm completely wrong, that you have developed a deep feeling for me. Those same feelings have grown on me as well. There are not many women I've come across who appeal to me in every way. You, babe, are just about as complete a woman that a man could ask for. Yes, I know that there are still things we need to know about each other but, at this point, I don't want another man coming between you and me. And don't think for one minute that I'm doing this because I feel sorry for you in your condition. It matters little to me one way or other. It's an engagement ring, so..."* Those were the last words that came out of his mouth before Stacy shouted, *"Yes! Yes! Oh, Jesus, Yes!"*

Tears had started forming the second she discovered it was a ring. Still holding on to his hands, she pulled him to her, hugged him as tightly as possible, still sobbing uncontrollably. She thought this had to be a dream. Stan, the smartest, kindest, most professional, and for sure, the most handsome man she had ever come across in her life – wanted her! She was hugging him so hard she was starting to lose feeling in her arms.

Finally, after letting him go, she tried to gather herself. Stan placed a handkerchief in her hand, which she used to dry her eyes. Stacy couldn't speak; she was utterly lost for words. Stan leaned forward and placed his lips onto hers. Her passion was ignited. Stacy put one arm around his waist and, with the other hand, placed on the back of his head, drew him in closer. She kissed him like it was the last kiss she would ever get. As if on cue, Stan did the same. It only lasted a minute, but that was the most intense kiss Stacy had ever experienced in her life. She had now fallen off the cliff in love with Stan.

Stan took the box from Stacy, who was still clutching it, took out the ring, and placed it on her finger. It fit perfectly. Stan pulled her close to him, and she melted in his arms. Neither said a word. Stacy felt so relaxed and comfortable that, within a few minutes, she started drifting off to sleep. Stan could feel her body going limp, so he woke her up. *"Honey,"* he said. *"You must be tired. You've had a most interesting day. I'll leave so you can get dressed for bed. I'll call you tomorrow to check in on you."* She didn't want him to leave, but he was right. The news from the eye doctor and just getting engaged had drained her of all emotions and energy.

Holding his hand, Stacy walked him to the door. Before leaving, Stan turned around and gave her another quick kiss. She felt herself blush. Then, he was gone. After climbing in bed, the day's activities kept re-cycling in her mind. Stacy touched her lips, remembering how his kiss felt. She kept feeling the ring to make sure this wasn't a dream. This was the second time in her life she had been engaged. She thought to herself, *"Mrs. Wallace! Mrs. Wallace. Mrs. Wallace!"* Stacy eventually drifted off to sleep with a smile, thinking about that.

When Stan got home, having climbed into bed, he also reminisced on what had just taken place. For some time now, the only thing that seemed to occupy his mind was Stacy. To him, she was an angel. He cared less what other people thought. To him, she was the perfect ten in every way. She had been through so much, yet she persevered. He felt that if Stacy loved someone, she would do it with all her heart. Stan knew why her mother was so jealous and envious of her –she was gor-geous, simply beautiful. As they used to say back in the days, she was "stacked, packed, and all that!" Stacy had a flawless dark complexion. He knew she caught the attention of almost every man's eye when she walked down the street. Stacy has class and was somewhat old-school, which is what he liked. The new-age woman really didn't understand how to let a man be a man nor how to please him. Stacy had no problem with it.

Stacy had already indicated to Stan that, from reading her Bible in the past, she had come to understand what it took for a woman to be a woman. He tried to find some reason not to like her – but couldn't. Of course, they needed to discuss and come to an understanding of things like kids, where to live, religion, money, and things of that nature.

But, knowing Stacy as he did, he hoped none of this would present a problem. Another thing he liked about her was her self-awareness of her figure. It was important to her that she kept herself in shape. He liked how dainty she was. She had a natural runway model walk. She kept her hair long and in order, pinning it up from time to time but never cutting it. Stacy wore bangs – a weakness of his. She wore very little make-up since she was naturally beautiful - light shades of lipstick only. She had thick eyebrows, which she kept trimmed, and long lashes. It was not the fake ones, but what you get by applying mascara. She was the perfect height, 5' 8", which complemented his 6'2" frame. But, one of the most fantastic character traits she possessed was her love of God and trying to live up to her biblical understanding. That was the foundation he looked for.

Stacy had no kids, and he didn't want any. However, he didn't know if this was going to cause a problem. From observing her and her apartment, Stan knew she was neat and organized. She had prepared dinner for him on several occasions, so he knew she knew her way around the kitchen. Other than her eyesight, she seemed to be in excellent health, didn't smoke or drink. He had never heard a cuss word come from her lips. She didn't mind working, which would add to their financial health. Stacy made sure the nail polish on her hands and feet matched. Other than a watch, a gold neckless at times, which was a birthday present from Christy, and small clip-on earrings, she wore no other jewelry.

When dressed, Stacy made sure she was color coordinated even when at home. Although she wore pants on rare occasions, he can't remember the last time he saw her in them. Stacy was a dress and heels girl. He knew about her past, but only what she felt free to talk about. Stan could care less about her past; all that interested him was the future – their future. If she needed help defeating those dark emotions from time past, he would be there by her side; no matter what. If she wanted to know something, she just needed to ask, and vice versa. He had been and would be truthful with her. He was glad he gave her a ring. Stan felt like he was the luckiest man in the world. He was glad she accepted. He had found his Eve.

CHAPTER THIRTY-SEVEN

When Stacy woke up the next day, it didn't take long for it to dawn on her what had happened the day before. News about her eyes was encouraging, but getting engaged was the real "icing on the cake." She reached down and caressed the ring on her finger. It wasn't a dream. It had actually taken place! Stacy immediately thought, *Christy! I have got to tell Christy!* She picked up the phone and dialed Christy. The phone rang and rang and finally went to voicemail. *"Christy, it's me. Girl, you have got to call me back as soon as possible! You are not going to believe what happened to me yesterday. Talk to you then. Bye."* Now that she was engaged to the most wonderful man in the world, her outlook on life changed dramatically. Although very much wanting to see again, it was now secondary to her engagement to Stan. She could live, just the way she was, as long as Stan was by her side.

Throughout the day, questions about Stan popped into her head. Did he want kids? Stacy was fortunate that she had not gotten pregnant by Mitchell. He had taken the precaution of putting her on birth control pills throughout their relationship. Once Stacy left Indiana, she discontinued the pills since she was no longer interested in forming a relationship. Did she want kids? She knew it was going to be a lot more work raising a child due to her visual impairment, but she concluded that whatever Stan wanted, she was fine with it. What about his religion? That was the easiest decision. Stacy never really had a religious church affiliate. Stan, on the other hand, knew a lot more about the Bible than she did and tried to live up to its standards and principles like her. She knew that, with his respect for her and the Biblical command, is why he had never attempted to have sex with her. Speaking of sex, Stacy wondered how he was in bed? She remembered the first time with Mitchell. If Stan was anywhere close to that, she knew she would be satisfied.

Would Stan move in with her, or would she move in with him? It mattered not to her. She would let Stan make that decision, and she would commit to it. Most all her decisions ended with, *"As long as Stan is by my side, I'm good with it."* Stacy knew what love was from her early experience with Mitchell. After meeting Stan, she realized that her need for love was still there. Stacy needed love; she wanted to love and be loved. She felt, deep in her spirit, Stan would fill her void.

Hours had passed while she was deep in thought. She felt her clock. Where had the time gone? It was 6:00 pm. She wondered why Christy hadn't responded. It was only then that the phone rang. It was Christy! Like Stan, Christy had her own personal ringtone, of course. *"Hi, Christy!"* Stacy exclaimed excitedly. *"Hey, Stacy. Girl, when I listened to your voicemail, it sounded like you were hyperventilating. What's going on? Should I prepare for good news or bad news?"* Christy replied. *"Girl, it's all good. No, better than good. I hope you're sitting down cuz you won't believe this."* Stacy continued as she laid out her trip to Dr. Browdy in detail. At every bit of good news, Christy screamed in joy for her friend.

When she was finished with that portion of the story, Christy asked, *"So, let me get this straight. You mean to tell me that there is a chance you will see again?"* *"Yep, that's exactly what I am saying. I am hoping for the best but preparing for the worse."* Stacy replied cheerfully. *"Now, let me put the icing on the cake,"* she continued. *"If you could see through the phone, you would see that I have a ring on my finger!"*

"Wait! Wait! Wait! What are you saying?" Christy asked, shocked. *"Believe it or not, my BFF, your BFF is now engaged!"* A scream, followed

by another, then another, then another. Stacy had to pull the phone away from her ear. After calming down, Christy said, *"I am so happy for you. I'm sure I don't have to ask who he is. But are you sure? Is he doing this because he feels sorry for you? Are you saying yes because he was the first man to ask, and you feel no one else would want you in this condition? Have you dated others to make sure there is not someone else out there for you?"*

"Christy," Stacy replied, *"You know I value your opinion and wisdom. Through all my ups and downs, you have been there for me, which feels like my entire life. It's hard to explain, but the love I feel for Stan is different than the love I first felt for Mitchell. Where I now know that I was attracted to Mitchell's charm, it's hard to explain, but Stan is the epitome of love. His love, compassion, and caring are genuine. Now, don't get me wrong, Stan is a real man, no pushover. But he has all the emotional skills that can satisfy me. Men don't like to listen. Stan will listen to everything I say, even if I'm just running off at the mouth. That is a rare quality to find in a man. And my heart. Girl, my heart skips a beat every time I hear his voice. And his touch, let alone his kisses, just sends electricity through my body. Neither one of those ever happened with Mitchell. And, believe it or not, Stan has never, ever asked me for sex. That is the show of ultimate respect to me. When I first started having feelings for Stan, I asked God to confirm it. Well, yesterday, I believe he did."*

"Well, baby girl," Christy said, *"If you're sure about this and Stan makes you that happy, then I'm happy. Maybe, one of these days, I will find someone like Stan."* *"Maybe,"* replied Stacy, *"But know this, you can't have Stan. He's spoken for!"* They both giggled. After a few more minutes of talking, they bid each other good night and hung up. Stacy was glad Christy had raised all of those concerns. Just the fact that she was able to answer them and defend her love for Stan reassured her that what she and Stan had was what love was meant to be – Mrs. Wallace. Stacy would be proud to be called that. Putting a hyphen in her last name?

That was not going to happen. She wanted the world to know she was Mrs. Stan Wallace. She loved how that sounded.

CHAPTER THIRTY-EIGHT

Stacy tried to stay busy the next two weeks trying not to think about her next eye appointment. She had talked to Christy several times during those two weeks, chit-chatting about girly things. Being curious, Christy asked her again to describe Stan's kisses. Christy partly judges a man by the way he kisses. Stacy told her that every time he gave her one, it sent shivers down her spine. Again, Christy wished Stacy well and hoped that, in Stan, she could find not only the love but the support she would need regardless of whether she regained her sight or not. Stacy had an immense platonic love for Christy.

Stacy had also talked to Stan several times during this same period but not as much as she would have liked. He was now working the second shift securing a government facility that was watched twenty-four hours a day. He would be there for a month then, hopefully, be returned to the bank. But every time he would call, he would ask, *"And where is the ring today, beautiful?"* She would reply every time, *"Exactly where my man put it."* They both got a kick out of that.

Even though they hadn't talked about the more important things that needed to be addressed, they did unfold a little more information about each other every time they spoke; this was by design. Stan had suggested they do this, and Stacy readily agreed. They needed to know more, not that it would change anything. On every call, each got a chance to ask one question that the other had to answer truthfully. Stan got to know about her mother, Christy, Mitchell, and why she was no longer married. Stacy got to know why his first marriage failed, why he chose to be an SDA, his kids, that the security guard position was only temporary, and that he was not a mushy romantic. Stacy knew what he meant by that last piece of information, and she was okay with that.

He had exhibited enough love, compassion, and concern for her from day one to convince her that he now truly loved her. When one gave the personal information, the other just patiently listened and could only as a question if something wasn't clear. They were not allowed to debate or give their two cents worth. Each would reflect on what was said and, at the appropriate time, they would sit down and discuss how the other felt toward each subject.

Stacy continued to pray and read her Bible. Whenever she became anxious or depressed, this would bring her comfort – along with Stan's calls. He just had a way of putting everything in perspective and left her feeling much better by the time they hung up. As the weeks went by, the closer her appointment date came, the more excited she became. She tried to get it out of her mind, but that was not easy to do. But again, as usual, she would accept the verdict. What was sure was her engagement, and nothing could change that. If she could have Stan and no sight, so be it. Besides thinking about her eyes, she had to be truthful. There was always a question in the back of her mind that she could not shake; always!

In fact, it came up even before the engagement, and that was, even though she was embarrassed every time she thought about it, how was Stan in bed? Her passion rose every time that subject came into her head. But now, it was only a matter of time when she would find out first hand. Hey, would there be a honeymoon? If he asked her where she would like to go, what would she say? To pass her time, she started to look at reasonable places she would like to go. If they couldn't, it was no big deal. They would do that later. She had Stan. But this gave her something to do to pass her time. Eventually, days had passed, and tomorrow was her eye appointment. Stacy felt confident that something would be determined. One way or another, tomorrow was a pivotal day for her life.

She got up the next day but was too excited to eat. So, she grabbed one of those smoothie breakfast drinks while waiting on her ride, which she had called for just before she got up. As expected, he arrived on time. On her way to the appointment, she made small talk with the driver. To her surprise, and by coincidence, this was the same driver who brought her back from her last appointment. He recalled how excited she was the last time they met and had remembered to say a prayer for her. She thanked him and said how appreciative she was. Pulling up to the office, he again got out and opened the door for her. She thanked him and started walking into the building. But, before she could get very far, he shouted out, *"Hey Miss, when you call for a ride home, ask for Jorge."* Stacy promised him that she would do that.

Once inside, she signed in and had a seat. Within minutes her name was called. *"Today must be a big day for you, huh?"* said the nurse. *"You have no idea!"* Stacy replied. In came Dr. Browdy. *"Good morning, young lady."* *"Hi, Dr. Browdy,"* Stacy replied. *"So,"* he said. *"Here's what we're going to do. We will do another test, like the last time, to see if there has been any progress before we continue. So I'll meet you in the examination room."* He left while the nurse came in and helped Stacy to the room. Once in, she went through the same routine as before. The doctor was silent throughout the exam. She still couldn't see any light. About five minutes later, she heard, *"OK, Stacy, the nurse will take to back to the room, and I will be in shortly."* Back in the room, she waited for what seemed an hour when, in reality, it was actually just fifteen minutes.

Dr. Browdy came in and had a seat. *"Ok, Stacy, here's what we've got,"* he stated. *"I have taken photos of both irises today and compared them to your last visit. I have shown both sets to several of my colleagues here today. They confirm, unanimously, that your irises have indeed repaired them-*

selves based on our combined knowledge and experience. Now, I say that tongue in cheek because we can only see the surface. Whether there is interior damage is unknown at this point. However, having said that, the way it is healing indicates that it is actually healed from the inside out. We have no idea if it has repaired itself to the degree that you will be able to see it again. But, before that is determined, as you know, there is a problem with your cornea. In order to know if you have regained any sight, we need to repair your cornea by transplant. A cornea transplant, known as keratoplasty, is a surgical procedure to replace part of your damaged cornea with corneal tissue from a donor. The surgery takes about two hours, at which you will be awake, but you will feel no pain. Or you can elect to have general anesthesia, which will render you unconscious. If all works well with your irises and cornea, you should be able to see almost immediately."

He continued, "However, every person is different, and it could take weeks, months, or even a year. There is no way for us to know. There could be several complications from this type of surgery but, based on your age, health, and the overall condition of your eyes, you shouldn't experience any adverse effects. You will be given eye drops to heal from the procedure and protect your body from rejecting the donor tissue. You will need to take the drops for about a year. It's vital for you to remember not to rub your eyes, no strenuous exercises for at least a week, and, for the first month, when you bathe or shower, be careful not to get water in your eye. All of this will be provided to you, so don't try to remember it. The transplant should last about ten years. And lastly, you should know that cornea grafts are the most successful of all tissue transplants. So, young lady, knowing all that, the question is, do you want to proceed with the procedure?"

It didn't take Stacy but two seconds to answer his question. *"Absolutely, without question,"* she said. *"OK,"* Dr. Browdy said, *"Do you have any questions?" "No! Not any that I can think of,"* Stacy replied. *"Alright, then. We will contact an eye bank and order a set of corneas. We will set up the procedure a week from today."*

By now, Stacy had a big smile on her face. Dr. Browdy left, and she was escorted back to the waiting area where she called for her ride, remembering to request Jorge. Once in the car, she couldn't wait to tell Jorge all about her visit. He was truly happy for her. It was one of the most pleasant rides home she had taken in a long time.

CHAPTER THIRTY-NINE

When Stacy got home, she was so excited that she couldn't contain herself – she had to tell someone! She called Christy. However, since she was at work, Stacy left a voicemail asking her to call her back. In her excitement, Stacy also called Stan and left him a voicemail to call her back as well. While she waited for a call from either of them, all kinds of things went through her mind. Would the surgery be successful? How would she feel if it wasn't? If she regained her sight, would Stan treat her any differently? If the treatment was a success, would she go back to the bank or look for another job? Who was the donor? Would she be satisfied with only half of her vision? What if the operation was unsuccessful? Would she try it again? Would her insurance company cover this procedure? Having asked that last question, she decided to find out.

Stacy called Mr. Stewart, the insurance attorney, who had stopped by shortly after her release from the hospital to talk to her about her financial options. He was in, but she was put on hold because he was on another line. A few minutes later, he answered the phone. *"This is Mr. Stewart. How can I be of service?" "Hi, Mr. Stewart, this is Stacy. How are you today?"* She replied. *"I'm doing well, Stacy. Nice to hear your voice. How are you doing? What can I do for you?"* Came the answer. *"I'm doing as well as I can be expected, thanks for asking. I have a question."* Stacy continued. *"No problem,"* he said. *"Ask away, and I will do my best to give you an answer." "Well,"* she said. *"There is a possibility that, with a cornea transplant, I might be able to see again. My question is, will that cost be covered?" "That's a reasonable question, and I have an answer for you. Give me a minute. I'll be right back."* He replied.

A few minutes later, he was back. *"OK, young lady. I've gone through your bank insurance papers, and it seems, other than a $175 copay, you're covered. You did not have MedPay insurance through us, which would have paid your medical bills. However, even if your work or auto insurance did not cover your expenses, we would still go after the driver's trucking company who hit you. So, I guess what I'm saying is not to worry about any bills stemming from this accident. Now, on a personal note, did you say you might be able to see again?" "Yes!"* Stacy replied excitedly. *"I can hardly believe it myself. There is more than a 50/50 chance of success, so I'm leaning more toward the success rate." "Well, I am so happy for you,"* he said. *"It couldn't happen to a better person."*

"If I may ask, are you a religious person?" Mr. Stewart inquired. *"Yes, I am; very much so. In fact, I doubt that this would have been possible had the Lord not intervened."* Stacy replied solemnly. *"I believe that Stacy. Even though I am not, what you call, 'a religious person,' I am spiritual. But please keep me up to date. I would like to know how it turns out," "I will. Thanks for the information,"* she said, *"have a good evening." "You too, Stacy. Talk to you later. Bye."* That conversation put her mind at ease. She would now try to keep busy around the apartment while she waited on Christy and Stan to call her back. Boy, did she have news for them!

Christy was the first one to call. After Stacy told her everything that went on that day, Christy was overcome with joy. She couldn't hold back her joy and broke down as Stacy repeated the event - thinking that her best friend had a chance actually to see again! She told Stacy that if she was blessed to regain her sight, she wanted her to spend a week or so with her since it had been quite some time since they were together, which would also give Stacy a chance to see where she lived and do some sightseeing. Of course, Stacy agreed. Meeting her best friend after so long would do her heart good. However, she also made Christy aware that she would not interfere with Stan's plans for them. Christy understood perfectly.

The rest of the time on the phone, they spent talking about the procedure, recovery time, the pain involved, medication needed, and if she would be able to see immediately. Stacy answered her as best she could, but a lot of answers would have to wait. After several more minutes, Christy said she had to run but for Stacy to keep the faith and that she knew where to find her if needed. Stacy thanked her, sent her a kiss, and hung up. Her mind started drifting back to when she had first met Christy. Stacy didn't know where her life would be without her; she owed her so much.

The phone rang. It was Stan's ringtone. *"Hey, Stan!"* Stacy exclaimed. *"Hey, little princess. Before we continue, I got a question for you. Where is the ring today?"* *"Exactly where my man put it,"* was her reply. *"Good enough. So, tell me all about your day, cutie."* As Stacy had done with Christy, she relayed the entire story to Stan, trying not to leave out anything. Midway, she started getting choked up with happiness to the point that she was gasping so hard it was difficult for her to finish the story, which she eventually did. *"Take your time, hon."* He said. *"Give me a minute, Stan,"* she said as she put the phone down. She needed a moment to gather herself. After a couple of minutes, she was back on the phone. *"I'm sorry, hon. Where were we?"* *"Babe,"* he said. *"Do you realize that's the first time you called me something other than Stan?"* *"Didn't I call you Stan?"* Stacy asked. *"No, young lady, you called me hon."* She thought for a moment. Indeed, she had. *"I'm sorry, Stan."* *"Sorry?"* he said. *"I've been waiting for you to call me something other than my name for the longest. Considering your history, I think I understand why you've continued to call me Stan. And that's OK. I knew it was only a matter of time when the love in your heart toward me would be expressed in words you would never say to another."* He was right; she could feel it in her gut.

Stan continued, *"Now, having said all that, I am just overjoyed at the good news of today. I do believe, wholeheartedly, that the Lord is behind this. There is no other way to explain it." "I feel the same way, Stan......No! I mean hon,"* Stacy replied as a big smile came onto her face. *"Hey, that's two 'hon's' on the same day. Boy, am I a lucky man,"* he said – they both laughed. Stacy and Stan wrapped up their talk with Stan promising to check up on her tomorrow – which would give Stacy something to look forward to. They gave each other kisses and hung up. After sitting there for a few minutes, Stacy realized she was emotionally and physically drained. She knew she would have no trouble sleeping tonight.

Stan called the next day, and almost every day after to check up on what he termed "His girl." During his call Saturday night, he asked Stacy if she wanted to go out Sunday night. She said, *"Honey, if it's all the same to you, can we eat in? I want to cook dinner for you." "You don't have to twist my arm, little sexy. What time do you want me there, and do you want me to bring something?"* Stan asked. *"How about 6 pm?"* She said. *"And as far as what to bring, there is something special I would like." "And that would be?"* Stan asked. *"One of your hugs and kisses,"* she said. *"Your wish is my command. That will not be a problem,"* he replied. *"But I am going to bring just a little something."* Stacy replied, *"I can't wait! See ya then, hon."*

CHAPTER FORTY

The next day, Stacy was busy making sure the apartment was neat and organized. She had picked out another one of her saved outfits to wear for Stan. It was a sleeveless, purple, and white form-fitting gown that nearly touched the floor. It had the back half out and the front held up by a fabric collar around her neck. She would normally have worn heels, but knowing the gown reached the floor, she knew Stan wouldn't see the heels anyway. First thing in the morning, she started marinating a thick, porterhouse steak – she wanted to make sure it was tender. She was going to do a slow bake, but, in the final two minutes, she would pour BBQ sauce on top and broil it until it formed a crispy glaze. But, she was having problems deciding what else to prepare. She knew Stan was not a picky eater. The only things he disliked were spicy foods and biblically unclean meats.

After much pondering, she decided on steamed garlic broccoli and creamy au gratin potatoes. For dessert, she had to think. Stan wasn't much for desserts, and she was too conscious of her figure, so she chose to skip it. If he did want dessert, she had ice cream in the freezer. After preparing everything, she took a shower and got dressed. Shortly after six, Stan arrived. After greeting each other, Stan kissed her on her forehead and stepped in. Stacy shut the door, took his hand, and walked into the living room. Once there, Stan grabbed her hands, held them at arm's length, and said, *"Girl, I'm tempted to forgo dinner and just have you for dessert. You are the epitome of beauty."* Stacy knew she was blushing and couldn't hide it. Snapping out of it, she told Stan to get comfortable, and she would serve. Stan offered to help, but she politely refused, saying, *"I got this."*

Stan got up, excused himself, and went to wash up. By the time he came back, Stacy had meticulously laid out everything on the table. She reached out her hand, Stan grabbed it, and she led him into the kitchen. *"Oh, my goodness, little gal! If I didn't know any better, I swear someone else prepared this exquisite meal. It looks like Gordon Ramsay made this! Are you sure you can't see?"* Stacy blushed again and said, *"Oh honey, stop it! You know it's not all that, but thanks for the compliment."* *"No, I'm serious."* He continued. *"In fact, I'm going to take a picture. I have faith that, one of these days, you will be able to see it."* As was his custom, he pulled the chair out for Stacy and made sure she was seated before taking his. They both said grace and began to eat. They ate quietly for the most part, but Stan ensured silence wasn't maintained every now and then, going "umph, umph, umph." Little did Stacy know that he was not only commenting on how perfect the meal was but also the way she looked – a picture of beauty.

After dinner, Stacy, again, would not accept any help from Stan as she cleaned up. She wanted to prove to him that, even if her eye surgery was not successful, she was able to provide for him, those things any other woman was capable of. She knew she had some limitations, but she would not let them get in her way with Stan. While Stacy was cleaning up, Stan turned on some slow jazz music – setting the mood. Once they were settled on the couch, Stan said, *"Stay right there. I'll be right back."* When he returned, he put a glass into Stacy's hand. He said, *"Now listen."* She heard a loud pop. *"Now, hold your glass still."* After he filled both glasses, he said, *"This is not champagne since neither one of us drink, but it's sparkling grape juice. I wanted to raise a toast to us, our love for one another and too many years of happiness together. And damn girl, you look good enough to eat."* Stacy couldn't stop smiling – butterflies going crazy in her stomach. He touched his glass to hers and said, *"Cheers."* Stacy took a small sip, not knowing what to expect.

It was all fizzy and cold, but it tasted good. She took a couple of more sips. *"This is good!"* She said. *"I've got to remember this. What's it called again?"* *"Sparkling Grape Juice,"* Stan replied.

They finished their drink as Stan took the glasses and set them on the coffee table. He had her face him then gave her a warm, passionate and heated kiss. By the time he broke away from her, Stacy was panting heavily. He waited for her to catch her breath. Now, he scooted over next to her, put his right arm around her shoulders, and drew her close to his side. By now, little by little, Stacy had lost her tension around Stan. She took full advantage of the situation and snuggled up against him. Stacy knew Stan knew about her drawback, but he never spoke about it. He knew that it was only a matter of time when she would conquer her fear. *"Babe,"* he said, *"I know you probably wonder, even though we are engaged, why I don't come over or invite you to my place like an engaged couple would normally do. Now, it has nothing to do with your eyesight and, quite frankly, has nothing to do with you at all. Well, that's not entirely true, but, in essence, it's me."*

Stacy was now starting to get worried. Where was this going? He continued, *"I have the utmost respect for you, and I would never want to hurt your feelings or disrespect you in any way. It's just that I find you so sexy and so beautiful and so desirable that the only way to contain myself was to not be around you. I'm not sure if I'm saying this the right way."* Stacy squeezed him tight. *"I get it, Honey, really I do. I have to admit that it did cross my mind every now and then, but I knew you had your reasons, and I would not question them. But that is so sweet of you to think of my emotions and protect my honor. And that's just one of the reasons I love you so much."* *"But, have no doubt, my sweet thang,"* he said, *"The time will come when I'm going to rock your world."*

Stacy had never heard it put that way before, but she was turned on by it. She squeezed Stan even tighter and pulled herself into him as much as possible. As they sat there, listening to music, she started to imagine how the first time would feel. Wrong timing! She was beginning to get hot. Unknowingly, she started squirming. Stan, saying nothing, just pulled her in tighter. She tried to stop thinking about it but couldn't. He was touching her, holding her, and that was just accelerating her desire for him. *"Oh, Stan,"* she moaned. He just held her, feeling her heart racing while breathing a bit faster. Stan patiently waited for her to go wherever her thought took her while he maintained his composure. It wasn't easy, but he managed. It took Stacy sometime before she was in control and herself again. She knew that, as long as Stan held her, she was never going to break away entirely from those thoughts.

She let go of him, sat up, and took a deep breath. Before she could speak, he leaned over, gave her a kiss, and said, *"That's my girl. All woman. Wouldn't want to have you any other way."* Stacy reached out, pulled him to her, and kissed him with all she had. They stayed there enjoying each other for a minute. Stacy's body began to react again; she began to lose control. Stan sensed her change, so he slowly broke away then just hugged her. Stacy was taking deep breaths, trying to calm down. She was a little embarrassed at how her body was betraying her. But, as long as Stan didn't mind, she didn't either. As he turned her loose, he said, *"Ms. Stacy, I have had a most wonderful evening with the most beautiful woman I have ever known. I hate that this evening will end but not soon forgotten. Now, if you would be so kind as to walk me to the door, I will bid you adieu."* As he opened the door to leave, he turned around, gave her a good night kiss, and said: *"Now I have to go home and take a cold shower."* And with that, he was gone.

Stacy just stood there, giggling. She closed the door and, as she was heading back to the living room, she was still trying to regain her composure. That's when she felt it. *"Oh, my God!"* She realized that her dress was wet. She rushed to her room and removed her panties; they were completely soaked. Terror struck her until she realized that, when Stan got up to leave, he was always in front of her, so he couldn't have noticed. *"Thank God. Now I need a cold shower,"* she said out loud. It seems their evening was a complete success with both of them leaving in the same condition. How wonderful!

CHAPTER FORTY-ONE

Two days later, her phone rang; it was the hospital. They told her that they had found a donor for her but, upon further investigation, that donor tissue had been in the eye bank for ten days. It was still considered acceptable, but the doctor decided that Stacy should wait for a fresher donor tissue since her procedure was not an emergency. Although disappointed, she understood. She did not want to take chances and rush anything for the sake of time. She had no problem waiting because she wanted everything to be perfect. However, two days later, she received another call telling her they had secured a donor tissue and she was to report to the hospital the next day, at 10 am, for the procedure. Stacy had already been given instructions as to what she could and could not do the day before the surgery.

The next day she called for her ride and asked for Jorge. On the way, she told Jorge what was about to take place. Jorge was genuinely concerned about Stacy's future. Before she got out, Jorge asked if he could have a word of prayer with her. *"By all means,"* Stacy replied. After praying, Jorge got out, opened her door, and wished her well as she made her way to the door. Before he drove off, Jorge said, *"Don't forget to call me to pick you up!"* After signing in and sitting down, she thought to herself, *"This is one of the biggest days in my life."* She said a little prayer that all things would work out fine.

A few minutes later, she was escorted to the room. *"Hi, Stacy. So, today is the big day!"* said Dr. Browdy. *"Yes, it's finally here. I'm a little ner-*

vous, but also very excited!" was her reply. *"Alright,"* he said, *"You have a choice. We can give you a local anesthetic or a general one. Local means you are still awake during the procedure. General means you are put to sleep. Do you have a preference?" "General anesthesia will be fine."* She replied. *"OK. So,"* he continued, *"Before we start, we have to, once again, do a thorough eye exam to make sure there are no unforeseen problems and that your eyes are still healthy enough for the procedure. Ready?"* Stacy nodded in agreement, and Dr. Browdy began the test.

After an extensive eye exam, Dr. Browdy said all was well and that the procedure could continue. *"Here's what's going to happen,"* he began. *"Because of the deep damage done by the shards, I will be removing the entire cornea. I will then replace both with donor tissue and stitch them in place. Once that is complete, I will place a shield over both eyes for protection. We will take you to the recovery room, where you will wait until the anesthetic has worn off and you are stable before sending you home. Any questions?" "Just one,"* Stacy replied. *"Will I be able to see like nothing ever happened?" "I can't say,"* said Dr. Browdy, *"everyone is different. Let's tackle that question later." "Alright,"* she said, *"let's do this."*

About two hours later, Stacy was wheeled into the recovery room. As she began to come out of her sleep, she was groggy and confused, moving a lot, not knowing where she was. *"Easy, Stacy,"* a nurse's voice consoled her. *"You just came out of eye surgery, and you're fine. Just lay there and relax. You'll be stable within the hour."* As her mind became clearer, she remembered that she had eye surgery. She opened her eyes and... darkness. She was disappointed and about to get upset when she realized the doctor had placed shields over both eyes for protection—knowing that, she settled back and relaxed.

After the anesthetic had worn off completely, Dr. Browdy came in to see her. *"Young lady, I'm glad to say that the procedure was a success. No complications. When you get home, lay on your back except for eating or going to the bathroom for the next two days. This allows the tissue time to seat itself. I've scheduled an appointment for you at 10 AM tomorrow to confirm all is well and remove the shields. You might notice some swelling and possible discomfort but, for the most part, no pain. We have given you a mild medication in case you need it for pain. We previously went over your care instruction, but make sure you apply the drops three times a day until you're told to stop. This is to heal your eyes as well as keeping your body from rejecting the donor tissue. Your stitches have to be removed at some point in time. It all depends on how well your eyes recover. Any questions?" "No doc. And thank you for what you have done. You have no idea how much I appreciate it."* Stacy replied. *"You're welcome, young lady. Make sure you go home and relax. See you tomorrow."*

Even though she had the shields on, she tried to put her sunglasses on, which didn't work. She was forced to leave them off even though she felt more comfortable with them. She wondered what she looked like with those shields on. Once in the waiting room, she called for Jorge to pick her up. Fifteen minutes later, she was in his car. *"Hey, can you see me?"* he asked excitedly. Stacy couldn't help but smile at his simplicity and said, *"No, Jorge. Unfortunately, it doesn't work that way."* She explained to him why as they continued to talk all the way home. She told Jorge that she had to be back in the doctor's office in the morning at 10 AM. Jorge told her not to bother calling in for a pickup. He would make sure he was here to take her.

After she got in and settled, she said a prayer of thanksgiving that the operation was a success and that the outcome would be as well. She felt a little queasy, so she just decided to lay down without eating, but she did have a few sips of Gatorade. She had dozed off when the phone rang. It was Christy. *"Hey, Christy."* She said with a rather tired voice. *"Hey girl, can you see?"* Christy asked excitedly. *"No, unfortunately, it's not like that."* Stacy went on to explain everything to her friend. *"So, you'll know tomorrow if you can see?"* Christy asked. *"God willing,"* Stacy replied. They talked for a few more minutes, with Christy promising to call her back once she got home tomorrow, which she agreed to, before hanging up.

She continued to lay there, as instructed, and waited for Stan to call, which he did several hours later. *"Hey, hon,"* Stacy said cheerfully. *"Hey sexy, tell me something good!"* He said. She gave him the same information she had provided Christy. *"So, it seems like we're going to have to wait until tomorrow, huh?"* He continued. *"Pretty much,"* Stacy replied solemnly. *"Do you need anything?"* Stan asked, concerned. *"Except for you, I'm good,"* she giggled. *"I'm only working a half-day tomorrow because I have some running to do. But I'll be over once I'm done. Just make sure you follow all the doctors' instructions,"* he said. *"Will do, my man,"* Stacy responded. *"I'll spring for dinner. Let me know what you decide,"* Stan continued. *"Got to run, babe. Hasta Manana!"* *"OK, Mr. Wallace!"* she tittered. After hanging up, now that she had talked to her man, she could relax. She planned to get up soon, eat something, prepare for tomorrow then go back to bed. She was excited yet apprehensive at the same time about tomorrow. Within a few hours, she would know, one way or the other. It was now in God's hands.

CHAPTER FORTY-TWO

Jorge showed up on time, and he honked the horn to indicate his arrival. Stacy had already readied herself to leave, despite not getting enough sleep, wondering what the outcome would be. She made her way to the car, and Jorge opened the door for her, *"So, today is the big day, huh?"* Jorge asked. *"Probably the biggest day of my life,"* Stacy replied. *"You know,"* he said, *"I told my wife about you last night, and she thought that we should all say a prayer for you. So, we gathered in a group, and each one of us took a turn saying a small prayer that God would restore your sight."* *"That was so thoughtful of you and your family, Jorge. You have my heart filled, thanks. I'm sure the Lord will bless you and your family for your concern."* Stacy said with joy.

Arriving at the office, Jorge reiterated to Stacy to ask for him for her return trip home. After waiting for around twenty minutes, she was escorted into one of the rooms. Her anxiety had been gradually building up, and now it felt like she was sitting on pins and needles – squirming in her seat. This was it. Everything led up to this very moment. Dr. Browdy entered the room and immediately noticed how fidgety she was. *"Calm down, young lady."* He said. *"I'm trying but, it's hard,"* she replied. *"Yeah, I'm sure it is. I've seen my share of patients go through the same thing but, take some deep breaths and try to compose yourself,"* he said. Stacy took a few deep breaths, and it improved her situation a bit, but not a lot. *"OK, sit back and let me take a look,"* he said. She closed her eyes as he removed the shields.

"Ok, Stacy, open your eyes." When she did, all she could see was very poorly lit, dark clouds. *"I don't see anything. It's like dark clouds. Why can't I see? What went wrong?"* Stacy asked Dr. Browdy while starting to panic. *"I will answer your question once I have finished conducting this exam,"* he said. A few minutes later, he added, *"Nothing is wrong, Stacy. Your prognosis was good from the beginning based on the healing of your irises. Adhering to a lot of scenarios, the recovery of sight differs from person to person. For some, they may be able to see perfectly within twenty-four hours while, with others, as I explained before, it can take up to a year. Please, don't get discouraged. Your eyes are healthy, and the donor tissue was quality, as good as we could expect. You now have to give your body time to heal itself. The better you are at following the aftercare instructions, especially the eye drops, the faster you will see results. It's a miracle that you can see at all, considering the condition your irises were in. I can't say if you will regain 20/20 vision again, but I assure you, you will see again. So, relax. Have faith."*

After hearing the doctor, Stacy felt considerably better. *"I'm sorry, doc. I didn't know,"* she said. *"It's alright. I understand. That is why I don't discuss how well a person will see until I get to this point. I want you back every week to note your progress. Lay on your back the rest of the day as much as possible. Tomorrow, you can resume your normal activities but, again, nothing strenuous. Any questions?"* Stacy paused for a minute, then said, *"Just one. Should I continue to wear my sunglasses?"* *"I think that would be a good idea at this stage,"* he said. *"But, whereas, your damaged corneas were very cloudy-looking; your new tissue is clear. So, if someone were to look at you, they would not know you had impaired sight."* That was another bit of good news to Stacy. Now, she wouldn't look like she was blind.

All in all, she was very thankful for what had taken place and her new outlook on life. She thanked Dr. Browdy again after giving him a big hug. In the waiting room, she called Jorge. Not too long after, he arrived. As soon as he walked into the waiting room to escort Stacy back to the car, he said: *"Hey, can you see me?" "No, Jorge, but I will explain on the way home,"* she said. Stacy gave him all the information on the way home. Once they arrived, Jorge opened her car door to get out and said, *"So, that means that you will be able to see me – just not right now, right?" "If everything works out as planned, I should be able to see who Jorge is one day,"* she replied. *"Well, don't worry. I'll be around till then!"* He said with a smile. With that, he returned to his parked car, got in, and drove off.

After Stacy got situated, she called Christy and gave her the good and bad news while she laid on her bed. Christy was happy and yet disappointed at the same time. Her break was about to end, so she told Stacy to make sure she did what the doctor told her to do and that she would call her in a couple of days to check in on her. Byes, kisses, and gone. After about an hour, Stacy got out of bed, fixed herself something light to eat, and started laying out the dress she would wear for her dinner date with Stan tonight. That's right! She almost forgot! Stan had asked her to pick out what they would be having for dinner. She had a taste for shrimps but knew Stan didn't eat Biblically unclean foods. She would have to think of something else. *"Pizza? Nah! Chinese! Nope! Tacos? Too messy! Think Stacy, what would satisfy you and your man?"* After some brainstorming, it dawned on her. *"Vegetarian! That's it. But what and where?"* She knew she had time to think about it, so she completed putting together what she would wear tonight and went back to bed.

About an hour later, she sat straight up in her bed. That's it! Leona's. She remembered once that Christy took her to Leona's, where she had a salad and Christy had a pizza, but she remembered Christy reading off the menu and mentioning something about a vegetarian burger. She didn't know how they tasted, but she was game. Stacy knew that would be something Stan could not object to. With that done, she put in her eye drops, laid back down, and waited for his call. Being in that position, she took an impromptu nap – only being woken by that familiar ring tone of Stan. *"Hey, handsome man,"* she said. *"Hey, sexy thing,"* he replied. *"You ok?"* *"Yes, I'm fine,"* she said. *"OH! I know you're fine,"* he said, *"but I was asking how you're feeling."* She burst out laughing. *"What am I going to do with you?"* *"Well, you certainly can't get rid of me, that's for sure!"* Stan said with a chuckle. *"Just one question, babe. Can you see?"* *"No, but I'll explain when you get here,"* she replied.

"Okay. Anyway, what's for dinner?" Stan inquired. *"I was thinking about a vegetarian burger from Leona's. I've never had one. Have you?"* Stacy asked. *"I have, and, to me, they are delicious."* *"OK, I'll try it, and you pick out the toppings. And how about some fries with it?"* Stacy asked. *"Not a problem,"* he said. *"I'm going home to change and will call them when I'm about to leave, so it should be ready by the time I get there. I'll call you when I'm on my way."* *"Sounds like a plan. Talk to you then. Kisses,"* she said, then hung up. About forty-five minutes later, Stan called. He was on his way. Stacy was ready. She had picked out a loose-fitting, red dress that had half-inch pleats, running the entire length, stopping just below her knees. The sleeves came down to her elbow. She decided to wear her strappy red pumps.

Since she now knew that her eyes were clear, she decided to keep her glasses off. The doorbell rang. When she opened the door, she struck a pose. Stan raised an eyebrow as he said, *"My! My! My! Will you look at this? And look at that sparkle in your eye. You look so good I'll kiss your daddy just to touch your hand. Let's just skip dinner. Can I just have you for dessert?"* as he walked around Stacy. *"Why sho' you can, mister. Come right on in and follow me,"* she said with an accent. They both had a good laugh.

Stan had ordered sautéed mushrooms, roasted red onion, avocado slices, and BBQ sauce on the veggie burgers, with an order of seasoned wedge fries. Stacy had chilled two bottles of lemonade. Throughout their meal, they mainly talked about what they were eating for dinner. They were some big burgers. Stan finished his, but Stacy could only eat half. She would save the rest for later. They retired to the living room with their drinks. Getting settled, Stacy began. *"OK, hon. I'll start from the beginning and try not to leave out anything."*

After telling him all that she could remember, she said, *"And here I am. So tell me, what do you think?"* He said, *"I think, young lady, that you have taken this in grand fashion. Only a woman with strong faith and what I call 'stick-to-it-iveness,' could have gotten this far. I am so proud of you. And, looking at you, one would not know you had sight issues. Just the simple fact that you can see any form of light at all is a miracle in and of itself. I do believe, over time, you will improve. Now, can I have my dessert?" "Mister, you certainly may!"* Stacy replied.

Stan moved closer, took her in his arms, and kissed her passionately`. Stacy melted in his arms. She hugged him with all she had. *"Damn!"* she said to herself, *"he really knows how to kiss!"* Then, she remembered what happened the last time they did this. Regretfully, she slowly backed off, panting, trying to calm herself. *"Honey, I'm telling you,"* she said, trying to catch her breath. *"Every time you do that, you take my breath away." "Well,"* he said, *"every time I finish, I guess I'll just have to give it back to you. Wouldn't want my gal to pass out." "Then you would have to do mouth to mouth resuscitation. That would be starting the cycle all over again."* She responded with a smile. *"Pretty much,"* he said. *"Or, we could just skip kissing from now on?"* Stan jokingly suggested. *"Not on your life, buddy,"* she said. *"You just keep it coming." "I love you so much little princess,"* Stan replied. *"And I love you more,"* Stacy responded.

They spend the rest of the evening listening to music and talking about the Bible. There were somethings, the Bible said, that were not easily understood by Stacy, but she knew she could always ask Stan. This was one of those times. She asked him about the Sabbath, where do people go when they die, are people supposed to understand Revelation, etc. Stan was a Bible instructor and had no problem answering her questions in a way that she could understand completely. Stacy admired how Stan used the Bible to back up everything he said.

Finally, he said, *"Babe, it's getting late, and I don't want to keep you up any longer, seeing as how you're supposed to be laying down today. But I'm still awestruck by your beauty. You, just wearing that dress... you are one magnificent creature. All I can say is, just wait."* *"And I will be waiting,"* she said, *"regardless of my sight, I will love you with everything I have. Without you, I feel only half alive. I am not complete without you by my side."* They kiss again but, this time, kept it short. They got up and made it to the door holding hands. At the door, he turned around and gave her a kiss on her forehead, then on her nose, and finally on her lips. Stacy thought that was very romantic. *"Bye, my love,"* and he walked away. She stood there for a moment thinking to herself, one of these days, they will not have to part. That was a day she was looking forward to. She undressed, got ready for bed, and climbed in, remembering to put her drops in. She had a full day. She had to admit, it didn't start off well, but Stan had a way of making everything alright. Within minutes, she was asleep.

Over the next few weeks, her sight did not improve. Stacy would go through her stages of depression, up and down. She kept her promise and talked to Christy almost every day, and that was good. But it was Stan who would call her every day without fail and, by the time they were done talking, her depression was gone. Stan was her medicine man. She had been back to see Dr. Browdy twice. He did routine checkups and said her eyes were continuing to heal. He gave her a refill on her drops and told her to have faith. She was trying to do that, but it wasn't easy. Having gone through all this, and nothing was frustrating. But she remembered what Stan said she had "stick-to-it-iveness". Once she re-membered that, it would take her back to the day he said it. And re-membering that day brought an immediate smile across her face. She had to continually remind herself that, no matter what happened, she had Stan. Stacy really felt, deep in her heart, that Stan loved her unconditionally. And the way they seemed to match each other's wish list perfectly was uncanny. They had pretty much, over the last couple of months, discussed everything except for where they were going to live after marriage and kids. Again, neither one of these presented a problem for her. Whichever direction Stan decided was fine with her. One thing she did hope was that Stan would not move in with her. Leaving there would seem like a new start in life. But, if he did, so be it.

CHAPTER FORTY-THREE

April 23, 2016. A day that is forever etched inside Stacy's memory. She woke up in the morning and upon opening her eyes, to her surprise, she saw something! Stacy immediately jumped out of bed and screamed, *"Oh my God!"* as her hands instinctively covered her mouth as if to muffle the scream. Stuck in that position, she turned her head, ever so slowly, gazing at the entire room. There was no color, just a grey background with darker grey, static images. She could see! She walked ever so carefully around the room. She recognized the rough, outline silhouette of her dresser, the nightstand, her chest of drawers, the standing mirror, the two pictures hanging on the wall, and the recliner in the corner.

She made her way out of her bedroom into the living room—same thing. In fact, going through every room, it was the same. She finally sat down on the sofa and cried. *"Thank you, God. I am lost for words. Thank you! Thank you! Thank you!"* she repeated continuously. She reached for a Kleenex to dry her eyes, remembering not to rub them. She continued crying for a long time, tears of joy. When she finally got herself under control, she realized she might have put a strain on her eyes with all that crying. She patted her eyes dry, then went back into her room, applied the drops, and lay back down with her eyes closed. *"I can see! I can see!"* She repeated over and over again in her head. Stacy was given a new lease on life.

Stacy laid there for about an hour to make sure the drops had worked, and her eyes were no longer swollen. Her doctor's appointment was tomorrow, and wouldn't Dr. Browdy be surprised. And not just Dr. Browdy. Christy and Jorge, but mainly she wanted to see Stan if only in this state for now. She got up, cleaned up, and fixed herself something to eat. After she was done, she was curious to know how the outside looked. Stacy opened her front door and stepped out. It was too bright. She went back inside, got her sunglasses, and went back outside. That was much better. However, the different shades of grey had changed because of her sunglasses. But, nevertheless, she could see. She heard a car approaching and, turning right, she saw it move from right to left—she could see.

Stacy went back inside and kept herself busy while waiting for Christy to get off of work so she could call her. The same applied to Stan. Stacy read her Bible to keep herself busy and, just by coincidence, ran across John 9:25, where Jesus healed the blind man. She knew she was led to that verse for a reason. As she continued to read, she came across the joy that the blind man felt having sight for the first time in his life. But, he did more than just have joy. He gave testimony of God's great love for him. At that instant, Stacy made a vow that she, like the blind man, would always give a testimony of God's love for her by what he had done. She would repeat the same words as he had *"One thing that I know, that, whereas I was blind, now I see."* She would praise him and give testimony about Him any chance she got.

The phone rang. It was Christy. Stacy had lost track of time. *"Hey girl, how you doing?"* said Christy. *"I don't know. Let me see."* Stacy replied, trying to suppress her joy as much as she could. *"What?"* Christy said, confused. *"I said, LET ME SEE! Seeing being the active word!"* she said with a small laugh. *"Wait a minute. Are you telling me you can see? You can see!?"* Christy asked with her voice rising in excitement. *"Not well, but yes, girl. I can see!"* Stacy replied. Screams! Screams! Nothing but loud, uncontrollable screams from the other end, which seemed to go on for hours. Stacy patiently waited for her BFF to get a grip. But she did understand her elation. *"Tell me, tell me. What can you see?"* Stacy explained to her that she was only able to see shadows at this time. She also told her about the blind man in the Bible and how she felt she was one of God's miracles. Christy agreed. *"Listen,"* Christy said. *"I want you to make me a promise. I either want you to come out here, or I'll come there as soon as you have recovered your sight or when you recover as much as you are going to get. We "HAVE" to celebrate. Deal?"* "Deal," Stacy responded cheerfully. They talked a few more minutes before hanging up.

Stan called about an hour later. *"Hey, pumpkin!"* he said. *"Hey, babe,"* Stacy replied, trying to control her excitement. *"Where is my ring today?"* Stacy was waiting for this. *"Well, let me seeeeeee..."* Stacy replied. *"See? Can my baby see? Really?"* *"Yes, honey. Not very well, but yes."* Stacy replied. As she did with Christy, she told Stan all about what happened after she woke up and also told him about the story she read in the Bible regarding the blind man. She started getting choked up again. *"Ms. Sexy, I am so happy for you. Let's do something tonight to celebrate. They have a carnival in the suburbs. Let's go there."* *"Why not?"* Stacy replied. *"Good! I'll pick you up in about an hour."* *"I'll be ready,"* she said. As soon as Stan hung up, she started thinking about what to wear. She had to decide whether to wear pants or a dress. She knew Stan fancied dresses, but they were going to a carnival. And, probably doing some walking, heels would not be too appropriate. She paced back and forth, trying to decide what to do. Finally, she had it. She had some yellow sandals with two-inch heels on them. She also remembered buying an outfit to match. It was a yellow and green, short sleeve jumpsuit, except that the pants only went as far as mid-calf. She had never worn it but now was a good time.

She found them in her closet, laid them out, and then took a shower. She had been ready for ten minutes when the doorbell rang. When she opened the door, she said, "Stay right there" then, she slowly extended her hand with a pointed finger and touched his forehead. *"Hey, Babe."* *"My baby can see,"* he said. Stan stepped forward and gave her a big kiss.

"You know, my sexy princess, you keep looking like this for me; once we are married, we may not leave the house, if you know what I mean." "Makes no difference to me, Mister. If that's what makes you happy," she said. "That's my girl. Grab your purse. Let's go!" he said, and off they went.

CHAPTER FORTY-FOUR

The carnival was very crowded. Stacy saw moving shadows every-where, which was somewhat disorienting for her since she was used to complete darkness for such a long time. As she walked around the carnival holding onto Stan's arm, it didn't take long before she heard some very positively reinforcing comments: *"Man. Look at the fox on his arm!" "You are one lucky man!" "Baby, if you ever leave him, let me know!"* She even heard, *"Girl, I wish I looked like you." "You must be a model or something."* In fact, one man just flat came up to them and said, *"Damn, girl! No offense, bro."* for everyone to hear. Stan took it all in stride as she clung to his arm. He was proud to know that he had such a stunning beauty cradling his arm. The more the compliments the couple, Stacy in particular, received, the more he knew he had a perfect 10/10. Stacy was a vision of God's handiwork.

They had a fantastic time. They rode on some rides, played games, and found various different things they enjoyed eating. They tried a dart game where they had to throw darts at balloons. The objective was to hit three balloons with three darts for a small prize – either a goldfish or a stuffed animal. Stan went first and got two out of three balloons. Stacy tried next and managed to get one balloon. Stan said, *"Here's what we're going to do. I'll throw the first two, and you throw the last one."* Stan expertly flicked his hand and hit two balloons. *"Bullseye!"* He added with vigor.

Once Stacy heard the two pops, she knew it was up to her. She could barely make them out, only managing to see a vague silhouette. Nonetheless, she took aim and let it fly. Pop! They won! The guy at the kiosk clapped slowly, then said, *"Alright, folks. You won a prize. What'll it be? A stuffed pony or a goldfish?"* Stacy thought for a minute, then decided on the pony. She cherished that pony and would never forget that night. As they continued to stroll around, Stan would buy any and all snacks they found. Hotdogs, cotton candy, popcorn, burgers, fries – you name it. They had eaten so much that they were about to pop open. A few hours had passed, and Stan, seeing how exhausted Stacy was, said, *"You ready to call it a day, hon?"* *"Yes, babe,"* she said. *"Let's go home."*

Arriving back home, they both flopped on the couch like dead weight. Stan reached over and pulled Stacy close to him. They stayed cuddled up next to each other for the longest time. *"Hey, honey."* Stacy said, *"I've been meaning to ask you this, and now is a good time as any. Have you given any thought about having kids? Do you want children?"* *"Well, sweetie,"* Stan replied. *"I am very fond of children. In fact, they seem to gravitate towards me whenever I'm around them. I have a way with them, but I prefer the kids at my church and my nieces and nephews as my kids. When I'm around them, it's a blessing. But, being married to you, I would prefer to devote all my time and attention towards you."* Stacy sat up and kissed Stan on the cheek. *"There's my answer,"* she said. Stacy had thought about it long and hard. There were pros and cons to both sides. She had never been a mother. The closest experience she had was when Vicky forced her to raise her kids, which was no easy task. She could take it or leave it. Some women were destined to be mothers. Stacy had no doubt she would probably make a good mother, but she didn't feel she was destined. She would be content devoting all her time to making her man the happiest man in the world.

When Stan received Stacy's kiss, he was relieved to know that his decision was fine with her. The only other major thing was the religious question. So he decided to ask her. *"Baby girl. As you know, I'm an SDA.*

The Bible says, 'don't be unequally yoked.' What's your take on religious affiliation?" Stacy thought for a moment, then said, *"Honey, I've read the Bible, and I know what it says about some things. You probably know more than I would ever know. But, everything you have taught me about your religion can be backed up by the Bible. So, as far as I'm concerned, you can't get any better than that"* *"Well, alrighty then,"* he replied and pulled her even closer. After some time, he got up and left – but not before kissing her good night. Stacy knew she would never forget this day. She went to bed, clutching her pony.

The next day, she called Jorge for a ride, but Jorge was not working that day. Hence, she had to settle for another driver. As courteous as this new driver was, Stacy thought of Jorge as a friend rather than a driver. Arriving at her appointment and going through the same routines, she escorted to the room to wait for the doctor. When Dr. Browdy came in, he said, *"Hi Stacy. How ya doing today?"* he said. *"Stay right there, doc, don't move!"* Stacy said excitedly. And like she did for Stan, she got up and slowly walked over to the doctor, extended her arm, pointed her finger, and touched his forehead. *"Oh, wow!"* Dr. Browdy exclaimed in joy. *"You have finally regained sight. That's wonderful! How much can you see?".* Stacy told him she could only see shadows, couldn't make them out, and no color. *"Alright. Let's take a look,"* he said.

After doing another thorough exam, he said, *"Well, young lady, everything seems to be coming along quite nicely. Even the stitched areas are healing much faster than I anticipated. Let's set another appointment for two weeks. How are you holding up with the drops?"* *"Since I won't be back for two weeks, maybe I should get a refill to be on the safe side,"* she replied. *"No problem,"* he said. *"Have a seat in the front, and I'll have my assistant bring it out to you. Congratulations, once again. I hope to hear of more improvement in two weeks. Take care."* Shortly after calling for her ride, she was given more drops. Ten minutes later, she was in the car, and soon after, home.

As Stacy went about her day, she reminisced about the date she had with Stan the night before. To her, he was all that and a bag of chips. She knew that women were trying to slyly hit on him all the time. She had even witnessed some of the bank customers try to get his attention. Stan would always say he was fortunate to have her, but Stacy felt just the opposite – she was very lucky to have him. Stacy would always say to herself, *"He's my everything!"* She had some errands to run, which would help her pass the time while waiting on Stan's call. Stacy made a few mental notes on what she needed to do and was out the door.

CHAPTER FORTY-FIVE

Four weeks had passed from the time Stacy first saw silhouettes, with no improvements, but that was about to change. That memorable Wednesday morning, when she opened her eyes, she looked into the mirror on her dresser, which had now become a daily habit of hers. She wanted to see if anything changed. To her surprise, Stacy could now see light; in various forms, etched into the shadows. This meant that shadows were coming more into focus. *"Yes! Thank you, Jesus!"* she exclaimed joyfully. Stacy bounced out of bed with a pep in her step. Dr. Browdy had correctly surmised that her sight would gradually improve. Her only question now was by how much. Her next appointment was still a few days away. She wondered if there would be more improvement by the time she would see the doctor again.

As she was preparing for the day, the phone rang –it was Mr. Stewart. *"Hello Stacy, this is Mr. Stewart from your insurance company. How are you today?" "I'm fine, Mr. Stewart. I know we haven't spoken in a while, but the update is, I have gained partial sight,"* she replied. *"Well, that is wonderful news! I know you had the operation since we received the bill. I'm sure you're very excited."* He continued. *"Absolutely. You have no idea,"* Stacy replied.

"Well," he said, *"I'm calling to give you an update from our end. We have successfully gone after not only the trucking company's insurance but the insurance company of the original driver that rear-ended you. Between the two, they will take full responsibility for all of your medical bills stem-*

ming from this accident. I trust you are still receiving checks to pay for your personal expenses?" "Yes, I am. Don't know how I would survive without it." Stacy replied – she was grateful for having a fixed stream of income. *"Perfect."* Mr. Stewart added. *"Once you have no more doctors' visits, we will wrap this up. We will have you sign off on this part of the case, but there is still the continued case of seeking damages from this ordeal, what we call tort. That may take a minute but know that we will stick with it."*

"Thank you for all of the help, Mr. Stewart. You are wonderful; I couldn't have gotten this far without your help," Stacy replied respectfully. *"That's what we are here for. I know that most people think that insurance is a waste of money, especially since they seldom collect but for an occasional accident or fender bender. But, in these incidences, they are lifesaving. Congratulations once again on regaining your sight. Once you've had your final doctor's visit, please give us a call. Have a good day."* With that, he hung up.

It just dawned on Stacy that they were filing a lawsuit against the insurance companies seeking damages on her behalf. When that would be and for how much was yet to be determined. But she wasn't concerned with that at the moment. Her sight was improving; that was her top priority. She planned to call Christy and give her an update after she got off work. Stacy would wait for Stan to call to provide him with the news as well. Things were looking up for her.

The day her appointment arrived, her sight had just slightly improved. This time, when she called for her ride, Jorge was back. Once she was in the car, Stacy inquired about what had happened to him the last time she called. Jorge told Stacy that there was a death in his family, and he took a week off to attend the funeral in Mexico. Jorge told her that he actually drove there. Stacy offered her condolences and said she was glad he made it back safely. They then discussed her improved vision for the remainder of the drive to her appointment. She proved it by reaching out to touch him. Stacy didn't know who was happier for her sight, her or him!

When Dr. Browdy came in, she gave him the update on her vision, which he had anticipated. Upon yet another thorough exam, he determined that her stitches needed to be adjusted. *"Stacy,"* he said. *"I'm going to adjust your sutures for optimal cornea alignment. I'll apply some anesthetic drop so you won't feel any pain, but you may feel a little pressure. You'll be awake when we do this. Ready?"* Stacy psyched herself up for the procedure and just nodded in agreement. The procedure didn't take long, and she was glad if anything. Stacy was willing to do anything to get her eyesight back. After relaxing for about ten minutes, she was ready to go. Once in the car, Jorge gave her all of the details about the funeral – it was his grandmother. She was eighty-nine, and her health had been failing for some time, so it was not a surprise to the family when she passed. Again, she gave her condolences and asked if there was anything she could do for him. He just asked Stacy to keep his family in prayer.

Arriving back home, she realized just how blessed she was. She was regaining her sight, and she had Stan! Stacy was a happy puppy. Knowing that her life was slowly getting back to normal, she now thought about her future. Stacy knew she didn't want to return to her teller job at the bank. She still did need a job, but where? She now took it upon herself to start contemplating her future career. Then, she had to ask herself something that never came up in their discussions. *"Did Stan even want her to work? What plans had he envisioned for them?"* With these questions in mind, she planned to ask him when he called later that night.

The phone rang – Stan's ringtone. *"Hello, my handsome man,"* Stacy answered, *"Well, hello, my beautiful fiancé,"* Stan replied. *"How did your day go?"* *"It went well,"* she replied. *"But I have some good news. You know how I would just see shadows and silhouettes? Well, now I can see *small images of light figures inside those images. Isn't that great?" "Babe, I couldn't be happier for you – you deserve to be happy," Stan replied enthusiastically. "And I want you to know, hon, that you are a huge part of my happiness," she added. "Which leads me to ask a question. If I were to recover to the point that I could actually work again, would you want me to?" "Sweetheart," he said. "I'm going to leave that entirely up to you. We won't have children, and I don't expect you to sit around the house all days if you don't want but, if you choose to sit at home, watch TV and munch on Bon-Bon's all day, I'm good with that so long as it makes you happy. Only, promise me, if that's the route you take, don't lose your health or that magnificent body and shape of yours. Either way, we are joining the health club; just thought I'd throw that in. I'm by no means rich, but I can afford to pay the bills and provide you with all the necessities of life. But, if you want more and want to work, I'm perfectly fine with that as well. Whether you choose to work outside or at home makes no difference to me."*

"You are such an angel!" Stacy replied cheerfully. "Actually, I have not made up my mind yet, but it's good to know that, whichever way I choose, you're in my corner. You are just perfect for me. I don't ever see us getting into a heated argument or disagreement." "I feel exactly the same way," Stan replied. *"But, if we ever get into something like that, no matter how we feel or how it ends, let's promise that the night won't end until we have make-up sex." "I promise!"* Stacy replied. *"But, I can't guarantee that I won't pick a small fight with you just so we can end up that way..."* She started giggling. *"I'm counting on it!"* He said with a laugh.

"However," Stan continued. *"There is something else for you to think about. What about furthering your education? Or, I could help you start a business?" "Now that's a thought that hadn't crossed my mind!"* Stacy replied, quite surprised. *"I'm going to have to really pray and think about this, but I have time. I still have to wait on my sight to significantly improve." "And, I have never mentioned this to you before,"* Stan added, *"But I do have a small business that I run online. I got tired of all the running and driving, which started affecting my health, so I stopped. I lost a lot of*

customers that way, but I still have a handful who are loyal to me. This security job I currently hold will suffice until I can figure out what I want to do next." "So, you're a businessman as well as an entrepreneur!" Stacy responded. *"God! I am so fortunate to have you."* They continued chatting for a few more minutes before deciding to call it a day. Saying good bye's and kisses, they hung up. After climbing in bed that night, the last thing that entered her mind was, *"I'm never letting that man go,"* before falling asleep.

CHAPTER FORTY-SIX

It had now been six months since that unforgettable day in April when Stacy saw for the first time. She had now regained about 90% of her vision. She was punctual with her eye appointments and applied the drops religiously. At her next appointment, Dr. Browdy decided it was time to remove her sutures, which he did, and gave her an eye examination to test her 20/20 vision.

"Now, young lady," he said, *"You will have some form of astigmatism which requires corrective eye rehabilitation. You have two options. You can either chose to wear glasses or contacts. If you were to choose contact lenses, we would do a topographical analysis of the graph shape of both eyes, which would help us in selecting a lens that exerts the least amount of stress on the eye. There are two types of lenses. A GP, or gas permeable, is an oxygen permeable lens that allows your eye to breathe. They will be custom fit; however, they do not flex or fold. Some drawbacks to a hard lens are its vulnerability to scratches or can be easily dislodged. The soft lens, being custom fit also, has an extended range of available fitting curves, diameter, and lens power. This type of lens also allows the eye to breathe. If not much changes over the next, say, three weeks, we'll proceed with the test and go from there. You good with that?"* After listening intently, Stacy replied, *"I'm good with that doc. Oh! And I need a refill on the drops"* *"Grab two bottles on the way out. See you in three weeks!"* Dr. Browdy replied as he headed out the door.

Before long, Stacy was on her way home. Stacy had kept Jorge updated on her eyesight improvement. She now knew what he looked like. He was about 35 or 40 with jet black hair, a thin mustache, with a medium build. He was tanned and rugged, a rather handsome man. Jorge seemed to always be friendly every time they met. Stacy knew she was going to miss him once she was able to drive again. Now that she could actually see things close-up – although it wasn't sharp and clear. But, if it was more than one foot away, even though she could distinguish the object, it was all blurry and fuzzy. She wondered if she would need a bifocal lens. That's an option she would check out on her next appointment. Arriving home, she settled in, waiting on the time to call Christy and Stan.

Three weeks passed, and she was now back in Dr. Browdy's office. After he performed the test, he talked over the options of lens vs. glasses with Stacy again. It seemed that she did need bifocals. However, bifocals only came in the form of a GP lens. Stacy had previously been informed of the drawbacks of these types of lenses. So, her options were the GP lens, knowing they could scratch and were not flexible, or regular graduated bifocal glasses. She had some idea of what she looked like in glasses since she still, occasionally, wore her sunglasses – but never a regular pair of glasses, as they were sold in places like America's Best, Lens Crafter, or maybe even Walmart. Stacy contemplated her options, then had an idea. She decided to spend some time trying on glasses in each, if not all, of those stores before she made up her mind. She also wanted to get Stan's opinion before deciding.

Stacy presented her idea to Dr. Browdy, who supported her decision wholeheartedly. But, he went on to say, *"Just so you know, a prescription for contact lens is quite different from a prescription for regular glasses. Here's why. Contact lens' sit directly on the eye. Glasses, of course, sit on your nose, about one inch from your eye. That distance makes quite a difference. So, make sure you're satisfied with your decision."* Stacy understood the importance of this, and this was a decision she would not take lightly. More than anything, she reasoned, Stan would be looking at her more than she would, and Stacy wanted him to be pleased with what he saw. Stacy sort of knew what he would say, but they would still talk it over.

She thanked Dr. Browdy and said, as soon as she made up her mind, she would set up an appointment to see him. On her way back home, it dawned on her that, after her next appointment, she was done—no more appointments except for the six-month checkups. After the corrective lens, she could start looking for a job – some form of income. She would see if Stan could come over this evening to talk about both subjects. *"Now,"* She thought. *"For dinner. What's for dinner?"*

Stan was able to come over that night. They decided on Harold's chicken with mild BBQ sauce, which came with fries. Stacy asked Stan to stop by a store and bring a bottle of sparkling grape juice with him. They made some small talk during dinner. Stan told her about his day at work, how a woman came in the bank trying to cash a forged check pretending to be someone else. When the teller said she would have to clear the check with her teller manager and while she was away, the customer slowly made her way to the exit and was gone. The two forms of ID turned out to be fake, of course, but that he had gotten a good description of her and gave it to the police, who were called in since the branch manager filed a complaint.

After finishing their meal and cleaning up, they relaxed on the couch with a drink in hand. *"Honey,"* Stacy began. *"I'm going to have to have some form of corrective lens. I can go for contacts or regular glasses. However, whichever one I choose, they will have to be bifocal."* Stacy elaborated on the pros and cons of the GP lens. Pros being she would look normal, cons being that the lens was rather delicate and prone to scratches. As another option, Stacy could just wear glasses and avoid all the upkeep of contacts but didn't know how she would look in them. *"It's really up to you, babe, since you have to look at me more than I have to look at myself,"* she added. *"Give me a second,"* Stan said. He sat there for a minute and just looked at her in deep thought.

Finally, he said, *"Well, sweetheart, it really doesn't matter to me. Of course, I love you either way. There are pros and cons to both. But, just an observation. Knowing you had eye surgery and how delicate your eyes are now, do you think it's a good idea to put something in them?"* That was an excellent point, something Stacy had not considered.

Stan was right; why risk it? *"Good point, mister,"* she said. *"That means you are going to have to take me around to several optical stores so I can pick out the perfect pair,"* She said as she snuggled herself up in his arms. *"Whatever my princess wants,"* Stan replied as he kissed the top of her head. Stan called in to dispatch and, after some negotiations, managed to get Friday off. *"We're all set for Friday,"* he said. *"One more thing, hon. Once I get my glasses, I'll be able to, hopefully, see enough to work. So, I'm going to start looking now to SEEEE what I can find."* Stacy said as she giggled. *"Go for it, boo. If you need my help in any way, just let me know; but it's going to cost you a kiss."* Stacy leaned over and gave him a kiss and said: *"You already did."*

"Now, what's on TV?" Stan asked. The rest of the evening was spent sipping on their fake Champaign, hugging with the occasional kiss. Stacy decided to grab a small pillow, placed it on Stan's lap, and laid down. Unintentionally, she soon fell asleep. Stan let her rest there until the movie he was watching was over. He gently woke Stacy up and asked her to walk him to the door. Still groggy and half-sleep, she managed. A last kiss, and he was gone. It didn't take Stacy long before she was in bed. Putting her drops in, she fell fast asleep in no time.

CHAPTER FORTY-SEVEN

Friday soon arrived, and Stan picked Stacy up at 9:00 A.M. But before they went on their "quest" to buy glasses, first, breakfast! They stopped by Valois Cafeteria for that. It was a bit crowded, and they had to wait in line for a few minutes, but it's not like they were in a hurry. They both ordered a veggie omelet with hash browns and a large orange juice. After enjoying their meal, they headed out in search of the perfect frame. They visited locals like Tropical Optical, Village Eyecare, Pearle Vision, and Lens Crafter, even ventured to the south side to visit Walmart, JC Penney, and America's Best.

After looking through dozens upon dozens of pairs – not to mention all the shapes and colors they browsed through, Stacy settled on a pair of Ray-Ban 5246 black frames. Stan paid for the frames, but Stacy preferred to have someone local put the lens in and do the fitting. That way, if she ever needed an adjustment or a repair, she wouldn't have to go far. By the time they were done with their search, it was well into the afternoon, and they were hungry. Stan asked Stacy if she had any place in mind. She thought for a minute, then said, *"Hon, you pick."* After going back and forth on a few restaurants, they settled on Outback Steakhouse since there were already in the suburbs. Stan happened to live in the south suburbs in a town called Lansing. He had a large, two-bedroom apartment on the third floor. He kept it neat and clean, with a distinctive taste in interior decoration – not something you usually get to see from a single man. He had taken her there several times but, since he worked close to Stacy, it was much easier for them to get together at her place.

When they finished with their lunch, Stan told Stacy that they were headed to the Orland Square Mall because he needed to pick something up. Stacy was greatly enjoying spending time with Stan, even if it was just running errands. With little details like this, she already felt like her wife! Walking down the mall, they turned into Zales Jewelers. At that point, Stacy was completely unaware of what was going on. Stan stepped behind her, put his hands on her waist, and nudged her forward, right in front of the salesman. *"Good evening, Stacy,"* he said. *"I've been expecting you. I understand you are presently engaged. Congratulations. However, I think it's time you considered a wedding ring. Don't you?"* In a mild shock, with her mouth half open and her eyes wide, she tried to back away from the salesman; but Stan was still behind her and held her in place. Stacy just stood quietly.

"Honey," Stan spoke. *"The gentleman asked you a question."* She quickly turned around and gave Stan a swift kiss. And, just as quickly, she turned back to the salesman and said one word, *"YES!"* – Still partly in shock. But, then she stopped and turned back around with a serious look. *"Babe,"* she said. *"We talked about wearing jewelry. Are you sure you want to do this?"* Stan looked at her and smiled, *"Sweetheart, that is my conviction. There may be somethings I insist on, but this is not one of them. Whatever you do, you have to do it for the right reason. In my case, some choose to, and some don't. The decision is yours to make. Whichever you choose, I still love you all the same."*

Stacy had always wanted Stan to put a wedding ring on her finger that would hide or cover up the memories of Mitchell. The engagement ring helped, but it was only temporary. She purposed in her heart that a ring would not break her relationship with God and would gladly display it, not for show, but to prove Stan was her husband and she was proud of it. If in time, she felt otherwise, she would do the right thing.

She turned back around and said, *"Please, show me what you have."* Stacy didn't want something small, nor did she want something very large and showy.

She turned around back to Stan and said, *"Honey, what price range should I stick to?"* *"Thanks, hon, but don't worry about that,"* he replied confidently. She sat down as the salesman brought several styles and sizes to show her from small, medium, and large. Stacy had to take each one and put it very close to her eyes to see it properly. After viewing the collection he brought, she asked to see several more in the medium-sized class. He brought her another half dozen to inspect.

Looking them over, one really caught her attention. *"Can I try that one on?"* she asked. *"But of course. Stick out your hand."* The salesman responded as he slid it on her finger. She held it at arm's length; it sparkled like a star. She pulled it closer to her so she could inspect it on her finger. She lct out a big sigh and said, *"It's beautiful. Simply beautiful."* It was a Two-Piece Bridal Set -2.30CT Princess Cut Diamond with 14KT Polished White Gold. But the cost? She forgot all about what it would cost. She slowly turned around in her seat and faced Stan wearing this big smile. She held her arm straight out in front of her to give him a closer look, all while batting her eyes. Stan smiled, then looked at the salesman and sort of lifted his head, slightly, up and down quickly. The motion was prearranged. The salesman wrote the price down on a piece of paper and handed it to Stan.

Stan looked at the price, handed the piece of paper back to the salesman, and said to Stacy, *"Will that add to your happiness?"* *"You have no idea,"* she responded. Looking back towards the salesman, Stan said: "So, you guys take Visa or MasterCard?" In an instant, Stacy leaped out of her chair, grabbed Stan, almost knocking him over, and started jumping up and down in pure joy. A few moments later, having calmed down, she rested her head on his chest and said, *"Thank You! Thank You! Thank You! You are the most wonderful man in the world!"* And gave him another kiss. Stan pulled out his wallet and handed the man his credit card. Stacy took the ring off her finger and handed it back to the salesman. After the transaction, he asked them to take a seat. He wanted to properly clean the ring and find a special box to put it in. When he returned, he had this small, fancy little shopping bag with the box containing the ring inside. They thanked him for his service and left with Stacy clinging to Stan's arm. On the way out, Stacy abruptly stopped and said, *"Hey, wait a minute. How did he know my name?"* Stan just looked at her, smiled, and winked without saying a word. After they were done, Stan drove Stacy back home. She immediately put on her ring when she got back and eventually drifted to sleep with her hand on the ring.

CHAPTER FORTY-EIGHT

The next day, Stacy called for an appointment with Dr. Browdy. Within two weeks, she had her glasses. Her vision wasn't exactly 20/20, and it would take some time to get used to the bifocals, but what she had was good enough. Stacy thanked God every day for the restoration of her sight. She now needed to see Dr. Browdy every three months just to make sure there were no complications and could discontinue the eye drops. Her journey of regaining her eyesight was over. She called Mr. Stewart and informed him that the file on her vision case could now be closed. Now, it was time for Stacy to decide what she was going to do with her time. Employment, of course, but what? From home? What was she good at? What were her skills?

That's when she realized that she never showed up for her appointment with the advertising company that fateful day. Even though it had been almost two years, Stacy decided to call Ms. Rogers and at least explain what happened. It took her a minute, but she finally located the number and called. To Stacy's surprise, Ms. Rogers answered the phone. To add further to her surprise, she still remembered her after all that time. After the usual pleasantries and introductions, Stacy began explaining why she had never made it to the interview. Ms. Rogers stopped her and stated that she remembered hearing or reading of a bad accident that day. She had no idea it was Stacy and, when she did not show up for the appointment, reasoned that Stacy had changed her mind. She had attempted to call her on several occasions, but it always went to voicemail.

Ms. Rogers was very curious about Stacy's wellbeing and how she was doing so; Stacy tried to sum it up as best she could. After listening intently, Ms. Rogers was amazed at her recovery. But what happened next, Stacy was not prepared for. Ms. Rogers indicated that there just so happened to be two office positions that would become available in two weeks and wanted to know if she was looking for work and would be interested in interviewing for them. Stacy didn't have to think long before giving her the answer. An appointment was set up for her to come in the next day. Stacy thanked her for her generosity, and after a few more minutes of conversation, the call ended. Of course, the minute she got off the phone, she called Christy and Stan and told them all about it. She also set up her ride, requesting Jorge as usual.

On the day of the interview, Stacy arrived right on time – prim and proper. Stacy thought the interview went well but, due to lack of experience and schooling, she had doubts about being hired. But, she left that up to a higher power. However, two days later, Ms. Rogers called and asked if she could come in for a second interview, which would include part of the management staff. Stacy immediately agreed. During the interview, Ms. Rogers basically repeated the same interview questions as she had before. Stacy answered, just as she did before. It was strange that not one of the management staff present asked a single question. They all just sat there, basically – looking at her.

After the interview was complete, Ms. Rogers turned to one of the officers and nodded her head. Finally, one of the men said, *"Thank you, Ms. Rogers."* Another man cleared his throat and said: *"I understand you like to be addressed as Stacy, am I correct?"* "Yes, if you don't mind. I sort of have my reasons,"* she replied. He continued, *"No problem, Stacy. It's true we have two positions coming up that need to be filled, and Ms. Rogers is considering you for one of those positions. And yes, those gathered here have an input into that decision. However, we are here for an additional reason. Have you ever considered becoming a model?"* "Who, me?"

Stacy responded, shocked. *"To be honest with you, that has never crossed my mind!"* *"Well,"* he continued, *"We think, with a little coaching, you would excel in that profession! Let's go back. I was the one who asked Ms. Rogers to set up the interview on the day of your tragic accident. I had previously informed her all about you. You see, it just so happens that I also live in Hyde Park. I've had the privilege of seeing you around town on several occasions back then. I hope you're not offended or think ill of me, but I even followed you a time or two. I concluded, by the way you walk and look, you were definitely model material. I did a little snooping around and found out your name. Then came the accident. The next time I ran into you, you were blind. So I chalked it up as a missed opportunity. You cannot imagine my delight when Ms. Rogers came to me, stating that you had called her. Neither one of us forgot. And now you can see. How is that?"*

Stacy was dumbfounded for a moment; all of it was a lot to swallow. Nevertheless, she kept it brief but gave them the whole story. *"Nothing less than a miracle,"* he said. He continued, *"It just so happens that this firm has part ownership in a modeling agency. So, here is our proposal. Suppose you land one of those positions, fine. But, we would somehow find the time, if you're ok with it, to work you into our modeling phase. And, if by some chance you are not given one of those positions, we would then like to hire you as a model, let's say, trainee until, of course, we try to make you a household name. Is this something you would consider?"* Stacy could hardly believe what was being said. *"Me. A Model. Are you sure?"* she said, visibly surprised. *"Oh! We're quite sure!"* he said confidently. *"We spent all day yesterday talking about you when Ms. Rogers brought you to our attention. And we couldn't agree more that you are a fabulous find.*

"If you need a few days to think about this, we understand." He added. *"I have one question,"* Stacy asked. *"If I want to continue my education, will the company reimburse my tuition?"* *"If you're a full-time employee, absolutely."* Came the reply. *"Well,"* Stacy continued, *"With all due respect, I would like to discuss this with my fiancé before I make a commitment. I presume being a model would involve traveling, and I need to get*

his take on that." "By all means," he said. *"In fact, you can bring him in, so he can look around and talk to us about any concerns he may have."* Stacy accepted that invitation and said she would call Ms. Rogers tomorrow with her answer. With that, the meeting ended. It took everything Stacy had to contain her excitement during the interview and on her way out. On her way home, she told Jorge all about it. He was just as excited as Stacy, if not more!

CHAPTER FORTY-NINE

Stacy waited until she knew Stan was off work and called him. *"Hey babycakes, what's up?"* Stan said, answering the phone. *"Honey,"* she said, *"You have just got to come over tonight. I'm so excited, but I want to know what you think about something." "Well, I'll be over in about an hour, but I can't stay long."* He replied. *"So you won't have time for dinner?"* Stacy asked, a bit sadly. *"Afraid not, little sexy,"* he said. *"Ok, babe. See you in an hour."* She replied.

Once Stan arrived and had been comfortably seated, Stacy told him all about her day having to stop several times to catch her breath. When she was done, she took a deep breath and exhaled. *"So, handsome, what do you think of that?"*

"I have to admit, never saw that coming. They seem genuine from what you've told me about them. The way he found you and remembered you all this time HAS to be divine intervention," He said confidently. *"I think so too,"* Stacy replied. *"They are a big firm, and I don't think they would have called me this quickly to waste their time or mine,"* she said. *"I don't think they could have made a better choice regardless of where you wind up in their organization,"* Stan continued. *"Do you want me to set up an appointment so you can check them out?"* Stacy asked. *"Thanks, but no, hon. You are quite capable of making that decision on your own. Whatever you decide to do has my approval."* He responded while taking Stacy into his arms and kissing her forehead. Stacy, looking up into his eyes, said, *"You're such a sweetheart. But, you know, modeling could in-*

volve traveling." "That's true." He added. *"Just another reason why I pre-ferred not to have children. But, if you do accept their offer, just remember what they say. Absence makes the heart grow fonder."* Stan replied.

"Hey," said Stacy. *"Maybe you could come with me?" "If that's possible and time permits, sure,"* Stan said. *"Okay! I'll call them tomorrow and tell them that I accept their offer."* Stacy replied cheerfully. *"That's my girl. If you need my help, just let me know."* Stacy leaned over and gave him a big kiss. *"Got to go, babe. Walk me to the door,"* Stan continued as he got up. Closing the door as he left, Stacy fell back against the wall. This was really happening! She had the opportunity to be a model. Who would have guessed that! Stacy was convinced that God had opened this door. Now, time to call Christy and fill her in. The next day, Stacy called Ms. Rogers and accepted the position, letting her know that a visit from her fiancé would not be necessary. Ms. Rogers told Stacy that she would not regret her decision. Since the opening would not be for a couple of more weeks, Ms. Rogers suggested she just take it easy until she called. Stacy wanted to celebrate. She left a message on Stan's voicemail asking him to come over for dinner after work; she was making a garbage salad. She also asked him again to pick up a bottle of sparkling grape juice – Stacy just loved that stuff! Stan called back during his break and said he would be over after work in uniform. Once he arrived, they sat down and had a peaceful meal together. During dinner, Stacy told him she had accepted the position.

After dinner, they retired to the couch with a bottle of bubbly and two glasses. Stan filled both glasses half full and made a toast, "Here's to the angel that fell from heaven. I am so proud of how far she has come when she could have easily given up. May the Lord bless her in all her undertakings and that, through life, she never lets go of His hand and continues to let Him lead her." They touched glasses and took a sip. Stan put his glass down and took Stacy's glass out of her hand, and placed it next to his. *"Honey, you are the love of my life. When you start working, I doubt you'd get time to take a vacation for at least a few months. Babe, let's get married before you start work."* Stan asked. Well, you can probably imagine what came next. A million "yeses", shouting, hugs, and kisses. It's a good thing she removed her glasses first. They probably wouldn't have survived the ordeal!

After she got herself under control, she asked, *"Where? When? How?"* Stan gently held her by her arms and said, *"Since there is no time to have an official wedding, I thought that we could fly to Vegas, get married and plan an official wedding, reception, and honeymoon when we get the time."* And here we go again! Stacy lost control once again! Absolutely ecstatic in joy! After she finally settled down, she flopped back on the couch beside Stan and kissed him. Stan continued, *"I'll make all the arrangements and get back to you. In the meantime, we'll stay for the weekend so pack enough clothes for the occasion."* Stacy was overwhelmed. In a few weeks, she would be Mrs. Wallace or, better yet, Mrs. Stan Wallace; she couldn't wait!

CHAPTER FIFTY

Ten days later, just as planned, they were in Vegas. They were married on December 23, 2016. Needless to say, I spent Christmas there. A little more than eighteen months after they first met and seventeen months since her accident.

Stan took care of all the arrangements. He even contacted Christy, who managed to be there as Stacy's maid of honor. Stacy was thrilled to see her even though she had to fly back out the next day. Christy couldn't have been happier for Stacy and knew, finally, she was happy and where she belonged. Stacy invited Sharon and all of the staff who helped her at Second Sense. Stan helped out with their airfare so they all could attend.

He even flew his kids in from California for the wedding. They immediately bonded with Stacy. Stan had arranged the ceremony at A Little White Wedding Chapel and ordered the Tunnel of Love Extravaganza package. It included: Bridal Bouquet 45, Rose Boutonniere, and eighteen professional digital photos. This did not have the minister's fee, which Stan took care of by slipping him a $100 bill.

Stacy wore a white satin gown, and he wore a black tux. Stan had booked the weekend stay at Harrah's. All throughout the wedding preparation, Stacy was smiling so much; her face began to hurt; prompting her to stop for a brief moment. She enjoyed every second of their weekend so far, including the flight, since it was her first time on a plane.

But, there was one thing, in the back of her mind, that got her a bit nervous. She knew, eventually, she and Stan would be in the same bed together for the first time in her life. Having already considered that as a possibility, she was now back on the pill. Stacy had no idea what to expect and began doubting herself since it had been so long. She knew she already longed for Stan, but could she satisfy him? What if she couldn't? She knew Stan would probably never say anything but, him being disappointed would break her heart.

The time came when they finished up with their whirlwind wedding and headed back to their suite. Stan showered first, followed by Stacy. When she came out of the bathroom, with just a towel wrapped around her, Stan was standing there to meet her. He handed her a note that said, *"Mrs. Wallace, you will find a long, pink charmeuse lace gown on the bed. Please put it on and join me in the living room."*

Stacy stood there for a minute before collecting herself, then headed to the bedroom. She found the gown; it was beautiful, but there were no panties. Stacy looked all over, but there were none. It finally dawned on her that Stan had not brought any for her. Stacy had to sit down and take a few deep breaths to calm herself. After putting it on, it fit perfectly. She headed for the front room. Stan was wearing a three-quarter length black silk robe.

When Stacy got halfway into the room, Stan asked her to stop and to stay right there. He walked over to a CD player and pushed the button. *"Tonight, I celebrate my love for you"* began to play. Stan walked up to Stacy and said: *"May I have this dance?"* He knew she was awestruck, so he stepped forward and took her in his arms. Stan started slow dancing, and, within a few seconds, she had matched his rhythm. As they slowly danced along to the music, Stacy suddenly froze when the song lyrics said, *"...When I make love to you..."* But Stan kept in rhythm. Soon, Stacy relaxed and began enjoying the first dance with her new husband. By the time the song ended, Stacy was already melting in his arms. Stan stepped back, took her hand, and, saying nothing, led her to the bedroom.

Once there, Stan said, *"Honey, I know you're a bit nervous, so I'll get on one side of the bed, turn my back and climb into bed. You can do the same from your side. Oh, and baby, lose the gown."* With trepidation, she slowly let the gown fall to the carpet and climbed into bed. Stan had already dimmed the lights and followed. Stacy just lay there, somewhat relaxed, but her heart felt like it would beat right out of her chest! She didn't know what to do next. After a few minutes, Stan rose up on one side, turned her face to his, gave her a big kiss, then laid back down. He said, *"OK. Your turn."* It took her a few moments, but she finally mustered the courage, rose up on her side, and kissed him. But Stan reached around her and pulled her on top of him. *"Good evening, Mrs. Wallace."* He said seductively. *"Good evening, Mr. Wallace,"* Stacy replied, after getting over the initial shock. He drew her head to his and began kissing her passionately.

He held on to her and continued for a long time until he felt her relax for a bit; but, Stan didn't stop. He kept it up until he could hear her start breathing a bit faster. Still, he didn't stop. Within minutes, Stacy's fuse had been lit – she started squirming, grinding her hips against his. Try as she might resist, her body completely took over; she had nothing stopping her now. And yet, Stan continued. Stacy could feel the heat rising and her heart beating louder. She started moaning uncontrollably. She became louder and louder. When Stan broke away, he saw that glazed look in her eyes. *"Oh, Stan!"* He said nothing. She was ready.

Stan quickly flipped her over on her back, climbed on top, and scooted down. Beginning with her belly button, he licked, kissed, and nibbled her warm flesh. Having spent a few moments there, he continued doing the same, moving from one side of her body to the other, never losing contact with his lips. Stacy was heating up. She closed her eyes, reached behind her, and grabbed the rails between the headboards, laying herself open for Stan. All her inhibition was slowly deserting her. He had now worked his way up to her breasts, where he continued to lavish them with licks, kisses, and nibbles; then started sucking each of her nipples until they were protruding and hard. He continued his assault, working his way up to her neck with more licks, kisses, and small, gentle bites. Then her ears, sucking each lobe. Stacy had been driven to a pure, euphoric state. He kissed her forehead, then her nose, then renewed his assault on her lips.

Stacy reacted. As if controlled by an outside force, her legs flew straight up into the air, wrapped them around his back, and locked them in place. At the same time, she wrapped her arms tightly around him. Stan was well built and strong for his size. *"Oh, Stan!"* Stacy moaned. She was now dripping wet. Stan slowly entered her but stopped halfway. Stacy winced and squeezed him even tighter with her legs and arms. It hurt a bit as she was being stretched open. Stan didn't wait very long for her to catch her breath. He began with a slow withdrawal immediately followed by a slow, methodical reentry. Stan repeated this for several minutes until he felt Stacy relax. He stayed with the same pace for a long time, plunging deeper and deeper, with every thrust, churning her to a frenzy. His rhythm. The feel of his body on her. Stacy was now delirious, being driven crazy.

All her built up passion and lust for Stan was now unleashed. Stacy couldn't control herself. She started pushing up as Stan was pushing down. Stan let her dictate the pace. Soon, her pace picked up, and Stan matched her. Stacy's mind and body were lost in raw desire. Her body trembled inside. Her insides were boiling. Now that she was matching his every thrust, Stan drove in deeper, reaching places that she had never been touched before. There were now no intervals between Stacy's moans; she was moaning near continuously – one behind the other. She was being pushed over the edge. It started with a small wave that intensified as it grew, building, and building. She held on for dear life. Within minutes, it reached its peak. A volcano ready to erupt. She burst like a balloon. The flood gates opened. *"Oh! Stan! Oh! Oh! Ugh! Ugh! Oh, God! Stan! Stan!"* Wave after wave ripped through her body. Pulsating again and again, and again. Non-stop. The intensity was tearing her apart. She thought she would pass out. Little by little, the waves died down and eventually subsided.

Stacy was still breathing heavily, emitting faint moans. She was drained and couldn't move. She stayed just like she was, clinging to Stan. After a few minutes, Stan lifted her head and gave her a small kiss. *"Is my wife okay?"* he asked softly. *"Oh, Stan,"* was all she could muster up. They made love three times that night.

They stayed in bed until about noon. All their guests had called to wish them well before departing for home. Stan had worn her out. Mitchell was good, but he was no match for Stan. Stan woke up every nerve in her body, something Mitchell didn't or couldn't do. And... Speaking of cunnilingus, we were talking about cunnilingus, right? NO? Well, we should be! Stan would torture her with pleasure for half an hour, at least. On each occasion, she had to plead for him to stop, but he was relentless. After a few minutes, she would beg him NOT to stop. Stan did some things to her to where she had to limit him on how often he performed that act of love on her. He drove her to a total loss of control and to the point of embarrassment on how she reacted. Stacy had to prepare herself for that enjoyment due to the intensity and how it left her afterward. After each mind-numbing session, she was spent for half a day. Yes! It was like that! Stacy knew she could become addicted to his lovemaking. To Stan, it was an art. He was not satisfied until his masterpiece was finished... that being her! He was never in a rush. He made sure that every part of her body got some attention. Her cup was full of love for him before today, but now it was overflowing.

They eventually got around to showering, getting dressed, and headed to the buffet for a late lunch. Stan had previously brought tickets to a Fleetwood Mac concert held at the MGM Grand. She could not be any happier. During the time there, they discussed where they would live. They agreed that Stan would move in with Stacy, for the time being, since he worked close by at that time, and she could easily drive to work or catch the train from there. Parking was always a problem in Hyde Park, but they would manage. They would make one car do for now. Flying back to Chicago on Monday, Stacy spent the time reflecting on what happened that weekend. Especially the lovemaking. She got chills just thinking about it. Many times, she would hold her hand up and out, just staring at the ring for minutes on end. Mrs. Wallace – she was now content. Stan had completed her life. In fact, he gave her a new outlook on life. A new life, a new husband, a new career – thank God. What more could a girl ask for?

CHAPTER FIFTY-ONE

Stan broke his lease and moved in with Stacy. They went over their furniture and decided to keep the best, and donated the rest to Goodwill. Stacy started working in the AP/AR department while they began grooming her to be a model. One day, Stan came home and told Stacy that he had to attend a funeral on Sunday. He wanted her to come with him if she had nothing to do. Of course, she accompanied him – why wouldn't she? It was held in a town in the south suburbs named Country Club Hills. Upon their arrival, Stan was greeted by several friends as he, in turn, introduced his new wife to them. It was a typical Christian service until the eulogy was said. The minister showered the deceased with accolades. No doubt, he sounded like a good man. He indicated that the young man had died from respiratory complications suffered from an accident that happened some time ago. It's what was said next that shocked Stacy.

The minister continued saying that the man also died of a broken heart, knowing that the very accident that caused him respiratory issues caused a young lady to be blinded for life; he never forgave himself for that. Even though he had eventually discovered who she was, he was so full of grief that he couldn't bear to see her in that condition. Stacy's eyes grew big, and her mouth flew open while her hand instinctively cover it. She let out a small gasp. She slowly turned to Stan with tears beginning to well up in her eyes. Stan just nodded slowly. This was the man that drove the truck that fateful day. Stan handed her a handkerchief as she began to cry. She continued in that state until the service was over, and Stan took her outside to get some air. *"Honey, was he...?" "Yes, my love,"* Stan responded solemnly.

He continued, *"A couple of months, after the accident, a friend and I were talking about his friend and how he was involved in a terrible accident downtown; how he T-boned a car with a young lady in it. After a little more research, it didn't take me long to put two and two together. I never knew how to tell you that. I never knew how you would react. But, when this happened, I thought it was time for you to know."* Stacy knew all about emotional hopelessness and despair. She had no anger or resentment left in her heart, only compassion. She could only imagine what he had to live through and how he must have felt all this time. Now that Stacy was nearly fully recovered, the family had talked it over about getting them together since Stacy had regained her sight. They felt it would relieve his guilt. They decided to do that once they got back from Vegas. Unfortunately, he had gone into a coma shortly before that and never regained consciousness.

Stacy had composed herself but couldn't help but break down again. Stan knew words wouldn't cut it, so he just hugged her. A few minutes later, she gathered herself. *"I have got to tell the family that I'm fine now,"* she said. Stan agreed, which was one of the reasons he wanted her to come. They made their request known to the pastor, who recommended that Stacy tell her story to the family members only. He volunteered to gather them up before the repass started. Once assembled in a back office, Stacy gave her condolences and told her story in a very emotional state, crying nearly nonstop. It took all she had in her just to complete the story.

When she was done, each of the man's family members came up to her, one by one, teary-eyed as they hugged her and thanked her for having the courage to let them know. The deceased man's name was Dowyne Reynolds. They thanked God for the miracle He had given her and said that Dowyne could now rest in peace. The pastor asked that they formed a circle and said a closing prayer before they departed. Stacy was an emotional wreck, so Stan took her home. From that day on, Stacy stayed in touch with the family, occasionally inviting them over for dinner or a cookout. They even got together for a girls' night out every now and then.

On the way back home, Stacy had time to think. She contemplated how blessed she was that God heard her prayers. She knew she was a walking miracle, not only because she regained her eyesight, but from what her mother and Mitchell had put her through. Stacy battled a lot of emotional drama and physical pain, but God saw her through. However, her thoughts went much deeper than that.

[What about those people who were not as fortunate she was? Most of those who are blind stay that way for life. There is no miracle coming their way. The courage it takes for them to deal with their situations day after day should be admired. Most of the blind people you meet are happy.

The homeless: They didn't start life off thinking they were going to be in that predicament. They have feelings and emotions, just like everyone else. Yet, most people look down on them with disgust and loathing. Who consoles their physical and emotional pain? A majority of the population gives it no thought once the blind or homeless have left their presence. They just get on with their lives. Somethings wrong with that picture. A change of heart is a fundamental necessity, to say the least. Not that you "have" to do something for them. However, lack of compassion warrants close inspection.

You should have empathy to the point that you, at least, pray for the comfort of those who find themselves in these situations. God hears all prayers. If you have the means for it, donate to a charity that assists these individuals. Practice not passing them without saying an uplifting word. A simple *"Good Morning"* works wonders. If they ask for financial assistance, give as you are led. Remember, they, too, are someone's child. If your son, daughter, or any relative was in this same type of predicament, wouldn't you want any person who comes upon them to have the same love for them as you do? This is the real purpose of this book. That you will, if need be, adjust your perspective in how you really see other people. Not just those who are in exceptional circumstances but everyone. No matter who they are, where they came from, or how they look. We are all equal in God's eyes. We are all in this together. No one is better than the other. Money, or lack thereof, doesn't make you any better or worse than the person right next to you. God holds you responsible for the development of your own values and those you bestow on others. As you adjust to this reform, you will understand the saying that it is better to give than to receive. Or, better yet, do unto others as you would have done to you. It's called golden for a reason.]

Stacy was now on her way to having an outstanding and successful career. Her hard work paid off, and she was a natural when it came to modeling – a real beauty. As her career improved, she eventually began flying back and forth across America for her agency. The company brought her a set of contacts, which she wore mainly on photoshoots, if necessary. Otherwise, she just removed her glasses. Stacy's contract gave her the option of not taking photos that she thought were too provocative. She did not want to tarnish her character or lower Stan's moral image of her in any way. She also couldn't disappoint God. There were times Stan went with her, on the company's expense, of course.

Stan had developed a different online sales business shortly after they had gotten married. This one worked. Within a year, he was self-employed, with the company financially sound. Stacy agreed to an out of court settlement, from the two insurance companies, for a considerable sum of money. They now never needed to worry about finances. She became a faithful financial contributor to many organizations that assisted the blind in any way, especially Second Sense. They planned to buy a house in the suburbs since they had had enough of the confinements of the city.

They never did have kids. Instead, she had a large aquarium with exotic fish and a solid black Pomeranian, who thinks she owns the place! Stacy never did reconnect with her family; Vicky was a distant memory, long forgotten. She kept the children Vicky adopted in her prayers always, hoping they ended up better than they started. Stan's family and friends became her family. Exactly a year after they were married in Vegas, they got remarried in a church with family, friends, and work associates. Stacy spared no expense. They spent a week in Hawaii for their honeymoon and, even though they had been married a year, still spent a considerable amount of time in bed. They were made for each other. What God has joined together, let no man separate. They were determined never to let that happen.

John 9:25 "He answered and said whether he be a sinner or no, I know not: one thing I know, that, whereas I was blind, now I see."

www.ingramcontent.com/pod-product-compliance
Lightning Source LLC
Chambersburg PA
CBHW071433200726

48294CB00002B/620